OTHER *Novels by Joan Johnston*

COLTER'S WIFE
THE SISTERS OF THE LONE STAR TRILOGY
FRONTIER WOMAN
COMANCHE WOMAN
TEXAS WOMAN

*SWEETWATER SEDUCTION

* Available from Dell Publishing

The Barefoot Bride

Joan Johnston

A DELL BOOK

Published by
Dell Publishing
a division of
Bantam Doubleday Dell Publishing Group, Inc.
666 Fifth Avenue
New York, New York 10103

ISBN: 0-440-21129-8

Printed in the United States of America

Published simultaneously in Canada

January 1992

10 9 8 7 6 5 4 3 2 1

RAD

This book is dedicated to my children
Heather and Blake,
whom I love very much.

Love has no reason.
Love just is.

1

Montana Territory
1868

"Fight! Fight! It's the doc's brat, Patch! She's whompin' the tar outta the preacher's middle boy!"

Fort Benton's rowdiest saloon cleared like a bedroll with a rattler in it. Miners, bullwhackers, and freightmen raced onto the muddy street to surround the two fighting children.

A ragamuffin twelve-year-old girl had a knee braced on the nape of a ruddy-faced boy. She held his arm twisted high behind his back. Her elfin features contorted as she raged, "You take that back, you varmint! Dang you for a durned pig-faced—"

"I won't take it back, 'cause it's true!" the boy bellowed. "Your pa's a yellow-bellied, lily-livered—"

That was as far as he got before Patch put

the full weight of her knee on his neck, shoving his mouth down and filling it with mud.

A pair of large hands caught Patch by her frayed collar and the seat of her britches, lifting her into the air. "That'll be enough of that, you runty little scapegrace."

The crowd laughed as Patch flailed ineffectually against the rough hands that had separated her from her victim. The preacher's middle boy quickly made his escape between a pair of legs at the edge of the circle of men.

Patch sputtered with fury at her helplessness. "I'll get you, Ferdie Adams! You better watch out you—you—"

"What's this all about?"

Patch looked over her shoulder to see who had hold of her. It was Red Dupree, the bartender at the Medicine Bow Saloon. Red must have had hair that color once upon a time, but now Patch winced at the sun's glare off his bald head. He was a huge, intimidating man, and Patch stopped struggling and hung limp in his grasp.

Nevertheless, she wasn't going to admit in front of all these leering, spite-faced men that she had been defending her pa's honor, because he couldn't—wouldn't—do it for himself. Her lips clamped tight, and her chin took on a mulish tilt.

Red sighed in disgust. "Let's go find your pa."

"Doc Kendrick's takin' care of some men got shot by Injuns," someone shouted from the crowd. "Down to the stage depot."

"Don't be too hard on her, Red," a bearded man said. "Kid's got guts—more'n her pa, anyway," he added with a snicker.

Patch stiffened in Red's arms.

Contemplating another attack from the feisty minx, Red tightened his hold. "Hold fast, young'n," he said in a quiet voice. "Don't take it so personal, what they say."

"But my pa ain't what they say," Patch gritted out through a throat swollen with hurt. "He ain't!"

Out west a man was judged by whether he stood up to those who challenged him or backed off. Doc Kendrick would as soon step aside as fight. Patch knew her father wasn't afraid, but she had no explanation for why he wouldn't raise his fists to another man or even carry a gun. So she had taken to fighting his battles for him.

People in Fort Benton knew better than to say a thing against Doc Kendrick. If they did, it was likely their horse might find its tail-hairs cropped, or their zinnias might start looking stark naked, or they might just find themselves locked in the outhouse. Patch had determined to be as ruthless as her father was mild-mannered. No one was going to say a word against her pa without answering to her.

She tried once again to tear herself from Red's hold. "There's no need to bother my pa."

"Sorry, kid, but this is the third time this week I've had to rescue some poor—"

"Dang it, Red! Didn't hit no one that didn't deserve it!" Patch argued.

Red surveyed the bruised swelling around Patch's right eye. "What was it this time?"

"He had no right to say what he did. My pa's the bravest, strongest—just 'cause he don't carry a gun don't mean he's a . . . a . . ." Patch couldn't say the word aloud, but it echoed in her head.

Coward.

Red snorted. "Can't fight the whole damn town, Patch."

"The whole dang town, the whole durned country if I have to. I—"

Patch shut her mouth as they entered the open-sided tent where her father was hard at work removing a bullet from the fleshy part of a man's calf. The wounded man was lying on a makeshift table created from two sawhorses and a few planks of raw lumber. A second man stood nearby, his arm already resting in a sling. A crowd of freightmen had gathered around to observe the doctor's ministrations.

"Took my whole poke of gold, them Injuns did," the man on the table said to the crowd that surrounded him. "Weren't more'n twenty mile south o' here when the stage was surrounded by shriekin' redskins."

"We'da been stone cold dead right now, if it hadna been for that masked fella," the man with the sling said.

Patch couldn't keep still. "Garn! Was it the Masked Marauder?" she asked in an awed voice. "Was it?"

" 'Spect so. Bravest thing I ever saw, how he rode up on that big black horse of his'n and started shooting from them twin pistols. Never missed a shot, that Marauder fella," the miner with the sling said.

"Was he wearing a black mask?" Patch asked. "Was he?"

"Sure 'nuff was, kid," the miner said. "With his black hat pulled down low, couldn't tell who it was for beans."

"But he must live around here somewhere," Patch guessed. " 'Cause he always arrives in the nick of time. Garn! I wonder who it is?"

The men looked around at each other. The identity of the Masked Marauder had become a burning question in Fort Benton. The man seemed to know whenever some gold-dust miner on the stage was about to be robbed and rode to the rescue with guns blazing. For some reason he had decided to remain anonymous. Over the past six months he must have rescued at least a dozen miners from Blackfoot renegades intent on relieving the men of their gold, which the Indians then traded for rotgut whiskey.

Patch looked at her father, his tall, broad-shouldered form stooped over the injured man. She wished he could be more like the Masked Marauder, brave and dashing and admired. She imagined he *was* the Masked Marauder. But her delightful imaginary bubble didn't last long before it burst.

"Say, Doc," one of the freightmen said. "These fellas here have offered a reward to anybody who can get their gold back. We're formin' up a posse to hunt down them Blackfeet. You wanta come along?"

Seth Kendrick's lips curved in a smile of self-mockery as he said, "I wouldn't be much use to you men. I'm not a good hand with firearms. Besides, I've got to be around to check on Mrs. Gulliver. Her bowels are acting up again."

There were several guffaws and a chuckle or two. While the laughter might have been directed at Mrs. Gulliver's uneasy bowels, Patch couldn't help feeling it was aimed at her father's feeble excuse for avoiding the danger of riding out with the other men. Why, oh why, couldn't he go with them just this once? Why couldn't he prove to them once and for all that he wasn't a—

Coward.

Patch mentally backed away from the word and in so doing inadvertently jerked in Red Dupree's grasp.

"Whoa, there, kid," Red admonished. "Your pa's about done. Once he's free—"

"I'm free right now, Red," Seth said. "You can let her go. Thanks. I'll handle things from here."

"You better, Doc," Red warned with a growl that was more bark than bite. "The kid cleans out the saloon every time she starts one of them fracases."

"It won't happen again, Red. I appreciate you taking care of my girl."

Seth laid a hand on Patch's shoulder and felt her flinch beneath his touch. He didn't want to start an argument with so many interested ears listening, so he let her go on the pretext of needing to pack up his medical supplies. He avoided his daughter's eyes as he closed up his black bag and left the tent. Patch followed him, feet dragging, as he returned to where he'd left his buggy.

"Get in," he said. "We'll talk later."

Patch climbed up to sit beside him on the cracked leather seat. Seth whipped the big buckskin gelding into a trot, then headed south toward the ranch he and Patch had called home for the past two years.

In the distance they could see the Highwood Mountains, an isolated range about thirty miles long. There, in the foothills about twelve miles from town, his ranch was nestled in a stand of cottonwoods along the river.

Seth spent the better part of the trip home staring at his hands. They weren't the hands of a doctor. They were big and callused and scarred from the calamitous events of long ago that had molded him into the man he was today.

Seth knew what was said about him in town. He had his suspicions about why Patch got into so many fights. He wanted to explain everything to her, to make her understand why he chose to walk away rather than to face down another man. But he couldn't. All the same, her fighting had to stop.

Seth wasn't sure how to confront his daughter. It seemed lately he couldn't talk to her without setting up her neckhairs. She was growing up. Soon Patricia Wallis Kendrick would be a woman. Only, at the rate she was going, Patch Kendrick—hoyden, tomboy, pugnacious brat—would be no lady.

The frustration Seth felt made his voice harsh when he spoke. "I thought we agreed you weren't going to fight anymore. What was it this time?"

Patch's lower lip stuck out in a stubborn pout. With the black eye rapidly forcing her right eye shut, it would have been difficult to argue that she hadn't been fighting. Nor could she admit to her father the real reasons she had attacked the preacher's middle boy. So she improvised. "That Ferdie Adams called me a flibbertigibbet, Pa. I couldn't let him get away with that."

"You know, Patch," he began, "the things people say—the words they use—can't hurt you."

"But, Pa! How can you stand it when somebody calls you a—a—bad name?"

There was a long pause before he said,

"Words aren't worth fighting over, Patch." He took another, even longer pause before he added, "When you're older, when you've seen a little more of life, you'll understand why—"

"I don't understand!" Patch cried in an anguished voice. "And I won't stand for it!"

Seth stopped the buggy abruptly and turned to grab his daughter by the shoulders. He shook her until her blond hair tumbled over her brow and hid her eyes. "Listen to me," he said in a hard voice. "This fighting has got to stop. You're getting too old to be wrestling with boys in the mud, coming home with black eyes and torn clothes."

He felt a band tighten around his chest at the sight of his daughter's quivering chin. Patch was blinking furiously to stem tears. As abruptly as he had grabbed her, he released her. With a shaking hand he reached out to straighten the bunched material at her shoulder.

Patch shoved his hand aside and straightened the shirt herself, clamping down on her teeth to still her chin. "Garn, Pa—"

"And that's another thing," he interrupted, both frustrated by and furious at her refusal to allow him to express the tenderness he felt for her. "I've heard about all the *garns* and *dangs* and *durns* I want to hear from you.

You have to start acting like a lady, Patch. You have to—"

"I ain't never gonna be a lady, Pa!"

Seth opened his mouth to contradict his daughter but snapped it shut again. No, not at the rate she was going. Didn't she want to be a lady? Another look revealed that it was despair rather than defiance he saw in his daughter's wretched blue eyes.

He wanted to pull her into his arms and hug her tight and tell her they would work things out. But he didn't think he could stand it if she pushed him away, as he was certain she would. So he sat without touching her and saw her back stiffen with resolve. No coward, his Patch. She had enough courage for both of them.

"You need a mother, Patch," he murmured. "A woman to show you how to be a lady. To comb this mop of hair"—he ruffled her tangled blond hair, which was as close to a caress as she was likely to allow, and tucked it behind a dirty ear—"to sew dresses for you, to teach you to cook and how to act."

"Dang it! We don't need anyone, Pa," Patch protested. "We manage fine by ourselves."

Seth didn't argue, just picked up the reins and started the buggy homeward again. He pictured the disorder that reigned at the

ranch house they called home. The barren
windows and walls, the dirty dishes stacked
in the sink, the laundry that grew in piles until Patch finally gathered it all up and boiled
it for an hour with homemade lye soap. She
was too young to have the kind of responsibility that had necessarily fallen on her
shoulders in a bachelor household.

But Seth had never been able to bring himself to marry again. He had loved Patch's
mother in a way he could never love another
woman. Nine years after Annarose's death,
his memories of her were as vivid as ever. He
was yanked from his reverie by an outburst
from Patch.

"Garn!" she exclaimed. "Why on earth do
you need a wife, Pa? Haven't I done a good
job of taking care of things? Maybe I ain't
such a good cook, but we haven't starved,
have we? The ranch house is a little messy,
but so what? We're hardly ever there. And
maybe I do dress in trousers, but with the
mud in town, a dress wouldn't be the least bit
practical. And I know ding-dang well you see
Dora at the Medicine Bow Saloon to satisfy
your manly lusts.

"See, Pa, you don't need a wife. And I don't
need a mother," she added in case he had
missed the point she really wanted to make.

Seth was appalled at Patch's knowledge of his visits to Dora Deveraux. He hadn't imagined she understood enough about what happened between men and women to even suspect what he was doing when he disappeared into town on Saturday nights. Which only served to convince him that something had to be done, and soon, or Patch would be lost beyond redemption.

Only, finding a wife wasn't as simple as it sounded. Not many respectable unmarried women traveled up the Missouri River on their own. Whenever one showed her face in Fort Benton, she was as popular as licorice at the mercantile store. Seth ought to know. He had advertised in the St. Louis paper three times in the past two years for a nurse to work with him. Each time, the woman had come up the river by steamboat and ended up being courted and married within a week of her arrival.

So why don't you advertise for another nurse, and when she arrives here, court her and marry her yourself?

Seth had no time to examine that astounding idea because they had arrived at the ranch. Patch bolted out of the buggy and raced toward the man who stood beside the corral.

"Ethan!" she yelled at the top of her lungs. "We're home!"

As if Ethan hadn't seen them driving up the road, Seth thought. He felt that constriction in his chest again as Patch allowed Ethan a quick hug of welcome. Seth quickly repressed the unwanted jab of jealousy. Ethan Hawk was his best friend and for the past six months had been his partner. Still, it hurt to see the way Patch smiled at the younger man as though he hung the moon. That sort of smile ought to be reserved for a girl's father —at least until she found a husband.

As Seth stepped down from the buggy, Ethan started toward him with Patch tucked under his arm and her arm firmly around his waist. They made slow progress because of Ethan's limp, and Seth met them more than halfway. Ethan's walk—long step, halting step, long step, halting step—was ungainly. But put him on a horse, and the man had all the grace of a centaur. Seth couldn't be sorry for Ethan's limp, tragic as it was, because it had been the cause of their meeting each other and the beginning of their friendship.

"The Masked Marauder has been at work again," Seth said. "He saved the bacon for a couple of miners on the stage from Virginia City."

"Oh, Ethan, can you just imagine it?" Patch asked in the reverent voice she reserved for anything having to do with the Masked Marauder. "Imagine him dressed all in black, mounted on his black stallion and riding to the rescue. Oh, how I wish I could meet him just once!"

"I trust you won't need rescuing anytime soon, little one," Ethan replied with a grin.

"Well, of course not," Patch retorted, pulling herself from his side. "You know I can take care of myself."

"Of course you can," Ethan agreed. "But there are some chickens out behind the house that can't. So how about spreading some feed for them?"

Patch grimaced. "Dang, I forgot. Sorry, Ethan. I'll do it right away."

Seth stared after his daughter, marveling at how quickly she had obeyed Ethan, and he fought another stab of jealousy.

"Anybody seriously hurt in the raid?" Ethan asked.

"A bullet in one miner's arm and in another's leg."

"You'd think the stage line would have heard enough about the renegade Indians around here to put another shotgun rider or two on board," Ethan said.

"There's an easier solution to the problem," Seth said.

"Which is?"

"Put Drake Bassett out of the illegal whiskey–selling business. If there's none of that coffin varnish available to buy, the Indians won't have any use for the gold they're stealing. And the raids on the stage will stop."

Drake Bassett owned the Medicine Bow Saloon, but he spent most of his time at his office in one of the several warehouses he owned along the levee. To all appearances, he was an honest businessman. It was through Dora Deveraux that Seth had learned about Drake's connection to the illegal whiskey-selling operation that was causing so much trouble.

"Unfortunately, to get to Bassett, you have to go through Pike Hardesty," Ethan pointed out.

There was a moment when neither man said anything. They were both thinking of the man Ethan had named. A gunfighter and a bully, Pike Hardesty was mean as a rattlesnake on a hot skillet. Thanks to Pike, there was no longer any law in Fort Benton to speak of. He had shot the sheriff in a supposedly fair fight eight months ago. Now the only restraint on Pike's viciousness was

Drake Bassett, a man without morals himself.

"I could take care of Pike," Ethan said.

"No."

"It would solve a lot of problems."

"No," Seth repeated. "The Masked Marauder seems to have everything well in hand. If the Blackfeet are unsuccessful in their raids, they won't have any gold. And without gold they won't be able to buy that tarantula juice Bassett is pawning off as whiskey."

They had wandered back over to the corral that held the few mustangs that remained to be gentled and delivered to the army at Fort Shaw.

Ethan braced his boot on the bottom rail of the corral and said, "I notice Patch is sporting another black eye."

Seth's gray eyes turned bleak. "I'm at my wit's end, Ethan. I've tried everything I can think of to keep her from fighting. I don't know what else to do."

"You could tell her the truth," Ethan said in a quiet voice.

Seth faced the younger man. Ethan had sandy brown hair that had bleached in the sun, green eyes above a straight nose, and a wide, full mouth. He should have looked as young as his twenty-five years. But there were hard edges to Ethan's face; lines bracketed his mouth, and those piercing green eyes had seen sorrow and disillusion and disappointment. Ethan was nearly as tall as Seth, but Ethan's shoulders weren't quite so broad, and he was lean and wiry, where Seth was all muscle and sinew.

Seth stuck his hands in his pockets. "You know I can't tell her anything," he said. "She wouldn't understand."

"I think you underestimate Patch," Ethan countered. "She's got a good head on her shoulders. She could handle it."

"No," Seth said. "She's got enough worries as it is, without adding any more. In fact, she's got way too heavy a burden for any kid to carry. She needs a mother, Ethan," Seth admitted with a sigh.

"That would mean you'd have to take a wife," Ethan said. "After Annarose . . . I didn't think you wanted to marry again."

"I don't," Seth said flatly. When Annarose died, he had felt grief so strong it had made him want to die too. For a while he had tried very hard to get himself killed. Then Ethan had come along and convinced him he had to live for his daughter's sake. Seth had been forced to build a stone wall around his heart to protect himself from the pain of living without Annarose. Over the years, his vivid memories of her had forced him to keep the wall strong. There was no way feelings of love for anyone besides his daughter could breach that barrier.

Nonetheless, Seth told Ethan, "I may not want to marry, but I think I need a wife—for Patch's sake."

"All right. Let's say Patch needs a mother. Let's say you need a wife. Where do you propose to find a woman to fill that role?" Ethan asked.

"I've decided to advertise for a mail-order bride in the St. Louis papers," Seth answered.

Ethan turned to stare at his friend. "You're joking."

"I'm perfectly serious. Patch needs the influence of a woman who can turn her into a young lady."

"Is that really fair to a woman, to marry her just so she can be a mother to your daughter?"

"I'd be giving her a home, feeding her, and clothing her. That sounds like a pretty fair trade to me," Seth argued. "My face wouldn't be so bad to stare at across the breakfast table." He cocked a brow and said, "A woman could do a lot worse."

Ethan smiled crookedly. "Yeah, I suppose so. What about . . . the personal side of things."

There was a pause before Seth answered, "I've got Dora. I don't need a wife for that." He took off his hat and thrust a hand through his hair in a gesture that betrayed his uncertain feelings about what he was contemplating.

"If you're bound and determined on this course, I have a suggestion," Ethan said. He waited for Seth to nod before he continued, "Put your advertisement in the papers back east."

Ethan didn't allow Seth to voice an objection, just kept right on talking. "Think about it," he urged. "You're a lot more likely to get a 'lady' if you advertise where there are a lot of them. By the time a woman's spent any time at all in St. Louis, the 'lady' gets ironed right out of her. You ought to put an ad in the Boston and New York and Philadelphia papers."

Seth pursed his lips in thought, then stroked his chin, feeling the two days' growth of whiskers. Having a "lady" for a wife was going to mean a lot of changes for him too. He wouldn't be marrying at all if it weren't for Patch. But for his daughter, he would make any sacrifice.

"All right," Seth agreed gruffly. "I'll take your advice. But just in case no one wants to travel that far, I'm going to put an ad in the St. Louis paper as well."

He was distracted by the sound of chickens squawking noisily. "What the devil?"

"Pa! Ethan!" Patch shouted. "Come quick!"

The two men raced toward the frantic cry that had come from behind the house. Ethan was slowed by his gait. Seth rounded the corner ahead of him, all his senses alert, ready to protect and defend his daughter. He stumbled to a halt when he saw her. Patch stood before him covered with a dusting of chicken feathers and grinning from ear to ear. Dangling by the neck in her outstretched hands was the obvious reason for the ruckus in the henhouse.

"I caught him, Pa!" she crowed with glee. "The raccoon that's been stealing our eggs! You can see he's still just a baby. Can I keep him, Pa? Can I?"

Seth didn't know whether to laugh or cry. Would anyone be able to turn his darling, adorable hoyden into a young lady? He opened his mouth to say yes to keeping the raccoon and snapped it shut again. Whoever heard of a young lady with a pet raccoon?

But he didn't have a wife yet, and he didn't have the heart to disappoint his daughter. "Sure," he agreed with a grin. "If you keep him fed, maybe I'll be able to have eggs for breakfast again."

"Oh, thank you, Pa!" Patch cried. "I'll just take him inside now and make him a bed."

Seth lifted a hand to say a raccoon didn't belong in the house, but she was gone before he could speak. He grimaced. Besides, the inside of the house, unfortunately, was eminently fit for raccoons. In that instant, whatever reservations he'd had about marrying simply to have a mother for Patch were put to rest.

At the same moment Seth reached that resolve, Ethan rounded the corner of the house and joined him.

"I saw the raccoon," Ethan said with a grin. "Looks like Patch has a new pet to add to her collection."

"At least for a while," Seth said.

"Surely you aren't going to make her get rid of it," Ethan protested. "Did you see her face? She's already in love with the poor thing."

"I'm not going to do anything," Seth said. "But I can't speak for the woman who'll be my wife." Seth's eyes turned flinty. But as he began mentally composing the advertisement for a mail-order bride, he added the words: *"Must like animals."*

2

"What are you doing, Mama?"

"I'm writing a letter."

"To Da?"

"No, sweetheart. Da is in heaven. This is a letter to a man in Montana named Seth Kendrick." Molly Gallagher set down her pen and pulled her four-year-old daughter into her lap. Nessie had lost the plump limbs and cherubic face common to all babies and was showing signs of the person she would become. Her brown eyes were still huge, but her nose had lengthened and straightened. Round cheeks had thinned to reveal the same strong Irish bones Molly possessed and a pair of charming dimples. Her chin was already a bit pointed, like her da's had been.

The little girl reached for the half-finished letter on the desk. She held it out in front of her with both hands, as though she could read the slanted script. "What does it say, Mama?"

"I'm telling Mr. Kendrick a little bit about myself."

"Why?"

"Because he wants to marry me."

"Why?"

Molly thought for a moment. What could compel a man to be willing to marry a woman sight unseen? He had given reasons; these she gave to Nessie. "He says he needs a lady to keep house for him and a nurse to help him do his work. He's a doctor, you see."

"You nursed Aunt Hattie."

"Yes, I did."

"But Aunt Hattie went to heaven. Like Da."

Molly sighed. "Yes, darling. Just like Da." It was the death of James's aunt that had caused the crisis in which she now found herself.

Molly had come to live with Aunt Hattie when she'd received word that her husband's whaling ship had been crushed in the northern ice and been sunk with all hands. James had already been gone to sea for nearly two years, and Molly had been living on the expectation of his share of the whaling catch. When word came that her husband had drowned, the mortgage holder had given her a week to vacate the home in which she lived with Nessie and her ten-year-old son, Whit.

Aunt Hattie's grand old New Bedford cottage, with its ladder leading through a trap door in the roof to the widow's walk, had been a refuge in a very bad storm. Molly had spent hours pacing the rectangular railed platform, coming to terms with her grief. She had looked out over the lonely sea and wondered . . . and wished . . . and worried.

Now, barely a year later, Aunt Hattie was dead, and James's cousin Rupert had inherited everything. Just as the crocuses were blooming, Rupert had written to say he had sold Aunt Hattie's house. Molly and her children now had to vacate the cottage by the first of June.

Cousin Rupert hadn't left her totally without recourse. He had offered her the opportunity to move in and be a companion to his mother in a small house on the outskirts of New Bedford. Living as Sadie Gallagher's companion would be a step up from the poorhouse, but it was not a choice Molly would have made for herself.

Molly hadn't minded nursing Aunt Hattie because she had truly loved the old woman. But Rupert's mother was another matter altogether. Sadie Gallagher was the worst sort of harridan, and the old woman didn't much care for children.

Thus, Rupert's ultimatum had left Molly feeling panic-stricken. James had been a good whaler, and a wonderful husband and father. But two of his three whaling ships had been sunk by the rebel cruiser *Alabama* during the war. That financial loss had been compounded by the increasing use of fuel substitutes for whale oil, causing a drop in the price of each hard-won barrel. They had continued to live well, but it had taken a toll on their savings. When Aunt Hattie died, Molly had finally realized how very little she had been left with at James's death.

Alone, she would have managed somehow. But Whit was ten, and already growing tall like James. His wrists and ankles seemed to sprout from his clothes. As for Nessie, Molly dreaded the thought of her four-year-old being regularly hushed to accommodate a crotchety old woman.

So on the day Molly got Rupert's letter, the words BRIDE WANTED had fairly leaped at her from the month-old Boston newspaper. She had carefully unwrapped the dampened paper from around the codfish she had bought for supper and read the rest. The ad was short and to the point.

BRIDE WANTED. Thirty-five-year-old doctor
seeks educated woman to work as nurse and
manage household. Must be lady of good
character. Also must like animals. Reply to
S.K. General Delivery Fort Benton, Montana.

It had taken her a while to find Fort Benton on the atlas she had used to track James's
whaling adventures. It seemed like the other
side of the world. Because she'd had nothing
to lose, Molly had immediately sat down to
compose a letter to the mysterious S.K. And
because she didn't think it would ever come
to anything, she hadn't mentioned the existence of Whit and Nessie.

Molly had been sure the doctor would have
so many replies that hers would be lost in the
confusion. She had been surprised, if not
pleased, when he responded.

Dear Miss Gallagher,
I'm a country doctor and live a very simple
life. It's good to hear you have nursing experience. That will be important here, where a
real nurse is desperately needed. My home is
a sturdy pine structure suited to the harsh
elements. It is set along a creek bordered by
cottonwoods.
    Out here, the sky is endless and the
prairies roll on until they meet the moun-

tains to the south. No one who sees this part of Montana can deny its beauty.

However, it's frigid in winter, scorching in summer, and the wind almost always blows.

It can be a lonely place.

You asked me to say a bit about myself. I try to be patient and understand the other fellow's point of view. Mostly, I succeed.

I can offer you my name and my protection. That may not sound like much. But out here, where there isn't much law and order, it's a lot.

> Your servant,
> Seth Kendrick

Molly had been disappointed that there wasn't a single word in the letter describing his appearance. She tried to imagine any man being as handsome as James and failed. But then, she wouldn't be marrying the mysterious S.K. for his good looks.

She felt a little guilty that her "nursing experience" amounted to no more than putting a cool cloth on Aunt Hattie's brow until she died of old age. But she didn't correct Seth Kendrick's mistaken impression when she wrote to him a second time. Instead, she explained that she was a widow, that she had loved James with her whole heart and soul, and that she didn't expect to find love in a second marriage. Molly also wrote that Montana sounded beautiful and that someday she would love to see it. For reasons she didn't wish to examine too closely, Molly still made no mention of Whit or Nessie.

Seth Kendrick's second letter intrigued her.

Dear Mrs. Gallagher,

I must say I was relieved to read from your most recent letter that you do not expect love as part of the bargain. I, too, am a widower, so I can very much understand your feelings. My heart isn't free either.

Will you marry me?

Your servant,
Seth Kendrick

P. S. Directions to Fort Benton are enclosed.

Molly had been composing her response to the Montana doctor's proposal when Nessie interrupted her. She still hadn't made up her mind what her answer would be. Over the months they had corresponded, the spring sun had done its work, turning New Bedford into a warm place full of color. Yellow lilies and orange poppies. Buttercups and violets. Always, everywhere, defiant clumps of dandelions. The wind-tossed sea provided brilliant blues and greens or stormy grays, depending on the weather. How could she even think of leaving it all behind? But the June day when she would be forced to leave Aunt Hattie's cottage was inexorably coming. She must move somewhere—and soon.

Molly wished she were daring enough to accept Doctor Kendrick's offer and go all the way to Montana to become his wife. But she had never been beyond the boundaries of Massachusetts in her life. She hadn't the courage to go haring off halfway across the country on a whim.

Maybe that was why she had fallen in love with a rough-and-tumble whaling man like James. Molly had seen the world through her husband's eyes as he sailed the seas. She had vicariously lived his adventures in the marvelous ports where his whaling vessel called. It had always been enough for her. But now James was dead. Any adventures she had in the future would have to be her own.

"Are we going to Montana?"

Nessie's question snapped Molly from her reverie and forced her to focus on the decision she knew must be made. She wanted to throw caution to the winds and say yes. But the words just wouldn't come. "I don't think so, Nessie."

"Good," Nessie said. "I don't want to go away. If we go away, Da won't know where we are. He won't be able to find us when he comes home."

Molly hugged her daughter tight. If she said nothing, Nessie would eventually realize that her father wasn't ever coming back. But that seemed more cruel than forcing Nessie, even as young as she was, to face the truth. So Molly said, "Do you remember how I explained that Da died and went to heaven?"

"Yes."

"Heaven is a wonderful place, Nessie, but when you go there, you can't ever come back. But Da can see us, and no matter where we go, he'll know where we are. And he'll watch over us from above."

Nessie's tiny brow furrowed. "Are you sure?"

Molly brushed the soft bangs away from Nessie's troubled brown eyes. "I'm very sure."

Nessie's face crumpled. "I want my da!" she cried. "Why doesn't he come home?"

Molly held Nessie and comforted her as best she could. But the little girl was inconsolable. Her tiny fists tightened in a death grip on Molly's dress as sobs wracked her body. Molly fought the welling emotion in her throat. She wasn't going to cry. She had done all her crying months ago, and tears hadn't changed anything. But still, one slid past her guard and fell in a hot stream down her cheek. And then another. Molly squeezed her eyes shut and buried her face in Nessie's silky black hair.

Molly sat in the growing darkness holding Nessie until the little girl finally cried herself to sleep. Molly was startled when she finally lifted her head to find her son standing by the parlor door staring at her.

"I was looking for you earlier," Molly said. "Where were you?"

"Down to the wharf," Whit answered. "The *Mary Lee* is taking on provisions for another whaling voyage."

A shiver raced down Molly's spine. The *Mary Lee* was the whaling vessel that had seen James's ship go down. Roger Sturgis, the captain of the *Mary Lee*, had been James's best friend. Molly felt queasy at the thought that someday Whit would want to go to sea and be a whaler like his father. She leaned back in the captain's chair in which she sat and arranged Nessie more comfortably in her lap, tucking the little girl's head under her chin.

"Did you say hello to Captain Sturgis?" Molly asked.

Whit's gray-green eyes sought out the seams in the planked wooden floor. "I did."

"What did he have to say?"

Whit's whole attention focused on the toe of his shoe, which he was trying to fit into a knothole one-tenth its size. "Not much. Only that the *Mary Lee* is ready to sail on the morrow."

Molly shook her head and smiled faintly. "He never was a talkative man, as I remember. Well, dinner will be ready soon. Go wash up."

Whit seemed reluctant to go. He stood there a moment longer, opened his mouth, shut it, then backed his way out of the room.

Molly had never understood the attraction of any man for the sea. The sea was so unforgiving, and it took as often as it gave. She had already tried to interest Whit in some other occupation than whaling, but so far, without much luck. She took comfort in the fact that Whit was an obedient child; she only hoped she could lead him away from a life on the sea.

Dinner was a quiet affair. Whit said few words. Nessie said nothing. Molly was too absorbed in her own thoughts to notice. She put Nessie down to bed right after they had finished eating and soon after came to help Whit get settled for the night.

When James was alive—and at home—he had helped Whit at bedtime while she took care of Nessie. Then they had changed places for a last good-night kiss. Now Whit depended on her to follow James's ritual. Molly wasn't James, and she couldn't ever take his place. But because she understood Whit's loss, she did as her son asked and ignored her own feelings of awkwardness.

She sat down beside Whit, gave him a quick hug, then helped him scoot down under the covers. She began firmly tucking the wool blanket around him, following the shape of his lanky frame down one side, as he had told her James used to do.

Molly was tucking her way up the other side when Whit stopped her. "Wait," he said. "You forgot to do my toes."

"What?"

"Da always used to go around my toes."

Molly took a deep breath and bit down on the cry that sought voice. *I am not your father. Your father is dead!* Instead, she forced a smile and tucked down Whit's side again and around his toes and back up the other side.

"Thanks, Mother," Whit said. "That was almost as good as Da."

Almost as good. Molly leaned over and kissed her son on the forehead. The ceremony was done. Not as good as Da. Not perfect. But all either of them had. And a constant painful reminder to both of them of all they had lost.

"Good night, Whit. I love you."

"I love you, too, Mother. Remember that. Whatever happens."

Molly frowned. She opened her mouth to ask what Whit meant, but he turned and tugged the covers up over his shoulder—in complete disregard of all those careful tucks —and said, "Good night, Mother."

She blew out the lantern and left the room to seek out her own bed. She could finish the letter to Seth Kendrick in the morning.

But in the morning, her son was gone. All Molly found was a note on Whit's pillow.

Dearest Mother,

I'm to be cabin boy for the *Mary Lee.* Please understand that I have to go. Da would expect it of me. I'm the man of the house now. I shall bring home my share of the whaler's catch to provide for you and Nessie. You don't have to cry anymore.

Your loving son,
Whit

Molly raced for the wharf that cloudy spring morning with her heart in her throat. She couldn't seem to catch her breath and held a fisted hand against the agonizing stitch in her side nearly the whole way. She half-laughed, half-cried in relief when she reached the wharf and saw the *Mary Lee* had not set sail. From the activity on deck, it appeared she didn't have much time to find her son.

"Hold! Please, hold!" she cried as she stumbled up the gangplank.

"Hey! You, there! No women on board ship!" a sailor cried, reaching out to stop her. "It's bad luck!"

She eluded him, shouting at the top of her lungs, "Whit! Whit! Where are you? Please, don't do this!"

A superstitious lot, the sailors turned ugly. The intruding woman might prove an ill omen for their entire whaling voyage. The men on deck formed a menacing circle to keep her from stepping farther into their domain.

Molly perched her fists on her hips and tipped her chin in the air. Her long black hair whipped in the brisk wind. "I'm not leaving without my son. Now please find him and bring him to me."

"Here, now. What's the trouble?" Captain Sturgis wasn't happy about being called on deck by the first mate to settle a disturbance. He couldn't believe his eyes when he sighted Molly Gallagher.

"Why, what's this, Molly? What are you doing here?"

Molly let out a heartfelt sigh of relief when she saw the friendly face before her. "It's Whit," she explained. "He's signed on as your cabin boy."

"Yes, I know," he said.

She waited for him to say more, but with dawning horror realized that James's friend approved of having her son on board his ship. "You can't take him," she said, her voice sharpened by anxiety. "I won't let you."

"The boy wants to go, Molly," the captain said. "You can't keep him a child forever."

"I don't intend to!" Molly retorted. "But I'll not lose another of mine to the sea. So bring him here, and I'll take him home."

"He wants to go," the captain said.

"I don't care what he wants," she snapped back. "I'm his mother. He'll do as I say."

Captain Sturgis turned to a nearby sailor. "Tell Whit Gallagher I want to see him on deck."

Molly's heart lifted when her son appeared. But from the defiant look in Whit's eyes, it was clear he wouldn't come of his own accord. She turned to the captain, her feelings bared for him to see. She said only, "Please, Roger."

"Come here, Whit," the captain said.

The tall, reed-thin boy obeyed immediately. The brisk sea wind ruffled the boy's collar-length black hair as he stepped forward. His fisted hands were hidden deep in his pockets.

"Your mother does not wish you to go, lad."

"I am the man now, sir," Whit replied. "I must earn a living for my family."

"No!" Molly said. When they looked at her she added, "It's not necessary. I've found a way to take care of us."

"Oh?" The captain arched a questioning brow.

Molly swallowed hard and said, "I'm going to be married again. To a man in Montana. That is why Whit must come with me *now*.

There'll be no one for him to come home to when you return in three or four years." Her throat had tightened so much in fear that the last few words came out in a raspy whisper.

"I see," the captain said. "Well then, lad, I think you had best go with your mother."

"But, sir—"

"I am the captain, lad. You will obey my order."

A flush began at Whit's neck and worked its way up to pinken his fair-skinned face. It was the only visible sign of his distress as he answered, "Yes, sir."

Molly reached out to put a hand on her son's shoulder, but he jerked away and started down the gangplank without a word to her.

"Thank you, Roger," she said to the captain. "Thank you for my son." She rushed after Whit.

The sun had come out, but the narrow streets of New Bedford did not feel it. The warmth was held at bay by giant oaks and hickory, bushy elms and pointy-leafed maples.

They had traveled more than halfway home before Molly finally caught up to her son. When she touched Whit's shoulder, he whirled on her. In his face was all the agony of humiliation and embarrassment a ten-year-old boy can feel when he is trying to act as a man before men, and his mother treats him as a child.

"I'll just find another ship," he said, his face flushed, his sea-green eyes bright with unshed tears. "Next time I won't leave you a note. Next time I won't give you a chance to stop me."

"Whit, I—"

"How could you lie like that?" he demanded. "Captain Sturgis would never have put me off the ship if you hadn't told that made-up story! There is no man to marry in Montana, is there? I mean, there couldn't be. You would never force us all to go so far from New Bedford—so far from the sea. Would you?"

Molly didn't know which accusation to answer first. But the thought of Whit running away again—and he could easily manage it with the number of whaling ships that would be leaving New Bedford over the next few weeks—made it clear what she must do. She struggled for the words to explain her decision to her son.

"It's true, Whit. I am to be married again. For the past several months I've been corresponding with a man in Montana who advertised in the paper for a mail-order bride."

"How could you do such a thing?"

"I don't know why I answered the ad. Yes, I do. I wanted something better for us. And Whit, he wrote me back, and he sounds like a very nice man. He's a country doctor and . . . in his most recent letter he asked me to come to Montana. He asked me to be his wife."

Whit was aghast. "You can't marry another man. Da is—Da is—"

"Dead." Molly spoke softly, but the word had a finality that was unassailable. She yearned to reach out and fold her son into her arms. But it was clear that even though he was a boy in years, he had a man's pride.

Whit scrubbed at his pooling eyes with the back of his hand. "You don't have to do it," he said. "I can earn a living for us."

"By going to sea? No, Whit, I shan't allow it. I've made up my mind. I'm going to marry him."

"You can't do it! You can't! Da is barely cold in his grave!" Whit whirled and fled toward home.

Whit's threat made it imperative that Molly act, and with all possible speed. Once her mind was made up, she didn't waste any time. A letter was posted that same day to Seth Kendrick, agreeing to marry him and promising that she would be heading west within the next several days.

Molly also wrote to Cousin Rupert saying she was "sorry not to be able to take him up on his kind offer."

Then she began packing. Among those items she couldn't bear to leave behind were her mother's rose-patterned china, a walrus tusk carved by the Esquimaux that James had brought home from a whaling trip to Point Barrow, and a ship in a bottle that James and Whit had made together the year James had been laid up at home with a broken leg—the year Nessie had been born. Last, but not least, was a painting of a sailor harpooning a bowhead whale amidst the icebergs of the Arctic. In the distance, a whaling ship—James's ship—was pictured in all its splendor.

All their warmest woolen clothes got packed, of course, since Doctor Kendrick had warned that Montana winters were harsh. She added a box of books—including an autographed volume by Massachusetts-born poet Emily Dickinson—because he had said the winters were lonely. Only they wouldn't be quite so lonely now, she supposed. Even less lonely than Doctor Kendrick expected, actually. Because he would be getting a little more family than he was counting on. An additional son and daughter, to be precise.

The three of them left New Bedford a mere two days later, during which time Whit was never out of her sight. The trip across country by train as far as St. Louis, and by steamboat from St. Louis up the Missouri River to Fort Benton, was as fascinating as it was frightening.

It wasn't so much the change in terrain that made Molly realize the momentousness of what she had done. Although the terrain did change tremendously. The lush, tree-laden hills in the east flattened out into grassy rolling prairies. More telling was the size and number of the towns they encountered. As they traveled farther west, the settlements became fewer and farther between and grew smaller. Finally, they were no more than mere whistle-stops for wood and water tended by a single man. That was when it dawned on Molly that she had left the civilized world behind and was heading into the wilderness.

They were in bustling St. Louis only a single day before the *Viola Belle* left on its journey up the Missouri. In contrast to the tiny Pullman sleeping car on the train, their accommodations on the steamboat more closely resembled those in a sumptuous hotel.

Molly had reserved one of the two staterooms aft, a spacious cabin with a four-poster bed, washstand, and built-in closet. A door with a curtained window in the upper half of it opened onto the deck, which ran completely around the boat.

They made about fifty miles the first day, at the end of which Molly saw her first Indian. He rode along the bank following the steamboat, practically naked on his pony. His posture was proud, erect—graceful and threatening at the same time. He was a Sioux, the captain told her, part of a tribe that expected them to be carrying flour and tobacco for tribute—tribute that wasn't on board. That night they anchored in midstream, and the captain left guards posted to keep a sharp lookout for attack.

Molly didn't close her eyes all night, terrified of being killed in her sleep. The next morning, the sun dawned bright and hot, and it was as though the threat had never existed. That day she saw her first herd of huge, shaggy buffalo, so vast they seemed to cover the entire prairie.

The places along the river had strange names—Rattlesnake Springs, Wolf Point, Alert Bend, Painted Woods, Devil's Race Ground, Mule's Head Landing, Osage Chute, Brickhouse Bend, Hole in the Wall, Elk Horn Prairie—all of which sounded as untamed as the land through which they traveled.

In the towns where they tied up at night, she met army wives who told of their loneliness. She saw it for herself when they steamed past log cabins where solitary women sat barefoot in rockers with children on their laps. Molly began to have an inkling of the immense difference in the life she and her children could expect to have on the frontier. As the unknown became known, her trepidation increased. In all-too-short a time, their journey was at an end.

Molly laid a hand across her brow to shield her eyes so she could better see the landing at Fort Benton. The town was easily visible from the upper deck of the steamboat *Viola Belle.*

It was situated on a flat piece of land right at the edge of the river. There were no docks, just a muddy bank leading down to the water, stacked high in places with machinery and other freight. A row of one- and two-story wooden buildings that appeared to be warehouses fronted the levee. Signs labeled some of the other buildings—Wells Fargo, Schmidt's Hotel, Carroll & Steell, North Western Fur, I. G. Baker & Co., and the Medicine Bow Saloon. At one end of town stood the crumbled adobe brick buildings that had been the original Fort Benton. Along the horizon, a butte rose about a hundred and fifty feet above the town and ran for several miles into the distance.

There were no bricked roads in the town, nor any sidewalks, nor even any grass that she could see. Just dirt. There was not a single tree, not one. The word that came to mind was *desolate*. But Molly shut out the stark picture before her. She denied the evidence of all those lonely miles she had traveled to arrive at this barren place. In her heart, she felt hope; in her mind, she saw a shiny new beginning.

"We're here, Mother! I can see the faces of the people waiting on the levee," Whit said.

Molly smiled at the excitement in her son's voice. It was the first emotion besides resentment or anger that she had heard him express during the entire trip from Massachusetts to Montana. She felt a tug on her skirt and reached down to lift her daughter into her arms. "We're here, Nessie," she said, playfully tugging one of the little girl's braids. "We've arrived at our new home. We'll start a new life here and put the past behind us."

The solemn-faced child said nothing. Ever since the night she had fallen asleep sobbing in Molly's arms, Nessie had been unnaturally silent. Molly had to believe that time and patience and love would restore the light to her daughter's once-laughing brown eyes.

"Be careful, Whit," Molly said. "Stand back from the rail. There's bound to be some jouncing when we tie up at the levee."

"Not nearly so much as on a real ship," her son responded with the disdain of a true sailor's son for a boat run by steam. Then, wistfully: "I should be cabin boy on a whaling vessel right now, Mother, if only . . ." His eyes narrowed as he turned back to gaze at the levee. "Do you think *he* is down there somewhere, waiting for us?"

Molly did not mistake the resentment in Whit's voice now, or the nervous pounding of her heart. Whit had made it clear he had no intention of liking, or even tolerating, the man she had come all this way to marry.

When the steamboat whistle blew their arrival, Whit headed on the run for the stairs.

"Wait for me on the main deck, Whit," Molly called after him. "Nessie and I will come down and join you as quickly as we can."

It wasn't that she thought Whit would purposely provoke a scene if he greeted Doctor Kendrick on his own. But it couldn't hurt if she was there by her son's side the first time the two males stood face to face.

Molly pulled Nessie close as the *Viola Belle* bumped against the levee at Fort Benton. Within moments she would be meeting the man with whom she had determined to spend the rest of her life. What would the kindly country doctor do when he realized she had not been entirely honest with him?

If he gave her a chance, she would explain everything. Molly thought of what her children had endured over the past year and vowed she would *make* him listen. Besides, the last of her savings had been spent getting here. She had no money to make the return trip.

There was little time to ponder her transgressions as the gangplank was lowered and people and cargo began moving from the main deck of the steamboat onto dry land.

Molly took her daughter's hand and led her downstairs to the main deck to join Whit.

"Can we go ashore now?" Whit asked.

"I wrote Doctor Kendrick that we would wait for him here."

Whit glowered and turned away to stare at the bustle of activity along the levee.

Molly set Nessie down, and the little girl grabbed hold of the narrow railing beside Whit and held on. "Be careful!" Molly cautioned. "Hang on tight so you don't fall in."

"I don't know why we had to come here," Whit complained. "It's dirty. And ugly. And there aren't even any trees. I hate it! And I hate him!"

"That will be enough of that, young man," Molly snapped. "Now stand there and be quiet. When Doctor Kendrick comes, I expect you to greet him politely. Do you understand me?"

Whit's sullen voice was barely respectful when he answered, "Yes, Mother."

Molly fought the nerves that had her hands trembling. Whit had clearly made up his mind that he was going to hate Seth Kendrick. Maybe she had been wrong. Maybe this wasn't the best choice after all. But it was too late now. In a matter of moments Doctor Seth Kendrick would be here to claim his mail-order bride—and her two children—from the main deck of the *Viola Belle*.

3

"Stay close, Patch," Seth admonished his daughter as they stepped onto the deck of the *Viola Belle*. "I want to introduce you to Mrs. Gallagher when I find her."

"I don't want to meet her, Pa."

Seth ushered Patch into a quiet corner where they could stand without being buffeted by the crowd. He put a forefinger under his daughter's chin and raised her eyes to meet his. "I want you to be on your best behavior today. We don't want to scare Mrs. Gallagher off before she even gets her feet on solid ground," he said with a smile. "I'm expecting you to make her feel welcome."

Patch's eyes flared with rebellion before her lids lowered, hiding her enmity for the dreaded Mrs. Gallagher.

But Seth didn't see. He was already searching the foredeck of the *Viola Belle* for the woman who had agreed to become his wife.

Snatches of Molly Gallagher's last letter

came back to him as he examined each of the women standing there. She had given him just enough information to identify her, without actually saying what color dress she would be wearing when she arrived.

I have long black hair. James said it was my crowning glory. However, I usually cover it with a hat to keep the sun off my nose. Otherwise I get freckles.

He eliminated every female who wasn't wearing a hat. That took care of a goodly number. Unfortunately, it was difficult to tell the hair color of those whose heads were covered. He wished he knew whether she wore her hair up or down.

I've become a mite too thin, but somehow food lost its taste after James died.

That left him only four women to choose from.

I hope you're not too tall, because I'm barely shoulder high to a grasshopper. Well, perhaps that is a slight exaggeration. But not much! James called me his "little darling."

He narrowed it down to two women.

Oh, yes. I have a small mole near my mouth. James said it was becoming. I hope you'll think so too.

Neither woman was looking at him at the moment. He marched up to the closest one and tapped her on the shoulder. She turned, and he exhaled the expectant breath he hadn't realized he'd been holding. It wasn't her.

As he approached the other woman, she turned toward him. Seth stopped in his tracks, stunned by her elegant beauty. Why hadn't she warned him? Her face was framed by a black straw bonnet trimmed with a fringe of black crystal beads that caught and reflected the sunlight.

He had an impression of anxious doe-brown eyes and alabaster skin—freckled across the nose—that flushed when she met his gaze. Even white teeth worried her full lower lip, but she held her chin in a defiant tilt. The mole was there near her mouth, just as she had described it. But it was more than merely becoming. It tempted. It tantalized. It invited.

His body tautened, hardening with desire that he had no wish to feel. This wasn't what he had wanted from a mail-order bride. Not a woman who made him long to possess her. Not a woman to make feelings he had thought long dead spring to demanding life. Especially since they had both agreed this was to be very much a marriage of convenience.

Seth took two steps toward her. As he reached out, she laid a delicate hand in his.

"Mrs. Gallagher?" he managed in a raw voice. When she nodded, he felt his gut tighten.

"Yes. Doctor Kendrick?"

"Yes."

He wasn't at all what Molly had been expecting. A doctor shouldn't have such disturbing gray eyes or such shaggy black hair. A doctor shouldn't be so fierce-looking or have such a powerful frame. A doctor shouldn't remind her of the savage on horseback she had seen along the river, or cause her whole body to shiver at the touch of his surprisingly callused hand.

Molly thought the crow's-feet at the edges of his eyes and the deep creases that bracketed his mouth gave his face character. She approved of his straight nose, his cleft chin, and his wide, sharp cheekbones. He was wearing a kind of hat she hadn't seen much in the east. It mostly covered his wavy black hair, except where it curled down over his collar in back. But it was his eyes—enigmatic, smoky-gray eyes—that drew her to him and held her in thrall.

One second they were standing on the main deck of the *Viola Belle* staring into each other's eyes. The next, Molly's hand was torn from Seth's as someone stumbled hard against her, forcing her over the short rail into the icy waters of the Missouri. She caught a fleeting glimpse of an impish face peering down at her before the breath was knocked out of her and her mouth was filled with muddy water.

Seth had a split second to register that *Patch* had knocked Molly Gallagher overboard before he too was shoved from behind and felt himself falling into space. He gave fleeting thought to wringing his daughter's neck before he hit the water with a resounding splash. He came up sputtering and quickly blinked his eyes, trying to clear them enough to spy the culprit who had shoved him over the rail.

Before he could get a good look, Molly broke the surface choking and cried, "Help! I can't swim!" and promptly sank again.

Molly's lungs felt as if they might burst, but she daren't take a breath. Was this what James had felt? This awful burning pain in the chest? The frigid cold of the water? Had he thought of her and Whit and Nessie in his last moments, as she was doing now? Molly struggled against her fate, her splayed fingers moving desperately through the murky water for the light at the surface. But the immense weight of her many layers of fashionable clothing forced her inexorably down. She felt dizzy. She couldn't last much longer. Soon she would have to breathe. Then her lungs would fill with water, and she would drown.

She couldn't give up. Her children needed her. She must live! She fought against the pull on her clothing, refusing to give up her life to the river.

Something tugged on her skirt and just as quickly let go. Someone had jumped in after her! *Save me! Don't leave me here.* She reached out blindly to grab hold of her rescuer's neck and promptly had her hands torn away. Which made her even more desperate.

A muscular arm snaked around her from behind, grasping her firmly across her breasts. She was so shocked at the intimacy of such a hold that she froze for an instant— which was time enough for her to realize that they had begun moving upward. She forced herself to remain calm, which was the only way she could aid her own rescue.

Molly gasped as she broke the surface of the water and immediately began coughing.

"You're safe now, Mrs. Gallagher," Seth said in her ear. "Just relax, and I'll swim you to shore."

By now, those on board the *Viola Belle* had been alerted to the fact that two passengers had fallen overboard. There were hands ready to take Molly from Seth as he lifted her up onto the levee, and to drag him out of the water as well.

Seth spied Ethan in the crowd that had gathered and said, "Take care of her while I get my medical bag from the buggy."

Molly lay on the ground with her eyes closed, grateful to be alive. The sun felt so warm, and she was so tired. She had no desire to move from this spot anytime soon.

"Step aside. Get out of the way. Give her some room to breathe," Ethan said.

When Molly opened her eyes, she saw a handsome man with sandy brown hair and bright green eyes kneeling beside her. He untied the soggy ribbons from under her chin and removed what was left of her best Sunday bonnet.

"Are you all right?" he asked.

Molly's mouth formed the words, "I'm fine," but nothing came out. She closed her eyes again. She felt the heat of a second body beside her just before she heard Seth's deep, rumbling voice.

"How is she, Ethan?"

"I can't tell, Seth. You better check her over."

Molly felt the buttons of her dress being undone and managed to drag a hand up to try and stop whoever it was.

"It's all right, Mrs. Gallagher," Seth said, moving her hand back down to her side. "It's me. Seth Kendrick. I'm a doctor, remember?"

"No." She didn't care if he was a doctor. He was a stranger. But his practiced hands made short work of the buttons on her bodice. Molly gasped as smooth, cool metal touched the skin above her left breast. The gasp set off a fit of coughing. Seth turned her over and patted her back. When she quieted, he laid her back down flat and once again placed the stethoscope so he could hear her heart.

Molly shivered at the slight touch of his fingers on her skin around the edges of the instrument. He moved the metal disc around as he checked her lungs. His fingertips left a spot of heat everywhere they touched. This had to stop. She didn't want to feel so—so— much.

"Doctor Kendrick," she managed to whisper, "please stop."

"I'm almost finished," he said, and continued what he was doing. "I don't think any permanent damage has been done," he announced at last. "Can you open your eyes, Mrs. Gallagher?"

Molly squinted her eyes open and quickly closed them to shut out the bright sun.

"Let me help you up."

Seth's arm surrounded her shoulders, and in short order she was nestled in the cleft created between his thighs as he knelt on the levee. As soon as she was upright, the bodice of her dress, which was still unbuttoned, fell open. She grabbed awkwardly to save her modesty, only to have Seth reach over her shoulders and matter-of-factly begin to button her back up again.

Molly closed her eyes, but she could do nothing about the flush that pinkened her skin and raced his buttoning fingers to her neck. There was no respite even when he removed his hands, for the heat kept on rising right up her neck to her cheeks.

"I . . . I think I can get up now," she said, anxious to remove herself from the embarrassing position between his legs.

Once again that muscular arm slipped around her. At the same time Seth rose, he lifted her effortlessly to her feet. Once they were standing, she saw that his sodden clothes—black broadcloth suit, white shirt, and string tie—conformed revealingly to the shape of his body. And she realized her wet bodice must be clinging to her like a second skin.

"Are you all right?" she asked, crossing her arms protectively to cover herself.

"Fine," he said with a brief, reassuring smile.

The smile softened his face but was too quickly gone. "It was courageous of you to jump in after me," she said. "You saved my life. I can't thank you—"

"I didn't jump in after you."

"You didn't?"

"I was pushed."

"Are you sure? Whoever would do such a thing?" But Molly had an awful, sinking feeling who it might have been. Suddenly she realized her children must be worried about her. She searched the spot on the main deck where she had been standing with the doctor. Sure enough, Whit was leaning over the rail with a smug look on his face. Well, he wasn't going to be looking quite so pleased with himself when he had to apologize to the doctor. She cringed at the thought of introducing them to each other. But of course it must be done. And the sooner the better.

Molly had already opened her mouth to speak when it dawned on her that she hadn't seen Nessie standing anywhere near Whit. She whirled around to look again. The little girl was gone. Her heart began to pound when another look did not reveal her daughter. Where was Nessie? Had she wandered off the *Viola Belle* alone? Was she now lost in the crowd?

Immediately, all thoughts of conciliating the man beside her fled. Molly didn't bother to explain where she was going, just lifted her soggy skirts in both hands and shoved her way through the gathered crowd toward where she had left her children.

"Wait!" Seth called. When Molly didn't even slow down, he hurried after her.

Molly hadn't a thought to spare for the towheaded waif in baggy trousers standing on the foredeck glaring daggers at her. She headed straight for the boy neatly dressed in knee-length trousers and a jacket, standing nearby.

"Where's Nessie?" she demanded of her son.

Surprised at his mother's question, Whit looked around in genuine consternation. "She was right here a minute ago."

"Was that before or after you pushed Doctor Kendrick into the river?" Molly demanded angrily.

"Before." Whit grimaced as he realized what he had just admitted. "I don't know where Nessie—" The boy snapped his mouth shut, scowling at something over his mother's shoulder.

Molly turned to discover that her husband-to-be had joined her. Had he heard Whit's confession? Her face paled when she saw the white lines of fury around his mouth. A quick look revealed bunched fists. For a moment she thought he was going to lay violent hands on her son. Every muscle in her body tensed to stop him.

But when his powerful hand closed around cloth, it was the small towheaded child dressed in a wrinkled cotton shirt and baggy corduroy pants that he held in his grasp.

"Would you like to explain what happened here?" he demanded of the child.

"It was an accident!" the urchin said. "I tripped."

"And just happened to fall against this particular woman?" the doctor asked in a sarcastic voice.

Molly suddenly recognized the impish face as the one she had seen leaning over the rail when she landed in the river. In the same moment she realized that the child was not a boy, as she had first thought, but a girl with her hair tied back with a string at her nape. She put a calming hand on Seth's sleeve. "I'm sure it must have been an accident, as she claims."

"You are, are you?" he snarled.

Molly drew back, astounded by the violence in his eyes and the harshness of his voice. She opened her mouth to tell him it was only a little water and that she would dry, but sneezed instead.

She watched through watery eyes as Seth turned his fierce look back on the rumpled girl and demanded, "Apologize to the lady."

The girl's chin came up pugnaciously. "No."

Seth's face was both furious and incredulous. "No?"

"I won't apologize." The girl's voice rose in distress as she cried, "I'm not sorry I did it. I hope she catches pneumonia and dies. She should go back where she came from. I don't need a mother!"

Confused, Molly turned to Seth for an explanation.

"This devil's helpmate is my daughter, Patricia," Seth admitted through clenched teeth.

"My name is Patch," the girl muttered.

"You have a *daughter*?" Molly asked in

amazement. "But you never said a word about having children."

"It's why I need a wife," he admitted in a gruff voice. "You can see she needs a woman's influence."

"It appears so," Molly agreed with alacrity. "Even so—"

Whit interrupted with, "She's the one who gave me the idea to push *him* into the water, Mother."

Molly felt her heart miss a beat as Seth turned his steely gray eyes on her.

"Did I hear the boy right?" he demanded.

"That depends," she hedged, lowering her lashes so she wouldn't have to deal with those piercing eyes of his. "What did you hear?"

"Are you the boy's mother?" Seth demanded with asperity.

Molly's chin came up, and her eyes met his. "And what if I am?" She shot a quick glance at his daughter. "Surely what's sauce for the goose is sauce for the gander."

"Look, lady—"

"Watch how you talk to my mother," Whit warned.

"Yeah, well you watch how you talk to my pa!" Patch retorted, putting herself toe to toe with Whit.

"Whit!"

"Patch!"

Both parents grabbed hold of their respective children.

"I'm sorry Whit pushed you in," Molly said.

"Out here a man speaks for himself," Seth said, his eyes meeting Whit's. "What have you got to say for yourself, son?"

"I'm not your son," Whit retorted. "And I'm not sorry. I'd do it again! I wish you'd drowned. I wish we'd never come here. You'll never be my father!"

Seth's steely gaze never left Whit's face.

Molly's dark brown eyes flashed at Seth.

Patch focused glaring blue eyes on Molly.

Whit's sea-green eyes shot daggers at Patch.

Any second, fireworks were bound to explode.

Molly nearly jumped out of her skin when she felt a hard tug on her sodden skirt. She looked down to see Nessie standing with her thumb in her mouth. Molly had completely forgotten about her daughter in the confusion. She reached down to lift the child into her arms. At the same time, she realized that if she held Nessie close to her, the child would get wet. She ended up holding the little girl the outstretched length of her arms.

Seeing her difficulty, Seth took the child from Molly and seated her in the crook of his arm. "And who might this be?"

Molly swallowed. "My daughter, Agnes. We call her Nessie."

"You have a son *and* a daughter?" Seth asked in a carefully controlled voice.

Molly's spine stiffened. She arched a brow as she stared him down. "Yes. It appears we have three children between us."

"Don't marry her, Pa!" Patch cried. "That boy of hers is a danged rowdy one, for sure. And that one you're holding—why, she's still a baby! She'll drive you crazy in a week with her whining and crying."

Patch's argument left something to be desired, since Nessie hadn't made a sound since she'd arrived on the scene. But Molly took one look at Seth's daughter and saw the genuine distress in Patch's blue eyes at the sight of her father holding the other little girl.

"Perhaps this isn't going to work out after all," Molly said.

"Why not?" Seth demanded.

Molly's eyes slid away from his steady gaze. "I should have told you about the children."

"Dang right you should've," Patch was quick to agree.

"I was no more honest than you were," Seth conceded. "And the fact that you have children doesn't change things. I still need a wife. And my daughter needs a mother."

"Dang it, Pa! I don't—"

"That'll be enough, Patch," Seth said in a warning voice.

"Send her home, Pa," Patch begged. "Send 'em all home."

Molly could see that Seth was torn. It was clear he would have walked over fire for his daughter. And Patricia—Patch—wanted them gone. But Molly needed a home for her children. If she had to fight Patch, she would do it.

Seth saw Molly's shoulders square for battle even as her black lashes lowered onto pale cheeks in exhaustion. A strong, inexplicable need to protect rose within him. He thought of a line in her second letter. After explaining that her parents and husband were all dead, she had written, *I am alone in the world now.* Now he knew she had meant that she alone was responsible for the welfare of her two children. Where would she go if he decided not to marry her? And after all, he had been no more honest than she had been.

He put a finger under her chin to lift her face up toward him. "Molly?"

At the sound of Seth's voice, Molly's lids lifted, and she saw that his hard gray eyes had softened. She let herself hope.

"Molly," he repeated, as though the name were foreign and not a perfectly ordinary Irish name. "I have a preacher waiting. If you'll still have me."

Molly refused to look at Patch. The child wouldn't have changed her mind, and Molly felt her pain too strongly to ignore it. "Seth, I think—"

She was interrupted by a cry from shore.

"Hey, Doc! Pike Hardesty gunned down a man in Bassett's saloon. Better come quick!"

Seth cursed under his breath. "I've got to go," he said, quickly handing Nessie over. "Hardesty doesn't often miss. It'll be a near thing at best, and if I don't hurry, I'll be no help at all. I'll meet you at the hotel in town when I'm finished."

"Say, Pa," Patch said. "Maybe she should go along." When her father frowned, Patch added, "I mean, maybe you oughta find out if she's any good at nursing before you agree to marry her. After all, you don't want a wife who faints at the sight of a little blood."

Molly swallowed hard. "Blood?"

Seth slanted a look at Molly, who had turned a little green at the gills. "I could use the help." He looked at Nessie in her arms. "But I understand if you can't leave your daughter."

"Whit can look after her," Molly said. Seeing the mutinous look in her son's eyes, she added, "I'll just walk them to our stateroom. I'll be back in a minute."

Seth watched her walk away, graceful despite the weight of the water-soaked skirt. He had taught himself to ignore women's bodies when he was doctoring them. But he hadn't been able to ignore Molly Gallagher's. He had seen the shape of her breasts through the wet cloth. Worse, the chill had made her nipples peak. He had been very much aware of her as a woman every moment he was unbuttoning her dress. Nothing with Molly Gallagher was turning out as he'd planned. How in the world had things gone so awry?

"You better be careful, Pa," Patch said.

"What?" Seth replied absently, unwilling to give up watching the widow Gallagher.

"She looks like more trouble than she's worth," Patch said earnestly. "And think about that whiny baby, Pa. It'll be a misery for sure having her around the house. And lord knows what mischief that boy'll start. I—"

"She's going to be my wife, Patch," Seth

said. "And she'll be your mother. Her children will become part of our family. You'd best get used to the idea."

Patch shook her head no. "I won't stand for it, Pa."

Seth hardened his voice against the pain he saw in his daughter's eyes. "You don't have any choice."

"Durned if I don't!" she cried. "Marry her if you gotta, Pa. But she ain't gonna be my ma. And they ain't gonna be my kin!"

Seth clenched his fists as he watched Patch thrust her way through the crowd on deck and scramble down the gangplank. He was doing this for her own good. Someday she would thank him for it. He shoved a hand through his damp hair in frustration.

"Shall we go?"

The sound of Molly's husky voice sent a shiver down Seth's spine. She hadn't taken the time to comb her hair, but she had grabbed a shawl to wrap around the bodice of her dress. He forced himself not to remember the way the wet material had clung to her figure. There would be time later to think about the hell on earth he had created for himself with this marriage of convenience.

"Let's go," he said tersely. "I have a bullet to dig out of a man's hide."

Molly extended her step to match Seth's stride. All in all, things hadn't gone as badly as she had feared they might. At least he wasn't sending them right back to New Bedford on the next steamboat. Now all she had to do was prove she could be a competent nurse. That shouldn't be so hard. Why, she had gutted fish all the time back in New Bedford. Could the sight of a little blood from a gunshot wound be so very different?

Molly had never seen so much blood in her life. It soaked the checkered shirt of the man lying on the floor of the Medicine Bow Saloon and stained the sawdust beneath him. She swallowed down the bile that rose in her throat and stayed as close as she could to Seth's side.

"Put him up on the bar," Seth said, setting his travel-worn medical bag down on the polished surface.

"Aw, come on, Doc. I'm trying to sell whiskey here," Red complained.

"I need a place where I can see to work."

Red grimaced. "You boys heard Doc Kendrick. Haul him up here."

Several bystanders hoisted the man from the floor onto the mahogany bar. Seth carefully pulled the fabric away from the gaping hole in the man's chest. Bloody bubbles of air surrounded the wound.

"Am I gonna make it, Doc?" the wounded man gasped.

"What's your name?" Seth asked.

"Wally Flanders."

"Just take it easy, Wally. I'll do my best."

Molly wasn't sure what she was supposed to do. So at first she did nothing, just stood and watched as Seth cut away the cloth from the wound. At Seth's command she supported the wounded man's head while the bartender held a whiskey bottle to his lips, then watched him pour whiskey from the same bottle over Seth's hands.

Seth motioned for several men to hold the wounded man down while he probed for the bullet.

Molly's hands gripped the smooth mahogany bar and held on as the man screamed and fainted.

"Thank God for that," Seth muttered. "Mrs. Gallagher," he said, "come over here and hand me my instruments when I ask for them."

"I don't know—"

"Come over here," Seth ordered. "I'll teach you what you need to know."

Molly sighed inwardly with relief. She could follow simple instructions. Seth need never find out she wasn't a real nurse.

Molly retained only impressions of the operation that took place over the next several minutes: Seth's large hands, strong and sure, yet gentle. An economy of movement and efficiency of action. The sickly sweet smell of blood. An urgency that hovered in the air around them as the country doctor fought death. And lost.

Molly knew it was over when she saw the slump of Seth's shoulders. He seemed to curl in around himself. His hands stopped their deft movements. And she heard the soughing death rattle as the man gave up breath and life.

"Shouldn't have wasted my time," Seth said in disgust. "Must have nicked the lung. Thought so when I first saw him, but I hoped . . ."

"You did the best you could," Molly offered.

"What I did wasn't worth spit."

Molly recoiled at the anger in his voice, the rigid tension in his body. "Was it something I did—or didn't do?"

Seth shook his head abruptly. "No. You did fine. A doctor couldn't ask for a more competent nurse."

Molly breathed an inward sigh of relief. Her deception had done nothing to contrib-

ute to a man's death. But she couldn't take
the chance that next time she wouldn't be so
lucky. She took a deep breath and confessed,
"Doctor Kendrick, I haven't ever assisted in
an operation before."

"I know."

"You do? What made you suspect—"

"You didn't stop shaking the whole time,"
he said with a wry twist of his mouth. He
took her hand and held it up between them.
It was still shaking. "But you did everything I
asked, when I asked. If you can follow instructions that well from now on, you'll do
just fine."

Molly pulled her hand from his and
clasped it with the other in an attempt to still
the tremors. She was appalled and amazed
when she realized everything she had just
done. Now she stood beside a dead body. She
had been exposed to nothing so grim in New
Bedford; it was going to be a very different
life in Montana.

Seth turned to the men who had already
resumed their various occupations in the saloon and asked, "Anybody see what happened here?" There was a restless shifting,
but no one spoke. "Red?"

Red shrugged. "Didn't see a thing."

Seth's eyes found Pike Hardesty, who had

never left his seat at the poker table in the corner. He sat with his back to the wall, his thumbs tapping a rhythmic tattoo on the table. The hand of cards the dead man had played still lay scattered on the green felt. A chair stood awry some distance from the table as though it had been shoved there. A trail of blood led from the chair to the spot where the unarmed man had fallen in the sawdust.

Molly read the truth of the matter, just as she was sure Seth had. For a terrified moment she thought Seth might say something to provoke the man at the table, whose left cheek was sunken and scarred as though skin and bone had once been crushed. He had a thick moustache that flowed beyond the edges of a narrow mouth. His shaggy brown hair hung over his brows, half-masking snakelike eyes that were simply black, with no distinction of pupil or iris.

Abruptly, the scarred man stood. Molly saw he was both taller and heavier than Seth and wore a gun tied down low on his right hip. His fringed buckskin shirt and leggings were stained and slick from wear.

Casually, as though he hadn't noticed the scarred man's actions, Seth turned his back and began wiping his medical instruments clean and repacking them in his bag.

Molly stared at Seth, a frown growing between her brows. What sort of man was this? James would have stood toe to toe with the scarred man and welcomed the fight. Many was the time she had nursed James's bruised and swollen face and bathed his bleeding knuckles after a barroom brawl. She wasn't averse to Seth not fighting, just surprised by it.

However, in the west it seemed a man didn't have to go looking for trouble. It found him wherever he was.

To Molly's horror, the scarred man sauntered over, leaned back against the bar, and hooked his bootheel on the footrail. "You got something you want to say to me, Doc?"

"Nope."

"He was cheating," Hardesty said. "Got what was coming to him." He surveyed the room, daring anyone to contradict him. No one did. He turned his attention to Molly. "Haven't seen range calico like you around here in a long while. Name's Pike Hardesty. Who would you be, purty lady?"

Molly shrank back until she came up against a solid wall of muscle. Startled, she glanced over her shoulder and saw the rigid line of Seth's jaw.

"She's no business of yours," Seth said in a quiet voice. "Come on, Mrs. Gallagher. I shouldn't have brought you in here."

"Hold on just a minute," Hardesty said, stepping in front of Molly. "I asked this here lady a question. I expect an answer."

"You got the only answer you're going to get," Seth said.

For a "patient man who tried to understand the other fellow's point of view," Seth's voice held a decided edge to it. Molly quickly said, "My name is Molly Gallagher. I came here to marry Doctor Kendrick."

There was a stunned silence in the saloon, and all eyes turned to stare at them.

"Well, now, Molly Gallagher," Hardesty said with a lurid grin. "You don't want Doc Kendrick. Why, he's got guts slack as old fiddle strings. Don't even wear a gun. Probably scared he'll shoot himself in the foot." Hardesty laughed at his own joke. "Why not try a real man instead?"

Molly had thought nothing of the fact that Seth Kendrick wasn't wearing a gun. No one in New Bedford carried a gun. In fact, anyone carrying a gun would have been highly suspect. But apparently things were different in Montana.

She wasn't sure afterward exactly how it happened. But Pike Hardesty took a step toward her, and the next thing she knew, he was lying flat on his back in sawdust.

"Sorry," Seth apologized, reaching down a hand to help Hardesty up. "Thought you saw my foot there. Didn't mean to trip you."

Hardesty knocked Seth's hand away and scrambled to his feet. Red-faced, he began brushing himself off. "If I didn't know you better, Kendrick, I'd say you did that on purpose." His voice was vicious as he finished, "But you being yellow-bellied clear through to your backbone makes that purely unlikely."

Molly watched as Seth's face paled. A muscle in his jaw jerked. Yet he made no move to strike the scarred man. He said nothing to defend himself. She was appalled and confused. Surely no man could tolerate such an insult and hold his head up high. But if anything, Seth's shoulders had squared more firmly. What manner of man was this who did not regard another's slander? Was he the coward Pike Hardesty had named him? She looked at Seth, and there was nothing in his face that told her one way or another.

"Let's go, Mrs. Gallagher," Seth said at last.

When Hardesty moved to intercept her, Red's shotgun barred his way. "Leave them be, Pike. You can be replaced. We only got one doctor hereabouts."

That explained their tolerance for a man with no backbone, Molly thought. In a land as violent as this was turning out to be, a doctor seemed a dire necessity.

Seth's hand at her elbow urged Molly out of the saloon. She walked beside him, her head held high, looking neither right nor left as they headed back to the levee. She felt the speculative stares of the townsfolk. What did they really think of Seth Kendrick? she wondered. Did everyone believe him a coward? How would they treat the wife of such a man? He had promised her his protection. But what was to keep someone like that awful scarred man from accosting her in the street if no one feared her husband's retribution?

Neither spoke until they reached the door to her stateroom on the *Viola Belle*. Then Seth turned to her and said, "Pike Hardesty is a bully and a braggart. I should never have taken you where you'd meet up with a man like that."

"Why did you let him get away with saying those things about you?"

"Maybe because they're true."

Molly frowned. "Are they?"

A bitter smile tilted his lips. "That's for you to decide."

"Were you afraid to fight him because you aren't wearing a gun?" she asked, the crease between her brows deepening as she sought to understand him.

"Let's just say that fighting wouldn't have proved me right, or him wrong."

"So you stepped aside."

His lips curled cynically. "That's certainly a kind way of describing what I did."

"You're an unusual man, Doctor Kendrick. I don't know what to make of you."

"Does that mean you've changed your mind about becoming my wife? Say so now, and I'll make arrangements to get you back to New Bedford."

Watching him closely, Molly saw him tense as if for a blow. She was tempted to take him up on his offer. She was frightened of what lay ahead of her. Seth Kendrick was so different from James, such a mass of contradictions. Strength and gentleness. Decisiveness and restraint. And though she didn't want to think him a coward, he had admitted he wouldn't willingly choose to fight. Would he be able to keep her and her children safe in this wilderness to which they had come?

She had to pray he could, because going back offered no solution to her problems. She must keep Whit away from the sea. And Nessie needed the security of a home.

It dawned on her that perhaps Seth hadn't made the offer of release out of consideration for her feelings. Perhaps he wanted out himself. That shocking thought gave her pause. "I haven't changed my mind," she said. "But now that you know you'll have two extra mouths to feed and care for, perhaps you've changed yours."

"Your boy looks like he'll make a fine man. And I won't mind having the little one around," Seth said. "Are you willing to be a mother to my daughter?"

She met his serious gaze and promised, "I'll treat her as though she were my own."

"And make her a lady," he added.

Molly tried to picture Patch as a lady and failed. "I'll do my best," she murmured.

"Then we have a deal. Shall we shake on it?"

Molly shivered with mixed fear and excitement at the touch of Seth's callused palm. She had just agreed to put her well-being, and that of her children, into the hands of this stranger. Only time would tell whether she had made a good bargain—or the worst mistake of her life.

"Change into whatever you want to wear to the wedding," Seth said. "There's a parlor in the hotel. I thought we could be married there. We'll have to hightail it out of town afterward if we hope to get to my ranch before dark."

"You don't have a house in town?"

His eyes slid away to the horizon. "No, I don't. I catch and break horses for the army. My ranch is south of town about twelve miles."

"But you're a doctor," she blurted.

"Yes. But I can't make a living that way."

At her quizzical look he explained, "This is a hard land. It's not just smallpox and typhoid that plague you. It's rattlesnake bites, broken bones when your horse steps in a gopher hole and throws you, and amputated joints when the woodsman's ax slips. Many a man gets shot by renegade Indians or outlaws like Pike Hardesty. A lot of my patients die, Mrs. Gallagher. And dead men don't pay. So you see, I need another way to make sure I can feed myself and my daughter."

Molly flushed. "I had no idea Montana

would be so—so violent. Even what you do
when you're not doctoring—breaking horses
—isn't that kind of dangerous?"

He flashed a quick grin. "It can be. But I
have a man who helps me, Ethan Hawk.
You'll meet him at the wedding. Anything
else you want to know?"

"Do we have neighbors?"

"Sure. Iris and Henry Marsh live about five
miles west of my place."

Molly's jaw dropped. "Five miles!"

Seth grinned. "That's a stone's throw here
in Montana. You can ride that distance in no
time."

"On what?" Molly asked with asperity.

"A horse."

"I don't know how to ride."

"Don't worry. I'll teach you."

They heard voices inside the stateroom,
and sounds like furniture being moved.

"We'll talk more after the wedding," Seth
said. "I'll be back to pick you up as soon as I
find Patch."

He bowed slightly before he turned and
walked away. For a moment Molly was too
stunned to do anything but stand there and
watch him. No wonder he had said Montana
was lonely. Imagine, neighbors no closer
than five miles away! And to be twelve miles

from the closest town was unthinkable. What had she gotten herself into? Why hadn't she asked more questions before she jumped into this with both feet?

To Molly's surprise, when she opened the door to her stateroom, Patch Kendrick was sitting cross-legged in the middle of the four-poster bed. The girl started guiltily and slanted a warning look at Whit, who wore an equally guilty expression. Molly stepped back outside to tell Seth she had found his daughter, but he had already disappeared into the crowd on the levee. When she came back in, both children looked as innocent as angels.

"Your father's looking for you," she told Patch.

"I told Red Dupree where I'd be, so Pa can find me. I was just getting to know Whit," Patch replied. "After all, we're going to be family."

Molly's eyes narrowed suspiciously. This reasonable speech didn't sound at all like it came from the same person who had mercilessly shoved a perfect stranger into the muddy Missouri. What was the girl planning now? Molly shook her head. What an imagination she had, to think that this freckle-faced child was hatching some plot against her. After all, there wasn't much one little girl could do to interfere with her plans. Most probably, Patch had simply accepted the inevitable.

Molly gave the girl the benefit of the doubt. "I have to get dressed now. You're welcome to stay and visit if you like. Your father will undoubtedly be back here in a little while to escort us all to the wedding."

Patch exchanged another quick look with Whit. "Uh, well, okay. If you don't mind, I think I will."

"Why don't I take Nessie for a walk?" Whit offered.

"That sounds like a wonderful idea," Molly agreed. "Just stay where you can hear me when I call you." She turned her back on them to sort through her trunks for the dress she planned to wear.

Molly carefully unfolded the dress of violet silk that she had packed as her wedding gown. It had been a gift from Aunt Hattie on her twenty-eighth birthday. The color was appropriate for the mourning she was still observing, but the hem was embroidered with a decorative design of grape leaves. It had a simple bodice that buttoned up the front with a foulard at the neck and a lilac mantilla scarf to be worn around the shoulders.

Molly stepped behind the screen in the corner of the room. Once she heard the door close, she began stripping off the still-damp gray silk dress that had been ruined when she fell into the river.

"Do you mind if I watch?" Patch asked.

Molly nearly jumped out of her skin. She had naturally assumed that Patch had left the room along with Whit and Nessie. Obviously she had not. Patch sat on the corner of a trunk staring at Molly with wide, innocent blue eyes.

Molly's first instinct was to shoo the girl out. But she had promised Seth Kendrick she would treat the child as her own, and Nessie had often sat and watched her at her toilette. After all, that was how a child learned, by example. What better way to begin to make a lady of Patch than to show her the proper attire she must soon begin to wear?

"Of course I don't mind," Molly said. She finished unbuttoning her dress, which was trimmed with black corded fringe and small pewter buckles. Perhaps she could salvage some of those for another garment, she thought as she set the dress aside.

"What's that thing?" Patch asked.

Molly followed Patch's pointing finger. "It's called a tournure. It's made of crinoline and supports the bustle of my dress, along with several petticoats."

"I know what a petticoat is," Patch said with disgust.

Molly arched a brow. "Then you usually wear one?"

"I didn't say that."

Molly gave an unladylike grunt of relief as she untied the white satin corset and let it fall. "I must say, I never did much appreciate the restrictions of a corset. But every lady wears one."

"I ain't gonna," Patch muttered.

Molly was left wearing a low-necked pointed basque-waist, lace-trimmed drawers and white stockings, all of which were a great deal the worse for their dip in the Missouri.

Patch appeared fascinated. "I had no idea you were wearing so much rig."

"There are certain rules of fashion that every lady must follow."

Patch snorted. "You won't catch me in none of that stuff. Couldn't hardly move wearing that durned getup."

"You'll learn," Molly said.

Patch grimaced but didn't argue.

"You'll have to get up a minute," Molly

said. "I need some things from that trunk you're sitting on."

Patch stood beside the trunk fidgeting while Molly sorted through it for fresh underthings.

"Uh . . . those shoes of yours would dry quicker if I put them out where they could catch the breeze," Patch offered.

Molly was touched by the girl's thoughtfulness. Why, Patch could be sweet when she wanted to be. Molly quickly closed the trunk and sat down on it to remove her black kid boots. "I appreciate you doing this for me," she said, handing the boots to Patch.

"It's my pleasure." She beat a hasty retreat before Molly had a chance to consider the reason for the brief appearance of that familiar impish grin.

Molly took advantage of Patch's absence to skin out of her underthings and put on new ones, blessing the foresight that had caused her to bring extras of the items she had thought might be harder to find in the west.

Once she was dressed except for her shoes and stockings, Molly came out from behind the screen and sat down at the dressing table to fix her hair. She parted it down the center and created two thick braids. The end of each braid was fastened under the beginning of the other and secured with hairpins. Small wisps of hair escaped around her face, softening what would otherwise have been a severe look. Last, but not least, Molly added a fetching crape bonnet the same lilac color as the mantilla scarf.

Molly was just adjusting the angle of her bonnet when someone knocked and the door was thrust open.

Seth Kendrick stood there. "Red Dupree said Patch was here." He looked around the room, but when he didn't see his daughter, said, "I should have known she'd send me on a wild-goose chase."

Molly hurried toward him. "She was here. She's just—" Molly looked past Seth out the door of her cabin and spied Patch standing at the rail of the steamboat. The girl held Molly's boots in her outstretched hand. While Molly watched in disbelief, Patch stared her straight in the eye and let go. Molly's precious kid boots dropped into the river like two big black stones.

There was not a speck of remorse on Patch's face. The little girl marched back to the door and stood beside her father, clearly daring Molly to say anything.

Molly was amazed at the sheer gall of the child. And devious! Patch Kendrick could teach a corkscrew to curl. She opened her mouth to vent her spleen and snapped it shut again when she realized she would be doing exactly what Patch wanted her to do.

Molly gritted her teeth and fought to control her Irish temper. Several words that James had brought home from the docks came to mind—but found no voice. Molly Gallagher wasn't going to let a mere child provoke her into making an unladylike scene in front of Seth. Neither was she going to let the fact that she and Patch could look forward to *years* of such confrontations change her mind about marrying the girl's father.

"Are you ready to go?" Seth asked, completely unaware of the war of wills going on between his daughter and his future wife.

"I'll just be a moment." Molly headed for the trunk where she had packed a second, older pair of boots. She had to take nearly everything out to get to the bottom of the trunk. When she did, the boots weren't there.

Molly's spine straightened with a snap. She whirled to confront a grinning Patch. The girl was positively *gloating*.

At that moment, Whit arrived in the doorway with Nessie and shared a conspiratorial glance with Patch. Then he turned and stared at Molly. One look at her son's outthrust jaw told Molly the whole story. Whit must have told Patch about the second pair of boots. He might even have helped Patch find them. How could he do such a thing?

Molly's throat tightened until it hurt to swallow. What chance did this marriage have if their children were so set against it? How angry they must be, how frightened and confused, to connive so desperately to prevent it! She looked around the room but had no idea what she was looking for.

She sought out Seth's gray eyes but found no answers there—only more questions. There was admiration in his gaze and, more disturbing, desire. His eyes were haunted, hungry.

Molly had no idea it was her breathlessness, her pinkened cheeks and the spark of fury in her brown eyes that had excited Seth. She felt a stirring deep within her, a response to his magnetism that was raw and primitive. It was unsettling to want a man—a perfect stranger—this way. She balled her fingers into fists to hide the fact they were trembling. The constriction in her throat eased, replaced by the thrumming of her pulse. She couldn't drag her eyes away from the man standing before her.

Seth gave her an encouraging smile and

said, "You look beautiful, Mrs. Galla—Molly. I can't imagine what more you could need to do. Shall we go?"

Molly curled her naked toes against the varnished deck. She couldn't very well admit she hadn't any shoes to wear without explaining what had happened to them. She couldn't do that without causing the confrontation Patch so clearly desired. For better or worse —and both despite and because of the children—she made her choice. She cleared her throat and said, "I guess I'm as ready as I'll ever be."

Molly felt the first stirring of satisfaction when she saw the astonished look on Patch's face. If Patch Kendrick thought being barefoot was going to slow Molly Gallagher down, she had another think coming!

Patch followed glumly behind her father and his mail-order bride as they headed down Front Street toward Schmidt's Hotel. Whit had been shooting dark looks at her ever since they left the *Viola Belle*. Dang it all! It wasn't her fault Whit's mother was still going to marry her father. Patch had done her level best to give Molly Gallagher a disgust of her, but the ding-dang woman had been too dumb to take a hint. She had thought pushing her father's mail-order bride into the Missouri would be enough to send her packing. That had backfired when Whit shoved her father in after the woman.

She had hoped Molly Gallagher might be one of those women who fainted at the sight of blood. But she hadn't been that lucky. From what Patch had been able to see through the plate-glass window of the Medicine Bow Saloon, Molly Gallagher had passed her nursing test with flying colors.

That was when Patch had devised the plan to leave the consarn woman barefoot, certain that no *lady* would ever think of crossing a portal unless she was completely dressed. Durned if that plan hadn't failed as well!

Patch was good at using her wits to get what she wanted. She had hoped to provoke the detested Mrs. Gallagher into making a scene about being barefoot. Her father would be disgusted by the woman's ranting and raving and change his mind about marrying her. But that Mrs. Gallagher was danged smart. She hadn't fallen for the trap.

Instead, at this very moment Molly Gallagher was walking barefoot up the main street of Fort Benton on Seth Kendrick's arm. And Patch couldn't say a word about it without getting herself into trouble!

Patch wasn't about to admit she had met her match. Molly Gallagher might marry her pa, but that didn't mean they had to stay that way. And they wouldn't. Not if she had anything to say about it. She would find a way to make Molly Gallagher call it quits. Before the brief Montana summer was through, those Gallaghers would be long gone.

Molly stared at the simple gold band on her finger in awe. She had worn James's ruby and diamond family ring for eleven years. Now it was gone, replaced by a circlet as elemental as the wilderness to which she had come. She looked up into the face of the man who had just become her husband. His gray eyes were somber.

"You can kiss the bride, Doc," Reverend Adams said with a wide grin.

Seth's hands framed her face, and she felt his breath on her cheek an instant before his lips brushed hers. Oh, the softness, the sleek dampness of his mouth! She stared, stunned, as Seth let her go and stepped back.

"Congratulations, Doc," the reverend said. "That's a mighty fine-looking woman you got for yourself."

"You're a beautiful bride, my dear," Mrs. Adams concurred.

Molly blushed as Seth murmured his

agreement. An instant later, she was gathered up in a bear hug by the man Seth had introduced as his partner and best friend, Ethan Hawk. She recognized him as the man who had removed her hat after her dousing in the river.

"Seth deserves a little happiness," Ethan whispered in her ear. He chuckled and added, "I'm sure you're just what the doctor ordered."

Molly found the young man so approachable that she led him aside to ask, "Do you think you could arrange to buy a pair of shoes for me?"

Ethan immediately looked down. From his startled expression, Molly knew he had detected her bare toes peeking out from beneath her skirt.

"What happened to your—"

"Shhh! I don't want Seth to find out."

Ethan raised a brow in speculation, then grinned and said one word: "Patch."

Molly couldn't help laughing. "How did you know?"

"I know Patch. How'd she manage it?"

"With great aplomb," Molly said. "I promise to tell you the whole of it later. Would you —could you buy me a pair of shoes so that when we leave here I don't have to do it barefoot? I have some money—"

"Keep your money. It'll be my wedding gift to you, Mrs. Kendrick. Just let me have another quick look so I can figure out a size."

Molly felt self-conscious as Ethan took her hands, stood back at arm's length, and looked her up and down.

"Don't worry," he said. "I'm a pretty good judge where these things are concerned. I'll be back in a heartbeat." He winked mischievously before he turned and slipped out of the hotel parlor.

Seth scowled at the sight of Ethan leaning close to his wife. His eyes narrowed when Ethan took Molly's hands in his. He knew Ethan with women. The man could charm the feathers off a duck. Well, Ethan could just find somebody else to charm. Molly belonged to him!

Seth snorted in disgust at his idiotic musings. The feelings of possessiveness that rose in his breast were unfamiliar and left him feeling foolish.

He had married Molly Gallagher to have a mother for his daughter, not to have a wife to warm his bed. And yet whenever he looked at her—at the curve of her bosom, the flare of her hips, the velvety brown of her eyes, and the soft, pink lushness of her lips—he found himself painfully aroused. He had visions of his body mantling hers, of holding her in his arms and feeling her soft breasts nestled against his chest, of his hips thrust in the cradle of her thighs.

He deeply regretted the inference in his letters to her that this was to be merely a marriage of convenience.

So why not renegotiate the terms of your agreement?

The thought hadn't been far from his mind since the moment he had laid eyes on Molly Gallagher. And why not? They were married. It wasn't wrong for him to desire her. Or for her to desire him.

He licked the small drops of sweat from his upper lip, conscious of the flare of excitement he felt at the thought of making love with his wife. He let his eyes find her again. She was beautiful in the violet dress, but he would rather have seen her in a brighter color. It had been nearly a year since her husband's death. Surely by now she was ready to set aside the memories of another man.

Only now that he thought of it, in her last letter to him, nearly every sentence had been written to reflect her relationship to her late husband: "James thought." "James believed." "James said." He had to admit that didn't sound like a woman who had permanently laid her first husband to rest.

But she would. He wasn't asking her to love him; he didn't expect to love her. His late wife held his heart in a grip that was as strong as it had been the day she died. No one could ever touch him that way again. Of that he was very sure. The stone wall around his heart was firmly in place.

But that didn't mean he couldn't *want* another woman. He very much wanted the woman he had made his wife. She might have memories of James Gallagher, but he would be the man sleeping in her bed tonight.

The tug on his pants leg surprised him. When he looked down, he met a miniature pair of brown eyes like Molly's. "Hello, Nessie," he said. "Is there something I can do for you?"

"Are you going to be my new da?" the little girl asked.

Seth cleared his throat to give himself time to think. "I suppose so," he said at last.

"Will you pick me up?"

When she reached up, he grasped her at

the waist and lifted her into the air. A burble of surprised laughter escaped her lips. Seth marveled at how light and fragile a four-year-old could be.

And felt a small crack in the stone around his heart as he settled her in his arms so they were eye to eye.

"Whit doesn't like you," Nessie promptly announced.

"He doesn't?"

"No. He didn't want you to marry Mama."

"Oh?"

"So he helped Patch find Mama's boots."

"Why would he do that?"

"So Patch could throw them in the river, of course."

"Of course," Seth said. His eyes sought out his daughter, and he found her sulking in a corner of the parlor. "Why would Patch want to do a thing like that?" he asked, afraid he already knew the answer.

"Patch said no lady would ever go barefoot to her own wedding."

Seth thought about that for a second and asked, "Are you saying that your mother is barefoot?"

"Well, of course she is," Nessie replied as though he were a particularly slow student, to whom things had to be explained twice. "Patch threw her boots into the river."

"Of course," Seth repeated in a slightly stunned voice. He searched for Molly and perused the hem of her skirt. He hadn't really thought much before about the fact that it dragged on the floor. Then Molly took a step, and he distinctly saw several toes beneath the violet fabric.

As he watched, Ethan returned to the room with a small brown-paper-wrapped package, which he handed to Molly with a grin.

Shoes, Seth realized.

A series of feelings assaulted Seth, leaving him shaken. First, there was embarrassment that his daughter would do such an awful thing, in defiance of all propriety. Second, there was disappointment that Molly would go to Ethan for help instead of coming to him. Third, there was certainty that he had chosen the right woman for his wife. Raising Patch to be a lady was going to be a considerable challenge. It appeared that Molly Gallagher would be equal to the task.

When Patch saw her father pick up Nessie Gallagher, she felt sick to her stomach. Nessie had attached herself like a leech, and her pa seemed more than willing to hold the little intruder. Patch couldn't remember the last time her father had held her in his arms like that. Not that she wanted him to, mind you. Or would let him if he tried. But he was *her* father. And she didn't intend to share him!

Patch glanced over to where Molly Gallagher Kendrick stood *barefoot* drinking punch and laughing with Ethan. For the first time, Patch admitted a grudging respect for the formidable adversary who was now her stepmother. Molly Gallagher Kendrick had gumption all right. But that didn't mean Patch had to like her—or obey her.

"I thought you said Mother wouldn't come to the wedding barefoot," Whit muttered into Patch's ear.

Patch turned wrathful eyes on him. "A *real* lady wouldn't have come."

"What are you saying?"

"Figure it out for yourself!"

"You take that back," Whit hissed.

"Make me!"

Patch was spoiling for a fight, and it appeared Whit was willing to give her one. She was two years older and wiser, but he was a good three inches taller. As far as she was concerned, that made them about evenly matched. Only, when she put up her fists, Whit just laughed.

"I can't fight a girl," he protested.

Her knuckles rapped him in the nose and rocked his head backward.

He yelped in surprise as blood spurted down his face. "Hey! Stop that!"

Patch walloped him in the stomach with a fist, bending him over double.

Whit forgot chivalry and fell on Patch like a tomcat in an alley fight. Only, when he swung, she stepped out of his path and his fist floated through thin air. He sagged as she belted him again in the stomach. He grabbed for her and used his greater weight to force her down. He heard her cry out in pain when her head hit the wooden floor.

Abruptly, the two combatants were yanked apart. Ethan held Whit by the shoulders, while Seth pulled Patch to her feet. Reverend Adams and his wife stood staring in disapproval. Molly was stuck holding Nessie, who'd been thrust into her arms by Seth as he ran to stop the fight.

"Oh, Whit! How could you?" Molly cried.

"What's going on here?" Seth demanded in a harsh voice.

"See, Pa!" Patch said. "I warned you he'd be trouble."

"She started it!" Whit shouted.

"I did not. I was minding my own business—"

"Liar!" Whit said.

"I am not! I—" Patch suddenly crumpled. If Seth hadn't been holding onto her, she would have fallen.

He lifted her limp body into his arms, thinking that she was pretending. But she couldn't be faking the total lack of response he now felt in her body. "She's unconscious," he said with astonishment. "What did you do to her?" he demanded of Whit.

"I didn't do anything," Whit said in a tremulous voice. "She hit her head when she fell."

"A concussion?" Ethan speculated.

Molly saw that Seth was rattled. He hadn't moved, and he hadn't taken his eyes off Patch's motionless, pale face. He was acting more like a parent than a doctor. Molly found that the most encouraging sign she'd yet seen that he would make a good father for her children.

"Seth," she said in a calming voice, "take Patch over to the settee and lay her down." Once she got him started in the right direction, he was fine.

Molly turned to the preacher and asked, "Reverend Adams, could you and your wife

please have the hotel manager arrange for
me to get a bowl of cool water and a cloth?"

As the preacher and his wife left the room,
she turned to Whit and said, "Go sit down on
that chair beside the settee. Tilt your head
back and pinch your nose until it stops bleeding. Ethan"—Molly tucked a stray wisp of
hair behind her ear while she thought what
else needed done—"can you find Seth's medical bag?"

"It's in the buggy. I'll go get it," he volunteered.

"What about me?" Nessie asked. "What can
I do?"

"You can give me a hug," Molly said. Nessie
was more than willing to comply. Molly
found the feel of Nessie's tiny arms around
her neck a comfort. She could imagine the
horror Seth must be experiencing as he
watched over his unconscious daughter.

"Nessie, it would be a big help now if you
would go and stand by Whit and make sure
he keeps his head tilted back. Could you do
that for me?"

"All right," Nessie said as Molly set her
down.

Within moments, the hotel parlor was bustling with people. The manager appeared
with the items Molly had requested, and

Ethan delivered Seth's medical bag. Once Seth saw the bag, he seemed to wake from his shocked stupor. He checked Patch's eyes and realized that although she might have a slight concussion, it wasn't serious. Ethan knelt beside the settee, his hand gently brushing Patch's tousled hair away from her forehead in concern.

Meanwhile, Molly put the damp cloth to work cleaning the worst of the blood off Whit's face and fingers.

Seth waved some hartshorn under his daughter's nose, and the ammonia smell brought her coughing and sputtering to life. Patch's first words, once she was fully conscious, were "I want to go home, Pa."

"That sounds like a good idea," Ethan said to Seth. "Unless you get started soon, it's going to be dark before you get there. I'll ride ahead and make sure there's a fire in the stove and some hot coffee waiting for you," he offered.

Molly met Seth's eyes across the room, and she nodded her agreement.

"I appreciate your offer, Ethan," Seth said. "We'll be leaving as soon as I can get the Gallaghers' trunks loaded on the buggy."

"I'll give you a hand," Ethan said.

Once the two men had left the room, a pall

descended. Molly had no intention of stirring up dust that had barely settled. She took advantage of the peace and quiet to rinse her muddy feet in what was left of the bowl of water.

Mrs. Adams stared bemused for a moment before asking, "My dear, is there some reason you came barefoot to your own wedding?"

Molly wasn't about to tell her the truth, so she made up a tale. "Oh, it's an old Irish custom, Mrs. Adams."

"It is?"

"We always start our marriages the way we intend to go on."

"I don't understand," the preacher's wife said.

Molly leaned over and gestured Mrs. Adams closer so she could whisper in her ear, "Barefoot and pregnant."

Mrs. Adams gasped and drew back from Molly as though she were contagious.

"Of course, I'm not in the family way," Molly explained, finding it hard to keep a straight face. "But with Seth being such a virile man, I'm sure it won't be long before I am."

Flustered beyond words, Mrs. Adams excused herself and left the room.

Molly looked up at Him and asked for forgiveness. Then she used the peace and quiet to open the package Ethan had given her. She smiled with delight when she discovered that besides shoes—a delicate pair of kid boots with patent leather tops—he had also purchased white stockings. And he hadn't lied. Both shoes and stockings were a perfect fit.

Ethan Hawk was obviously a man who knew a lot about women. He had made her feel perfectly at ease from the first moment she had met him. She wasn't a tenth so comfortable with the man she had just married. Whenever she got near Seth, she felt a strange tension, a feeling of expectation, of excitation, that she couldn't explain. Molly hoped that as she and Seth got to know each other, these inexplicable feelings of agitation would ease.

Molly ushered the three children outside, where Seth and Ethan were just finishing.

"There's plenty of room for everyone in the buggy," Seth said. "You might have to sit close."

Patch scowled at Whit, and he frowned back.

Seth didn't miss the exchange and said, "I don't want to see any more fighting between the two of you. If you've got differences, find a way to settle them peaceably, or I'll settle them for you. Do you both understand me?"

"Yes, Pa," Patch muttered.

"You're not my father," Whit said. "And I don't have to do what you say!"

Rather than say anything, Seth simply walked away to make sure the buggy was hitched up properly. Seth knew he couldn't win that kind of argument. So he refused to engage in it. He fiddled with the harness until he was ready once again to face his new family.

But he found it hard to believe the situation in which he now found himself.

When Seth had first imagined the drive home from Fort Benton with his mail-order bride, he had thought it might be an awkward trip. After all, he'd be sitting in the front seat with his new wife, and his daughter would end up being a twelve-year-old chaperone in the buggy's back seat. As it turned out, the drive was every bit as awkward as he had expected, but for a very different reason.

In order to ensure peace on the trip, he put Patch beside him in the front seat. Whit, Nessie, and his new bride sat in back. At first Seth tried to carry on a conversation with Molly, but he was forced to turn around to

hear her reply or let her talk to the back of
his head. Neither alternative was comfortable, so he soon fell silent.

Every time Seth turned to check on them,
Molly gave him what she hoped was a bright
smile but knew must look more like a grimace. So many feelings were struggling for
dominance within her that she only felt anxious and wished the trip were over. The
grassy prairies were endless, and the mountains seemed very far in the distance.

Molly thought she heard Seth sigh with relief when a peak-roofed log cabin came into
sight. A thin stream of white smoke drifted
from a stone chimney at one end of the
house.

"We're almost home," Seth announced. "It
won't be long now."

The time went more quickly when they
could see their destination, and very soon
Seth was helping Molly down in front of her
new home. As his letter had promised, it was
nestled in a copse of cottonwood along a
creek. There was also a pond not far from the
house.

"I know it isn't much," Seth found himself
saying.

"It's fine," Molly replied as she took the

three steps up onto a shaded front porch that ran the length of the cabin in front.

Seth opened the door, but before she could walk through it, he scooped her up into his arms.

"Every bride should be carried over the threshold," he whispered to her.

Molly lowered her eyes, moved by his gesture. Then he set her down, and it was a good thing she was feeling in charity with him. Because what she saw was enough to make any woman turn tail and run the other way.

The house was split in half. A log wall to the left had two doors built into it that were closed. The righthand side of the house, the one onto which the front door opened, was all one room. It apparently served as parlor, dining room, office, and kitchen combined.

In the center of the room stood a scarred maple table and four mismatched chairs. The sideboard on the righthand wall was filled with an odd assortment of half-empty medicine bottles. A rolltop desk had been shoved half-open to reveal a clutter of papers and medical books. It was situated on the front wall and looked out a window that provided a vista of the mountains.

Along the back wall was a sink with an indoor pump—a real luxury, Seth assured her.

There was also a new four-hole stove he'd
had shipped up from St. Louis when he'd
found out she was coming. To the right of the
stove was a window with a view of the cottonwoods that lined the creek. To the left of
the sink was a back door leading to what she
could see through the window was another
shaded porch.

There was no decoration in the room,
nothing on the walls, nothing to ameliorate
the bleakness of the place and label it a
home. The crackling fire Ethan had lit in the
stone fireplace was the only spot of cheer in
the room.

"Pa and I neatened up the house for you,"
Patch said.

"I can see that." Dirty dishes were stacked
neatly in the sink. A heap of dirty clothes
were layered neatly over a dining-room
chair. A pile of dirt had been swept into the
corner of the wooden-planked floor and hidden neatly behind the broom. "You did a fine
job of neatening things up," she said with a
perfectly straight face.

"We sure don't need you," Patch pointed
out belligerently.

"But two hands make the load lighter,
don't you agree?" Molly asked.

As she focused on the two closed doors on

the opposite side of the room, it dawned on Molly that the house had only two bedrooms. Where were they all going to sleep? As Seth opened the door to what he described as "his" bedroom, the same thought seemed to occur to him.

As he stepped to the other door he said, "This is Patch's room." He looked at the three children who stood huddled before him, then back at the room. Daylight was fading fast. A decision had to be made. So he said, "Nessie can share with Patch."

"Durned if she will!" Patch retorted. She ran to stand protectively in her doorway. "I don't want that baby in here breaking my things, Pa."

"Look, Patch—" Seth cajoled.

"What about Whit?" Molly asked, trying to keep her growing apprehension out of her voice. "Where is he supposed to sleep?"

Seth was silent a moment. "I guess he can sleep in the barn until—"

"The barn!" Whit and Molly shouted together.

"Just until I get another room built."

"Absolutely not!" Molly said. "My son sleeps in the house."

"Where?" Seth asked pointedly, his eyes going first to one bedroom door, then to the next.

Molly folded her arms across her chest. "You and Whit can share one room. "Patch, Nessie, and I will share the other."

"The hell you will!" Seth retorted.

"That's telling her, Pa!" Patch chimed in.

Seth marched over to stand in front of Molly. "You're my wife. You'll sleep with me."

"And Whit will sleep where?" Molly asked.

"He can go stay with Ethan," Seth suggested, trying to rein his temper.

"And where, exactly, is that?"

Patch piped up, "Ethan has a cabin just beyond the trees. It's about a five-minute walk from here."

Molly met Seth's gaze and said flatly, "No. That's too far away. My son stays in the same house with me."

Seth shook his head in disgust. "Hellfire."

Molly put her hands on Nessie's ears. "Remember you are in the presence of children of tender years," she admonished.

"Hellfire and damnation!" he roared, at the end of his patience.

"That's telling her, Pa!" Patch chortled with glee.

Molly opened her mouth to give Seth a piece of her mind and let out a scream instead. Something furry had just rubbed against her leg! She jumped straight up in the air and threw her arms around Seth's neck. "There's something"—she gasped—"something's in here! Let me go! I have to save Nessie. Run, Whit!"

Nessie began to cry, and Whit backed toward the front door, eyes wide for the demon that had frightened his mother.

"Hellfire and damnation," Seth repeated. "Patch, get that raccoon out of here."

Molly gasped. "Raccoon?"

"Come on, Bandit. It's about time I put you to bed." Patch scooped the perfectly tame animal up into her arms. Its bushy, black-ringed tail promptly curled around her neck.

Molly watched in amazement as Patch disappeared into her room with the small, black-masked creature. She turned stunned brown eyes to Seth. "She keeps a raccoon in her bedroom?"

"It was sucking eggs in the henhouse," Seth explained.

"So she made a pet of it?" Molly asked incredulously.

"Can I see the raccoon?" Whit asked. "Do you think Patch will show it to me?"

"I want to see the raccoon," Nessie said.

Molly shook her head in disbelief.

Seth took command of the situation, ushering her two children into Patch's room. "The Gallaghers want to meet Bandit. Why don't you introduce him while I talk to their mother?"

Seth didn't really give his daughter any choice, leaving the room and shutting the door behind himself. He marched over to Molly and took her by the elbow, then walked her over and sat her down in the chair behind his desk. Then he went around the room lighting lanterns to stave off the dark.

"I think we better have a talk," he said. He took a spread-legged stance in front of the stone fireplace.

Molly sat stiffly on the swivel chair, her hands folded tightly in her lap.

"I hadn't counted on you having any children," Seth admitted. "If I'd known about them, I might have made some arrangements." He raised an accusing brow. "However, since I didn't, it appears we'll have to manage as best we can until Ethan and I can get another bedroom built."

Molly took a deep breath and let it out. "I won't be able to sleep unless I know my children are under the same roof as I am."

"So what do you suggest?"

"You and Whit can share your room. Patch, Nessie, and I will manage in Patch's room."

Seth shook his head no. "I don't think Patch will go for it."

"Patch is a child. She'll do as she's told," Molly said, exasperated.

"That's what you think," Seth muttered.

Molly folded her arms across her chest. "That's my final offer."

That was her *only* offer, Seth thought ruefully. He was more frustrated than he could remember being in a long time. He wanted Molly in *his* bedroom *alone*. It wasn't that he'd been that long without a woman. He'd seen Dora Deveraux not more than a week ago. But he wanted Molly. And his best estimate on building another bedroom onto the house was a good two to three weeks. He had no intention of waiting that long to bed the woman he had just made his wife.

So be it. There were other places they could use for a marriage bed. A stack of hay in the barn or a grassy spot beneath the cottonwoods would do just as well. He would find the time and choose the place. And make her his.

"Shall we go tell the children our decision?" he said.

"All right."

When Seth opened Patch's door, he wasn't sure what to expect. To his surprise, Nessie was sitting cross-legged on the foot of Patch's four-poster bed. Whit and Patch were hunkered down in the corner beside the raccoon's box.

"Patch. Whit."

The two of them stood and faced Seth. "Molly and I have talked it over, and we've come to a decision. Whit and I will share my room, while Molly and you girls will sleep in here."

"This is my bedroom!" Patch protested.

"Don't argue," Seth said in a no-nonsense voice.

"I won't stay here with them," Patch said. Before Seth realized what she was going to do, she slipped out the open bedroom window and was gone.

"Aren't you going after her?" Molly asked.

Seth shrugged. "She's just going to Ethan's place. She'll come home when she gets over being mad."

Molly put a hand on his arm and felt his muscles tense beneath her fingers. "I'm sorry for all the trouble. I'll make it up to you. I promise."

Seth sighed. "I'll go get the trunks." A few minutes later he was back. Molly marveled at his immense strength as he set two huge trunks down lightly on Patch's floor. Seth crossed to the door, then turned and said, "You come when you like, Whit. But once I'm in bed, the lanterns go out, and it'll be dark finding your way."

A second later Whit followed Seth out the door.

Molly was in awe of the way Seth had manipulated her son without forcing a confrontation. But then, as she was quickly learning, that was his way.

"I'm tired, Mama," Nessie said, yawning hugely.

"I'm not surprised, darling. It's time we all went to bed. If I'm not mistaken, morning comes very early in Montana."

Molly found a nightgown for Nessie and tucked her in, all the time wondering how Whit was getting along. She knew he would be mortified if she came and tucked him in, but all the same she missed the traditional bedtime ritual. How quickly their lives had changed!

Once Nessie was settled, Molly undressed and put on a warm flannel nightgown. She honestly tried to sleep, but the foreign night sounds she heard through the open window kept her awake. After shifting and tossing for an hour, she decided enough was enough. The house was quiet, and as stealthily as a thief, she stole from her bedroom out the front door to the porch. She had just sat down on the steps when a hand clamped down on her shoulder. Another hand quickly clamped over her mouth, cutting off her scream.

6

Molly fought like a wildcat, writing and clawing and kicking against the hands that held her. At last she began to tire, and the hissing sounds she had been hearing through a haze of terror took form as words.

"I'm not going to hurt you. Settle down before you wake up the whole house."

Molly shuddered. It was Seth. Good lord. She'd been fighting her own husband. Her knees felt like jelly. He helped her to sit as her legs collapsed under her, then joined her on the steps.

She covered her face with her hands and fought to hold back a sob of relief. "I thought you were—I don't know what I thought."

"I didn't want you to scream and wake everyone up," he said. "I'm sorry I frightened you. What are you doing out here?"

"I couldn't sleep." She met his concerned gaze and raised a sardonic brow. "I thought it might be relaxing to sit on the porch for a while, maybe take a walk."

"It's not safe for you out here alone."

"So I found out."

His smile flashed white in the moonlight. "Come on. I'll walk with you."

"That's not necessary. I—"

He took her hand and pulled her up and without looking back started off toward the pond. He stopped abruptly when he heard her yelp in pain. "What's wrong?"

Molly stood on one foot and lifted the other to expose a huge sticker.

"Don't you ever wear shoes?" he asked with amused exasperation.

"Believe me, I will from now on," she responded tartly.

"Here, let me help."

Before she could object, Seth lifted her into his arms and headed back to the porch. He set her down on the top step and sat down near her, but on the lowest of the three steps. Gently, he lifted her foot into his lap and turned it so he could see the burr in the moonlight. A moment later, he had it out.

"That wasn't so bad, was it?"

"Not nearly so bad as the beesting I got running in a field of clover when I was seven," she agreed.

He smiled again. "So going barefoot is an old habit with you?"

She laughed. "When I was little, my family had a farm in Ireland. I can still remember the feel of grass between my toes and the cool softness of new-plowed earth. Funny, I haven't thought about that in years."

His hand surrounded her foot. His thumbs pressed into her arch, causing a disturbingly erotic response.

Molly tried pulling her foot away, but he not only held on, he reached for the other one and rested them both on his thigh. "Your feet are like ice. Let me warm them up."

"No, really, I—" She gasped as he pulled up his long-john shirt and set her feet against his bare flesh. She instinctively curled her toes into the wiry black hair that covered his chest.

He chuckled and grabbed her toes to hold them still. "You're liable to tickle me to death if you aren't careful."

Instantly Molly stilled, abashed. In all the years she had been married to James, they had never done anything quite like this.

"So how does an Irish farmer's daughter become a Massachusetts lady?" he asked as he began to caress her feet again under the pretense of warming them.

Molly was slightly breathless as she answered, "Like so many others, my father brought his family to America, looking for the pot of gold at the end of the rainbow." She shivered from the touch of his hands and hid it with a shrug. "He found it—selling whiskey on the waterfront in Boston."

With her feet situated where they were, Molly felt Seth stiffen. She didn't know what she had said to offend him, but guessed, "Is it spirits in general you're against? Or those who sell them?"

He stopped what he was doing and searched her face a moment. "For married folks I guess we really don't know much about each other," he admitted ruefully. "As a doctor, I've seen too many hurt by bad whiskey—and good whiskey, for that matter. In Fort Benton there's a man named Drake Bassett who's selling the bad kind. He's hired Pike Hardesty to back him. I guess my neckhairs just naturally came up when you mentioned the subject."

He began stroking her feet again, his thumbs pressing into the tender flesh of her arches, his fingers caressing her toes. It was the most exquisite, the most sensual experience Molly had ever had. But it wasn't only the soft soles and arches of her feet that caught fire. With every titillating brush of his fingers there was a corresponding flare deep within her. She knew it had to be wrong to let him do this to her. They'd only just met, for heaven's sake! But he made it seem a mere kindness. And after all, it was only her *feet*.

"About this man selling bad whiskey," Molly said. "Why doesn't the law stop him?"

"There isn't any law to speak of in Fort Benton right now. Pike Hardesty shot the sheriff eight months ago—in a fair fight—and no one else has been willing to take his place. Pike has everyone too scared to make a move." He paused and added, "Except the Masked Marauder."

"Who?"

Seth grinned. "The Masked Marauder. Nobody knows for sure who he is or where he comes from. But he's on the side of the law, which makes him Bassett's enemy. Whenever someone is in trouble, the Marauder rides to the rescue, guns blazing."

"He sounds like a very brave man. Why do you suppose he keeps his identity a secret?"

"He has his reasons, I'm sure."

"I'll bet he's well known in town," Molly guessed. "And if people saw him, they'd recognize him."

"Maybe," Seth said. "And maybe he's nobody and wants to stay that way."

Molly angled her head so she could see Seth's face. His features had hardened, along with his voice. She caught her breath and said, "You know who he is."

Seth abruptly stopped rubbing her feet. "Nobody knows who he is." And to make sure she knew the conversation was at an end, he said, "Are you about ready for bed?"

With Molly sitting on the top step and Seth on the bottom, they were almost eye to eye. She reached up a hand in an unconscious action to smooth the hair from his brow, as she might have done with one of her children. He grabbed her wrist to stop her, then changed his mind. His hand dropped to his side.

Self-conscious now, Molly met his piercing gaze as she finished what she had started. His black hair was thick and surprisingly silky. She felt him shiver as her thumb brushed his temple. Then her hand fell away, and they sat there staring, totally aware of each other.

"I don't love you," Seth said in a quiet voice. "I'm not sure I can ever love another woman. But I want you—desire you—with every breath I take."

"Seth, I—"

He began murmuring words he might have used to soothe a frightened colt, because he could tell she was skittish. He had never suspected that simply caressing a woman's feet could arouse her. It had started innocently enough. But as her lids had lowered over her eyes, as her mouth fell open to draw shorter, panting breaths, and as her toes curled sensuously against his flesh, he had realized she desired him. His hands circled her ankles, and slowly, languidly, he began to draw her legs around his waist.

As she slid down onto his lap, his hands traveled up the velvety length of her legs, pushing her flannel nightgown up and out of his way so that her bare legs could surround him.

Moments later, she was sitting on his lap facing him, the heart of her snug against the heat of him. Her hands rested tentatively on his shoulders. Wide-eyed, she stared at him as his hands slowly curved around her naked buttocks and lifted her up and more fully onto him.

Molly couldn't breathe, the feelings were so exquisite. She could feel him. He was hard. And there was a throbbing heat. Molly laid her head on his shoulder but could not

bring herself to do anything to further his seduction of her.

Seth framed her face with his hands. He
forced her head back and looked deep into
her eyes to see what she was feeling. And
then his mouth closed over hers. It was a kiss
of possession.

His voice when next he spoke was hoarse
with need. "Come to bed with me, Molly."

Molly blushed scarlet. "But Whit—"

"We can go to the barn or—"

"I can't! I never intended—"

"I want you, Molly Gallagher Kendrick."

"I can't! James—"

"You're my wife now!" he said fiercely.

Seth's mouth was hard, and his embrace
nearly crushed the breath out of her. His
need, raw and honest, spurred her response.
She thrust her fingers into his hair and
opened her mouth under his. His tongue
plundered, his hands ravished. He grasped
her hips and pulled her hard against him.
The cloth of his jeans abraded her tender
skin, sending small tremors of pleasure rolling through her. Molly couldn't catch her
breath; she felt out of control and couldn't
catch up with the turbulent sensations roil-
ing through her body.

"Mama?"

Seth and Molly broke apart like two teen-agers caught spooning when the preacher comes to call. There was a mad scramble as Molly tried to scoot out of Seth's lap. He just grabbed her at the waist and stood. Her bare feet dropped to the ground, and the flannel nightgown surrounded her once more. He held her tight against him for an instant. Then with a monumental effort of will and a gusty sigh of resignation, he let her go.

A moment later, Nessie shoved open the front door.

"I couldn't find you, Mama," the little girl said. "I got scared."

Molly scooped the child up in her arms as she tried desperately to regain her equilib-rium. Her breathing was still ragged, her pulse thrumming. "I couldn't sleep, Nessie. I just came out to sit for a while on the porch with Seth. Come on. Let's go back to bed."

As she stepped inside the house, she threw a quick look over her shoulder. Seth stood in the shadows, tall and forbidding. It had been a narrow escape. She might even now be ly-ing beneath him on a bed of straw, had Nes-sie not interrupted them. And how would she have felt tomorrow morning if she had?

Wonderful! It would have been wonderful! a voice cried.

But the grieving widow was appalled at what she had nearly done. It was nearly dawn before Molly closed her eyes at last.

Seth didn't have much more success getting to sleep. He hadn't stayed on the porch much past Molly's departure, just long enough for his blood to slow and his body to settle down. When he finally returned to his bedroom, he found Molly's son sitting up in bed waiting for him.

The whites of the boy's eyes showed his fright. "Who's there?" Whit asked in a small voice.

"It's me, Seth."

He watched the boy visibly relax.

"I woke up," Whit said, "and no one was here."

Whit didn't admit he was scared. With what Seth had seen of the kid's pride, he knew the boy probably would have been appalled to know Seth even suspected such a thing.

"I just stepped out for some fresh air," Seth said. "You'd better get to sleep. We've got a hard day ahead of us tomorrow."

Whit lay back down, but his body was stiff. Seth pulled off his boots and socks, then skinned out of his jeans, leaving him in his long john underwear. Normally he would have removed that as well, but in deference to the boy, he left it on. He slipped under the covers and lay as stiff as the youth on the other side of the bed.

He closed his eyes, which made his other senses more acute. He heard Whit's indrawn breath and the muffled sound of what might have been a sob. And felt the small jerky movements of the body beside him. Seth wasn't sure what he could, or should, do. To notice at all would be to humiliate the boy.

Suddenly, Whit rolled over and pulled the pillow hard against his mouth. His legs drew up into his stomach. Seth felt Whit's desolation; he couldn't ignore it.

"I lost my father when I was only a little older than you," he began. "I was fifteen. My mother died when I was born. Pa always told me if I wanted to see her, I could look in the mirror, because I had her eyes."

The sobbing stopped abruptly, and the small form on the other side of the bed was still. Seth kept on talking.

"Pa and me, we had a small place southwest of San Antonio with a few head of cattle. Texas had been annexed by the States, and Mexico decided to make an issue of it. I wanted to join the army and fight Mexicans. Pa absolutely forbade it."

Seth paused, remembering the ferocious argument they'd had, the harsh words that had been spoken.

A small voice from the other side of the bed said, "I wanted to go to sea, to be a whaler, like my pa. I left a note when I ran away, but Mother came and made me get off the ship. She brought me here to keep me away from the sea."

Seth smiled in the darkness. That explained why Molly Gallagher had accepted his offer of marriage so promptly. "That story sounds a lot like mine," he said.

"One night, I took my hunting rifle and a bag of food and set out to enlist in the army. I didn't get far before I ran into a band of cutthroat Mexican outlaws. Those bandidos had my rifle and my horse, and I was saying my final prayers when my father showed up to fetch me home.

"I'd never been so glad to see anyone in my life. He'd been a Texas Ranger, my pa, and he knew how to fight bandidos. When the shooting stopped, what Mexicans weren't dead had turned tail and run. But my pa had been mortally wounded. He died on the trip back home."

Seth didn't say that he'd always blamed himself for his father's death. Or that remorse over that one incident had shaped a great deal of his life. "My pa was one brave hombre," he murmured.

"I saw my da fight once on the waterfront," Whit said in a wistful voice. "He was a brave man too. I want to grow up to be just like him."

"That's a good goal, Whit. A man can't wish for more than to have his son grow up following in his footsteps."

Only Whit's father was dead. And the only footsteps for Whit to follow would be Seth's. Suddenly, the immensity of what he had done, the responsibility he had accepted, struck Seth. Would the boy see who he really was? Or would he only see the man Seth must pretend to be?

"I miss Da," Whit admitted in a choked voice.

"You always will," Seth said. It wasn't much, as comfort went, but it was all he could offer. "It'll get easier as time goes on. You'll always have your memories of him, of the good times you had together. They'll stay with you the rest of your life."

"Da used to tuck me in at night."

Seth held his breath. Was Whit asking him to do that? Would he let him? Not if Seth asked. The boy had too much pride for that.

Seth didn't say what he was going to do, didn't ask permission that the boy couldn't, or wouldn't, give. He just sat up and leaned over and tucked the covers firmly around the boy, up one side, and down the other.

"You forgot my toes."

Without a word, Seth leaned down and tucked the blankets firmly under Whit's long, narrow feet. Then he lay back down and turned on his side away from the boy. "Better get to sleep. Dawn comes early."

Whit closed his eyes, unaware of how he had found solace, only knowing he had. *Almost as good as Da,* he thought as he drifted off to sleep.

When Seth walked into the kitchen the next morning, Molly greeted him with a smile that took his breath away. He remembered the night past, the taste of her, the feel of her lips. He wanted to kiss her good morning, to start the day with the feminine softness of her in his arms. But she had turned back to the stove the instant she saw him, sending a message loud and clear without saying a word.

She was wearing simple clothes this morning—a white shirtwaist and dark brown broadcloth skirt, covered by a faded red apron that he recognized as one from the sideboard—that made her seem more approachable. But though she was apparently not angry over what had happened last night, she was keeping her distance.

When he started to sit down at the kitchen table, she asked, "Aren't you going to shave?"

Seth felt the day's growth of whiskers. It was a small sacrifice. "Sure. I'll be out back."

But as he started out the door, she handed him a bowl of warm water. "For shaving," she said.

Seth stared down at the bowl and then back up at Molly. "Thanks," he said as he took it from her. He would never have heated water for himself, but as he held a warm-water-soaked cloth to his face to soften his beard, he realized there were a lot of things about having a woman in the house that he'd forgotten about.

When he came back inside, Molly smiled at him and waved him to the table. "Have a seat. The coffee's nearly ready. I had to scrub the pot before I could start. There must have been three days' worth of grounds in it."

Seth opened his mouth to say it took three days' worth of grounds to make a decent cup of coffee but snapped it shut again. It was another of the changes he'd have to accept.

But there were compensations, he thought as he watched his wife busy herself at the stove. Her absent-minded humming made a nice accompaniment to the sounds of coffee perking and the sizzle of frying bacon. He loved to watch her move, enjoying the feminine grace of each gesture.

"What's that I smell?" Seth asked, sniffing the air. "Are you baking something?"

"You must mean the biscuits," Molly replied. "I found some flour and I thought—you don't mind, do you?" She lifted the lid on the Dutch oven on top of the stove. Seth got a glimpse of the most beautiful, fluffy golden-brown biscuits he'd ever seen in his life.

At that moment, Patch appeared in the kitchen doorway and announced, "I always make Pa's breakfast. And he hates biscuits."

Seth couldn't deny that he hated Patch's biscuits. They were hard as shoe leather and half as tasty. His mouth watered as Molly served up a dozen aromatic biscuits into a straw basket and set them on the table in front of him. He wanted one of those biscuits so bad, he could already taste it, loaded down with butter and blackberry jam. But eating one of those biscuits was going to be a diplomatic nightmare, after the way he'd disdained Patch's efforts.

"I . . . uh . . . think I ought to have one just to be polite," he said to Patch, grabbing one from the basket.

"That's not necessary," Molly said, lifting it right out of his hands and setting it back in the pile. "I'll toast some bread for you instead."

Seth swore under his breath. "No, really," he said, picking up another biscuit. "I don't want to put you to any extra trouble. Biscuits'll be just fine."

This time Patch took the biscuit out of his hands. "You know you can't abide these things, Pa."

Patch sat down to the right of her father and began to slather the biscuit with butter.

"What can I get for you to drink with that?" Molly asked Patch.

"A cup of coffee."

Seeing Molly's surprise, Seth explained, "We don't have a milk cow." He found himself adding, "But there's no reason why we couldn't get one."

"Good. Then I could make some buttermilk," Molly said.

Seth shuddered at the thought. He couldn't think of a worse-tasting thing to swallow, but he kept his mouth shut and counted his blessings—her biscuits—instead.

"Look what I found out back." Ethan stood in the kitchen doorway holding Nessie. The little girl was still dressed in her nightgown and curled up like a teddy bear in his arms.

"Can't that baby even walk by herself?" Patch snapped. Her chin jutted in response to Ethan's frown of disapproval. "Durned Gallaghers," she muttered. "Troublemakers. All of them."

"Patch," Seth warned. "Watch what you say."

Ignoring the hostile undercurrents in the room, Ethan asked, "Is breakfast ready? Something sure smells good." He looked around the table and saw that there were only five chairs—the swivel desk chair had been pulled up to the table. Clearly, Molly had made accommodations for her children but hadn't been expecting him.

Seth tensed, unsure whether Ethan's presence at the table would result in another confrontation with Molly, like the one they'd had the previous day over sleeping arrangements.

"Ethan always has breakfast and supper with us," Seth said cautiously. "We're usually out working at noon, so we take something along to eat while we're gone."

"That's fine," Molly replied, equally cautiously. "I'll be sure to set an extra plate from now on."

Ethan set Nessie down in one of the three empty chairs at the table. But the child was too small for the chair. Her chin barely reached the edge of the table.

Seth reacted first. He simply leaned over and lifted Nessie into his lap. As though it were the most normal thing in the world, the little girl settled back against his chest and accepted the biscuit he handed to her. "Go ahead and sit down, Ethan," Seth said. "There's room now for you at the table."

Patch stared at Nessie in disbelief.

So did Molly.

Within moments, Molly turned back to the stove; Patch turned purple. She jumped up and said, "Pa, I told you that baby would be a bother."

"She's no bother," Seth replied as he met Patch's troubled blue eyes. "She hardly weighs a thing."

Patch struggled for words, but nothing came. Her lips thinned as she watched her father dandling the Gallagher girl on his knee. "I've got to go feed my animals," she said at last.

Seth looked at the nearly untouched plate

of food sitting before his daughter. "You didn't finish your breakfast."

"I'm not hungry." Patch turned and shoved her way past Whit, headed for her bedroom.

Seth wondered how long Whit had been standing in the doorway like that. "Come in and sit down, Whit."

"I'd rather not," he retorted.

Apparently, in the bright light of day, their bedtime talk was forgotten.

"It's a long time betwixt breakfast and supper," Seth said. "We'll be working hard. You'll need some vittles to make it through the day."

"I'm not hungry," he insisted, eyeing his mother's biscuits with the look of a starving coyote.

"Suit yourself," Seth said with an apparently careless shrug. But a muscle in his jaw worked as he gritted his teeth against saying something provoking that he would regret later.

The tension eased some when Molly suggested, "I'll pack a few biscuits for you, Whit. You can eat them later when you're feeling hungry."

"That's not a bad idea," Ethan said as he slathered blackberry jam on a second biscuit.

"I wouldn't mind having a few extra of these myself for a midmorning snack."

Seth sighed heavily. Not only was he being denied Molly's biscuits at breakfast, he was going to have to watch Whit and Ethan enjoy them later in the day. He threw down his fork and said, "I've got work to do. The sooner I get started cutting down logs to build that extra bedroom, the sooner it'll be finished."

Seth handed Nessie to Molly on his way past. At the kitchen door he turned and said, "Meet me out in the barn when you're done, Ethan. Bring Whit with you. And tell Patch I expect her to work inside today with Molly."

Molly took one look at her son's rebellious face, handed Nessie to Ethan, wrapped several biscuits in a cloth napkin, and started out the door after Seth. She was breathless by the time she caught up to him in the barn. He was leaning back against a stall, his spread legs braced out in front of him, the heels of his hands pressed hard against his eyes.

"Seth?"

His hands came down immediately and rested in balled fists on his thighs; his gray eyes looked bleak. Molly walked up to him and stood between his outspread legs. "I'm sure things will get easier as we go along."

Seth snorted. "They couldn't get much worse."

"Perhaps not," Molly agreed with the beginning of a smile. She laid a hand on one of his fists, and it unfolded and his fingers entwined with hers. She brought his hand up and drew his knuckles across her cheek. "Thank you for being so patient with Whit."

"He doesn't make it easy," he grumbled.

"I know." She brought his hand down from her face and opened his fingers, setting the napkin in his palm.

"What's this?"

She grinned. "Biscuits. For someone who doesn't like them, you seemed awfully anxious to have one."

"I was. I am." He grinned wryly. "Thanks." He leaned over and quickly kissed her on the mouth.

Startled, Molly's hand came up to caress the dampness on her lips. She looked up into his eyes and saw the hunger there—and not for biscuits, either.

Slowly, carefully, Seth curled his hand around her nape and drew her face up to his. Slowly, gently, he laid his mouth on hers, feeling the softness of her lips under his.

Molly felt her body tensing, felt the slow curl of desire wind its way upward. She parted her lips slightly and felt him do the same. She opened her mouth wider, and—

"Pa! Where are you?"

Seth snapped upright as though a bullet had hit him. He looked down at himself, and then up at Molly. There wasn't any hiding how his body had reacted to her. And his daughter would be here any second.

Molly hid her trembling hands in the apron. She turned her back to him, letting the width of her skirt over several petticoats conceal Seth's problem. Moments later, Patch came hurtling around the corner and into the stall.

"I don't want to stay in the house," she said to her father. "I want to work with you."

Seth put a hand on Molly's shoulder. "I want you to help Molly in the house."

"But you need me," Patch protested.

"Ethan and I will manage. And I've got Whit to help."

"Whit Gallagher doesn't know a blamed thing about anything."

"He will by the end of the day," Seth said, cutting her off. He turned his back on her to take down two axes and several wood saws that hung on the barn wall.

Patch was just getting warmed up. "Why, that boy couldn't tell skunks from housecats! He's grass-green and brain-shy. He'll be no good to you at all, Pa. Why, he's a scatter-brained lumpkin, a want-wit who—"

Seth took one look at Molly's shocked face and realized maybe he'd been too tolerant of Patch's tirades in the past. "Go back to the house, Patch," he said firmly.

"But, Pa—"

He ignored the desperation in her blue eyes and said, "I want you to spend the day with Molly and watch what she does. It's time you stopped acting like some tomboy and started acting like a lady. I'll see you at supper, and you can tell me what you've learned."

Molly thought for sure Patch was going to argue. Instead, the girl hung her head and said, "All right, Pa. I'll see you at supper." She ran out of the barn as abruptly as she had entered it.

Molly turned to Seth and said, "She's very attached to you. Maybe it isn't a good idea to change everything all at once."

"I want her to be a lady. A lady doesn't spend her day chopping down trees." He hesitated, then gave Molly a quick, hard kiss on the mouth. A moment later, he stepped into the sunshine carrying an assortment of lumbering tools.

Molly stood in the barn, which smelled of hay and horses, and stared at her husband's retreating figure. She didn't understand her strong attraction to him. And she couldn't help feeling guilty for it. James had been everything to her. She could never love a man the way she had loved him. So what, exactly, was it that she felt for Seth Kendrick? Molly was very afraid it was something much less honorable, much more visceral. What kind of woman did that make her? A woman very much alive, who must learn how to survive in new and very different circumstances.

One of the most difficult of those was being a stepmother to Patch Kendrick. The most Molly realistically hoped for was some sort of truce between herself and Seth's daughter. Seth seemed to think Patch would accept her banishment to the house. Molly wasn't so sure. Patch's head had been bowed when she accepted her father's will, but her lips had been pressed flat and her arms had been rigid at her sides. Was it any wonder Molly had the feeling Patch wasn't going to be anywhere near as agreeable as her father thought?

As Molly crossed to the house, she passed

Ethan and Whit on their way to join Seth. Ethan had a hand on Whit's shoulder and was speaking in a voice too soft for Molly to hear. Whit was listening so intently, he didn't even see her as they passed each other. Molly felt suddenly bereft. James had been gone to sea so much that she had often had Whit to herself. It appeared those days were gone. Molly knew she could not cling to the past. She must allow Whit to change and grow, and she must change and grow as well.

But that brief, wrenching moment when it felt as if she were losing Whit gave her tremendous insight into what Patch must be feeling. And made her much more tolerant than she might have been of the situation she found when she arrived in the kitchen.

7

Molly's daughter was sitting cross-legged on the kitchen table with the raccoon in her lap, while Patch fed it scrambled eggs from her fingertips. Molly's immediate fear was that the wild animal would bite Nessie. But as she watched, her heart in her throat, she realized the raccoon was not the only threat. Sitting beside Patch was a huge wolflike creature. It turned its head to stare at her. Though it made no sound, it bared ferocious teeth at her, freezing her where she stood.

"Bandit here never bites unless he gets scared," Patch said as she fed the raccoon a bit of egg. "Now Maverick, my dog—he used to be real mean." She absently patted the wolflike creature on the head. "That's because he belonged to this man in town who was real mean to him. I talked to Maverick and asked him if he wanted to come home with me. He said he did, and he's lived here ever since."

"Dogs can't talk," Nessie said.

"You just have to know how to listen," Patch explained. "Like Bandit here. He just said he's had enough and he's ready for a nap."

Molly noticed the raccoon had curled up into a ball in Nessie's lap.

Patch stood and scooped the furry animal into her arms. "It's time to put Bandit to bed." As she rose, she saw Molly, who was still frozen in the doorway. "Don't move," Patch warned, "or she'll attack."

Molly's eyes were riveted on the dog Maverick, so she was aware when the hackles of fur rose on its neck. It growled low in its throat.

Patch quickly dropped the raccoon back into a delighted Nessie's lap and turned to face Molly. "She's right behind you in the window, and her tail is twitching, so it isn't going to be long now. I'll to try to get to her before she leaps, so stay perfectly still."

Molly's mind raced to assimilate what Patch had told her. In the window? *Behind her?* The eerie scream Molly heard was almost human and made the hairs stand straight up all over her body.

Patch shoved Molly aside as she intercepted the yellow blur that launched itself from the window. Molly screamed as Patch fell, entwined with the animal that had attacked her. The two of them—Patch and a golden brown beast with teeth and claws—went tumbling over and over on the floor. Horrified, Molly screamed at the top of her lungs, "Seth!"

It was over as quickly as it had begun. Patch was sitting on the floor with what looked like a lion stretched out on its back in front of her, its paws dangling in the air. Patch grinned up at Molly while she scratched the great cat's stomach. "Her name is Rebel. Somebody shot her mother. I raised her myself. She likes to sneak up behind you and try to surprise you."

Molly was still gasping for air, her jaw gaping, her eyes wide with fright that had not yet turned to relief, when Seth arrived at the door on the run. He was followed closely by Whit, who was trailed by Ethan. Molly flew into Seth's arms and buried her face against his chest.

"What happened?" Seth demanded of Patch as his arms tightened around his terrified, trembling wife.

"I think Rebel scared her," Patch said innocently.

Molly tore herself from Seth's arms, her

fear rapidly evolving into fury. "You could have warned me!" she hissed at Patch. "You could have simply told me that . . . that . . . clawed monster is as tame as a tabby cat. Instead, you scared the wits out of me!"

"Now, Molly," Seth said. "I don't think Patch intended—"

"Oh, she intended it, all right," Molly retorted.

"Is that true, Patch?" Seth asked.

A crocodile tear appeared in Patch's left eye and rolled down her cheek. Her lower lip stuck out like a buggy seat. "I swear I didn't do it on purpose, Pa. Don't you believe me?"

"Of course I do," he said.

Patch shot Molly a sideways look of triumph beneath lowered lashes.

The girl was a formidable foe, Molly realized. "Nevertheless," Molly said through tight jaws, "that cat—"

"Mountain lion," Seth corrected.

"That *cat*," Molly repeated, "has no business being in my kitchen." By now, Molly's fists were perched on her hips, and her legs were spread wide in an unmistakably militant pose.

Discretion was the better part of valor, Seth decided. "Maybe you'd better take Rebel outside, Patch." He realized the dog-wolf was also in the room. "And Maverick too."

"And keep them out," Molly said.

"Now, Molly," Seth cajoled. "Patch's animals—"

"Belong outside," Molly said firmly. "Not in the house."

"But—"

"Do you want her to be a lady or not?" Molly demanded.

The expression on Seth's face was ludicrous. He had been well and truly hoisted by his own petard. Molly wanted to laugh but forced down the impulse, afraid it would come out sounding as hysterical as she felt. She refused to look at Patch, taking no chances that the girl's wiles would work on her as well.

Patch rose from the floor with a grace and dignity that Molly thought many a lady might yearn to emulate. She put one hand on Rebel's yellow fur and another on the silver gray hackles that rimmed Maverick's back. Ethan held the kitchen door wide as Patch made an exit worthy of a queen.

Molly shook her head in disbelieving admiration.

"I guess I should have warned you about Patch's pets," Seth said.

"Are there any more surprises I should know about?"

"If by surprises you mean animals, there are a few more—Outlaw, Tramp, and Hermit come to mind."

"Don't keep me in suspense. What are we talking about here?"

Seth looked sheepish. "A bear cub, a crow, and a snake."

"Maybe you should have been a vet."

Seth smiled, relieved to see that Molly had a sense of humor. "I have been known to treat the occasional four-footed patient. In fact, most of Patch's animals have come to her through some kind of tragedy. In most cases they would have died if she hadn't adopted them. Except for the raccoon, Bandit. He was eating my eggs."

Molly turned to where Nessie still sat on the table with the satiated raccoon in her lap. "I hate to be the one to tell you this, but he's still at it."

Seth grinned. "Yeah, but I get first crack at them."

Molly laughed and shooed Seth toward the door. "Go back to work. Now that I know what to expect, I'll be fine."

He hesitated. "Patch—"

"Don't worry about Patch. We'll be fine."

When the ragtag girl made a reluctant reappearance at the kitchen door, Molly said, "I want to do some unpacking today, and a little cleaning. I could use your help."

"Do I have any choice?" Patch asked, glancing up at her father.

"No," he said.

She shrugged. "Fine. Tell me what to do."

Seth glanced quickly from Molly to Patch. "Guess I'd better get back to work." He beat a hasty retreat with Ethan and Whit.

All afternoon, Patch was a model of cooperation. But Molly didn't underestimate Seth's daughter. She knew the clever child hadn't pulled the last rabbit—or should she say wolf, raccoon, or mountain lion—from her hat. But Molly was determined to make a lady of Patch Kendrick if it was the last thing she ever did. With the array of wild animals at Patch's disposal, she realized it very well might be.

She and Patch worked side by side through the afternoon. Molly cleaned and straightened, and it was helpful to be able to ask Patch whether something belonged to Seth or to her, or had somehow found its way into the house through one of its animal inhabitants.

Molly removed the medicines from the

sideboard and carefully restacked them in a box beside Seth's desk in the corner, where Nessie would not be able to get to them. Then she placed her mother's rose-patterned china on the upper shelves of the sideboard. The painting of James's ship in the Arctic sea she hung above the fireplace. With just those small changes, the room looked more like a home.

However, it was the two very personal items she had brought to Montana that fascinated Patch.

"What is that?" Patch asked, pointing to an ivory-colored object.

"It's a walrus tusk, carved by the Esquimaux to look like a whale," Molly said. A spout of water shot from the whale's blowhole, and the impressive width of its tail flukes curled up behind it. It didn't surprise Molly that Patch didn't ask, simply reached out and caressed the carving.

"It's so smooth! And it feels cool, like maybe there's ice inside or something."

"You know, I've always thought the same thing. But I felt a little silly saying it."

Patch looked suspiciously at Molly. It was clear that she didn't want to be on the same side as her stepmother regarding anything.

Molly put the whale on the chest in her

bedroom, where she could see it each morning when she awoke. She would transfer it into Seth's room when she moved there. She didn't want to think about how soon that might be.

But it was the ship in the bottle that sent Patch into raptures. Molly placed the bottle on one side of the pine mantel above the fireplace.

"Garn!" Patch said. "Just look at that! Garn! How did that ship get inside there?"

"You'll have to ask Whit," Molly said with a smile. "He made this with his father."

That option obviously didn't appeal to Patch. "Don't you know?"

Molly shook her head. "James wouldn't let me watch. He said it's a sailor's secret. He taught Whit because he expected him to become a sailor."

"Durn. I sure would like to see how that's done."

"You'll have to ask Whit," Molly repeated.

Although Molly had definite plans for what she could do to the house to make it more of a home, she was less certain what steps she ought to take to make Patch more of a lady. Two obvious things came to mind. First, the girl needed a bath. Second, she needed to be dressed in some feminine clothing.

But when Molly suggested the idea of a bath to Patch, she got the quick response, "Don't need one." And when she asked where Patch's dresses were, so she might iron one for her, Patch said, "Don't have any."

Molly considered trying to manhandle Patch into a tub or getting her to stand still while she was measured for a dress. *I'd probably come off better tangling with the mountain lion,* she thought.

But throughout the afternoon, Molly put her mind to ways she could accomplish those first two goals. She felt like a general, planning a major campaign. It took the better part of the afternoon to devise her strategy. She put her plan into action that evening after supper.

While everyone was eating dessert, she put several kettles of water on the stove to heat.

"What are you cooking now?" Seth asked, imagining something as wonderful as the dried-apple pie he was finishing.

"Nothing. I'm heating water for Patch's bath."

"Don't need a bath," Patch said, looking warily at Molly.

"When was the last time you had one? A bath, I mean."

Patch frowned. "Don't remember."

"Then it's time for another one," Molly said firmly. She had found a large wooden tub outside the back door that looked like it doubled as a bathtub and had cleaned it earlier in the day. It was situated now in the corner by the stove. She began to fill it with warm water.

"I ain't taking a bath. You can't make me," Patch said to Molly.

"I don't plan to try," Molly replied. "I expect your father to do the honors."

Patch and Seth spoke at the same time. "What?"

"Your father can do for you whatever needs done. All I'm concerned about is that you get clean. Later, I need to take your measurements so I can make a dress for you. Come on, Whit, Nessie—let's go for a walk."

Ethan grinned at Seth and said, "Much as I'd love to stick around and see the fireworks, I think I'll join them."

A moment later, the house was empty except for Patch and Seth.

"Are you going to let her get away with this, Pa?" she demanded.

Seth tugged one of Patch's ears forward, revealing the grime there. Then he took her chin in his hand and angled her face one way and then the other. With his thumb he brushed at a stubborn smudge on her cheek. He took her hands and held them out in his. Molly had insisted Patch wash her hands before supper, but dirt was still crusted under her broken fingernails.

"She's got a point, Patch," he said at last. "You do need a bath."

"I ain't gonna do it, Pa."

Seth's eyes narrowed. "I say you are. Now take off your clothes and get into that tub without any more of this nonsense."

The blood bleached from Patch's face as it became clear her father had no intention of leaving the room. "I won't," she rasped. "And you can't make me."

If it had only been the two of them, Seth might have let it slide. But he shuddered at the thought of Molly's reaction if he couldn't get his daughter to bathe. He remained unyielding. "Get in the tub, Patch."

She glared at him, defiant. He rose from his chair and started toward her. She jumped up and took several steps backward until her legs came up against the tub. Staring at him the whole time, she pulled off her boots and socks and then stepped, fully clothed, into the tub. Before he could get to her, she sat down.

"There. I'm in the tub."

Seth was furious—not only at the fact that she'd thwarted him but at the way she'd chosen to do it. He didn't think, just reacted. An instant later he was beside the tub and had pulled Patch to her feet. One jerk downward in front sent buttons pinging across the wooden floor. A second jerk at the collar in back, and he had the shirt off her. Her arms immediately curled around her chest.

The only sounds were Seth's grunt as he wrapped an arm around her waist and hauled her into the air, and Patch's yelp of dismay as he yanked both trousers and drawers down and off over her kicking feet. Her pants landed on the floor at the same time he dumped her back into the tub with a resounding splash.

Patch moaned and immediately curled in on herself. Her head bowed as she drew her knees up to her chest and surrounded them with her arms.

"Now wash yourself," he commanded.

"Go away," she mumbled against her knees.

Seth didn't hear the plea in her tone, only the words of defiance. "By God, if you won't bathe yourself, I'll do it for you!"

Patch's head snapped up, and her panicked eyes sought his. "No! Pa! Please!"

He had already gone down on one knee and grabbed the washcloth Molly had left on the side of the tub. Grasping Patch by the wrist, he pulled her arm up over her head so he could wash under it. And stared, stunned at what he found.

Hair.

Because he was holding her arm up out of the way, he could see what else she had been hiding in that protective fetal position.

Budding breasts.

Patch's face flushed an agonized red, and she moaned again.

Seth let go of Patch's hand, which she immediately used to hug her knees tight against her breasts. He sat back on his haunches and exhaled a deep breath. "I had no idea, Patch," he said. "I knew you were becoming a woman. I just—I didn't realize you had . . . It's nothing to be ashamed of," he said.

"Please don't talk about it," she said, mortified.

"Look, Patch, I'm a doctor. I see bodies all the time. I—"

"Pa!" she wailed. "Go awaaaaay!"

Seth didn't know what to do. He wanted to stay and talk to her, but he was all too aware that her father was the last person she wanted there. "Be sure to wash your hair," he said, and rose and left the room.

Seth didn't know he was looking for Molly until he saw her with the children and Ethan coming toward him. When he met up with them, he said to Ethan, "Why don't you take Whit and Nessie and show them that spot down by the pond where the frogs congregate and sing?"

Ethan raised a brow in speculation. One look at the taut lines around Seth's eyes and mouth told him there was trouble. "Sure, Seth." He headed Molly's children toward the pond and said, "You kids have a real treat in store for you."

Seth started walking beside Molly back in the direction of the house.

Sensing his distress, she asked, "What's wrong?"

Seth stopped under a cottonwood and stared out toward the mountains. He looked for words to explain what had happened that wouldn't make him sound as bad as he felt. "It's Patch," he said at last. "She wouldn't take her clothes off and get in the tub. That is, she got in the tub with her clothes on. I lost my temper and stripped her down and—"

"And what?"

"She's got breasts!" he blurted.

Molly put her hand before her mouth and coughed so Seth wouldn't see her smile. "That explains her resistance to a bath. She's probably been hiding the fact that she's growing up from you for some time. A bath would have given her away."

"I acted like a fool and an idiot."

"None of us is perfect," Molly said with a teasing smile.

Seth groaned. "What can I do now?"

"Just keep doing the best you can." She thought for a moment and asked, "Do you think she'll take the bath?"

"She'd better."

"Then I think the best thing is to leave her alone long enough for her to finish in private. Then you act as though this never happened."

Seth looked relieved. "I can do that?"

Molly grinned. "I don't see why not. Next time she takes a bath, we can arrange for her to have the privacy a young lady needs. I'll have plenty of time when I take the measurements for her dress to find out if there are other questions Patch needs to ask or have answered."

Seth felt better, but he couldn't have said why. Nothing had changed. He had still embarrassed his daughter. She still had those budding breasts. Only somehow, Molly had made everything all right.

But over the next several days, it was clear the battle lines had been drawn. Molly was determined to introduce Patch to the womanly arts; Patch was equally determined to thwart her; Seth was caught in the middle.

To Molly's chagrin, Whit was being equally troublesome to Seth. Seth held his ground; she was caught in the middle.

Molly wasn't sure what she could do to make them a family, but she was determined not to give up or give in.

About a week after their arrival, Molly decided that things were enough under control in the house that she could surprise Seth, Ethan, and Whit with a picnic lunch. She made fried chicken and mashed potatoes and packed it up in a basket. Just before noon, she and Nessie and Patch set out for the stand of pines where the men were working.

When she arrived, Ethan was cutting limbs off a downed tree, but Seth and Whit were nowhere to be seen.

"Where's Seth?"

"He's farther up the mountain, chopping down another tree."

"Is Whit with him?"

"I suppose so."

That sounded too uncertain for Molly's peace of mind. She left Nessie and Patch in Ethan's care and went searching for Seth and her son.

When she saw Seth, she just stopped and stared. He had taken off his shirt, and dappled sunlight danced on the muscle and sinew in his shoulders and back. A trickle of sweat started down the crease in his back and eventually dampened the cloth at his waist. The sculpted beauty was marred by two large scars, one on his right shoulder and one on his lower back, just above the waist of his pants. She watched in awe as he lifted the heavy ax gracefully over his head. The echoing sound of the ax hitting wood brought her to her senses. She realized Whit wasn't with him.

There were reasons why her son might have left here momentarily. There was no reason to panic, so she didn't.

"Hello," she called.

When Seth turned, she caught her breath. He was truly a magnificent man. A smile flashed white in his tanned face. She smiled back and asked, "Where's Whit?"

Seth leaned against his ax and mopped his forehead with a red kerchief that had been hanging out of his back pocket. "Don't know," he admitted. "He decided he was tired, so he quit. He left here a while ago."

"Where was he going?"

"He didn't say."

Molly's heart began to pound. "You just let him leave?" She looked out at the dark expanse of jack pine and juniper, evergreens and leafy birch trees. "Why aren't you out looking for him?"

"He knows where I am," Seth said.

"But he may be lost. There are Indians out there, and wild animals and—"

Seth drew an arm-waving Molly into his embrace and held her there. "Molly," he said, trying to cut her off.

"—and buffalo and mountain lions and—"

"Molly."

"—and desperados and—"

Seth shut her up with his mouth. She had kept her distance from him ever since that night a week ago on the front porch. He had watched her, and wanted her, every moment of every day. But there had never been a time when their children were not around. Now that he had her in his arms, he took full advantage of whatever moments of privacy they might have.

He pulled her up snug against him, fitting

himself in the cradle of her thighs. He could feel her breasts against his chest through the thin cotton material of her dress. He grunted his disapproval when he discovered her waist was corseted. One hand held her head so she couldn't escape his kisses, and he plundered her mouth, taking what he needed.

Molly was overwhelmed by the astonishing heat of his passion. Hands that had come up to push him away, roamed his sweat-slick shoulders instead, feeling the muscle beneath smooth skin. When his tongue slid along the edge of her lips and she opened her mouth to protest, he thrust inside. He compelled a response from her, and her body gave what her heart would have withheld.

His mouth left hers to seek the flesh of her neck. She gasped at the curl of desire she felt as he sucked on tender skin. She hid her face against the muscle at his shoulder and accidentally tasted the salt on his skin. As his ardor increased, so did hers, and when he nipped her shoulder, she bit him back. And discovered it was pleasure, not pain she had caused.

With some sixth sense necessary to the frontier, Seth realized they were being watched. He abruptly pushed Molly behind him to protect her.

Molly gasped when she saw the look on her son's face.

Whit turned and ran. She started to go after him, but Seth stopped her.

"Let him go."

"I have to talk to him!"

"What can you say that he doesn't already know?" Seth asked.

Molly stood apart from Seth, refusing to let him draw her back into his arms. "I don't know," she said. "But for him to see us . . ."

Seth's lips flattened. "What he saw was a husband kissing his wife. There's nothing wrong with that."

But they both knew there had been more to it than that. It had not been a matter of simple kisses. There had been raw, explosive passion between them. And James Gallagher had been dead for less than a year.

"I brought a picnic," Molly said. "I'll leave it for you and Ethan . . . and Whit. I'm feeling tired all of a sudden. I don't think I'll stay to eat with you."

She turned and ran. Molly was breathless when she got back to the spot where Ethan was working. She grabbed Nessie and, with a quick excuse about the little girl's nap time approaching, headed back to the house.

Molly lay down on Patch's bed with Nessie

and read her daughter a fairy tale—one with a happy ending. As the little girl drifted off to sleep, Molly tried to make some sense of her confused emotions.

She couldn't deny her attraction to Seth. It would be foolish to try. Molly simply didn't understand how it was possible to feel so passionate in another man's arms when she was still grieving for James. Only, when she was in Seth's arms, she didn't think about James. Something magic happened. And the only face she saw, the only man she wanted, was Seth. She needed time to understand her feelings. But she was very much afraid Seth wasn't going to give it to her.

When Molly woke up, Nessie was gone. Something else had taken her place.

Molly stared wide-eyed at the snake on the pillow beside her and forced herself not to scream. She wouldn't give Patch the satisfaction. The rest of Patch's menagerie, once she had become acquainted with them, had all turned out to be harmless. Surely her snake —what was its name?—wasn't poisonous. Molly looked at the head to see whether it formed the triangle Seth had warned her meant a snake was venomous. It didn't look deadly. But better safe than sorry. She would just lie still. Patch would soon tire of waiting for her terrified reaction and come and collect her pet.

Only Seth showed up first.

"Don't move," he said.

His caution surprised Molly. Was he afraid of snakes in general? Or just this particular snake? He crossed slowly to the window and pushed it all the way open. She lay perfectly still as he reached for the broom standing in the corner. He slipped the wooden handle under the dark brown snake, which opened its mouth, revealing sharp fangs in a huge white expanse. In one continuous movement, Seth flipped the snake off the pillow and out the window, where it slithered away.

Seth pulled Molly up into a hard embrace. "Are you all right? You weren't bitten?"

"No. I—I thought it belonged to Patch."

Seth laughed shakily and hugged her tighter. "Oh no, my dear little tenderfoot. That was a cottonmouth."

"Venomous?"

"Very."

"How did it get in here?"

Seth nodded his head toward the open window. "Most likely through the window. Mostly the cottonmouths stay down by the water, but we're close enough that they sometimes wind their way up to the house looking for frogs. You have to be careful."

Molly began to shiver, a delayed reaction to the danger she'd been in.

Seth felt her reaction and rubbed her back to calm her. "You're all right. There's nothing to be afraid of now."

Molly shuddered. At one point, she had actually considered picking up the snake and confronting Patch with it. Imagine the child's reaction if she had! Molly laughed. It was her first genuine laugh for a long, long time. But really, enough was enough.

Misunderstanding Molly's hysterical laugh, Seth murmured soothing words of comfort. "Take it easy, sweetheart. You're fine. I won't let anyone, or anything hurt you. Relax, Molly. Relax, little darling, I—"

"What did you call me?"

Seth's stream of words was halted by the touch of her fingertips on his lips.

"Sweetheart? Darling?"

"Little darling," Molly said. "You called me little darling. James used to call me that."

Seth stiffened and started to release her.

"Please don't let go," Molly said. "I—I'm still feeling a little scared, if you want to know the truth."

Seth's arms closed around her again. He

put one hand under her hair to rub her nape. Her head eased forward to give him greater access, and her cheek rested against the chambray shirt he had donned.

"What are we going to do about our children?" she murmured.

"I don't know," Seth said. "I'm doing everything I can think of to make it easier for Whit, but he doesn't seem to want to cooperate."

Molly stiffened at his criticism of her son. "He's only ten. You can't expect him to be able to do such hard work."

"Out here, a boy learns to do a man's job in a hurry, or he doesn't survive."

Molly's head came up. "Well, he's not a man, he's a boy," she protested.

"You expect a lot from Patch, and she's just a little girl," Seth said.

"She's twelve!"

"She's a kid."

"She's a—" Molly cut herself off.

Seth grimaced and stood. Neither of them felt very loverlike at the moment. "I only came by to say I have to make a trip into town to get some window glass tomorrow, and to invite you to come along. I thought maybe you'd like to get some curtain material or something."

Molly opened her mouth to continue the discussion—all right, argument—they'd been having about their children, then shut it again. It was a long ride into Fort Benton. She would have plenty of time, and privacy, to talk with Seth about his daughter—and her son. "I would very much like to go," she said.

"Fine. You might want to ask Ethan to keep an eye on Nessie."

That evening at supper, Seth announced that he and Molly would be driving in to Fort Benton the following day.

"Can I come, too, Pa?" Patch asked.

Molly's heart sank. If Patch came, they wouldn't have a chance to have that heart to heart talk. To her surprise, Seth said, "I'm taking the buckboard so I can get supplies. There won't be room for you."

"I can sit up front with you," Patch said.

"Molly's sitting up front."

"Oh."

Molly waited for further complaint from Patch. When it didn't come, she eyed the girl suspiciously. Patch never gave up when she wanted something, she just went about it another way. Molly decided that it wouldn't hurt to keep watch over her shoulder when they left, to see if they were being followed.

8

Ethan's nose twitched at the heavy smell of perfume in the darkened room. "Dora?"

"Over here, Ethan. I'm at the window."

He lit a lantern before trying to cross the room and then was glad he had. Dora collected dolls. They were all over the room, on shelves, on the dressing table, on the bed, and even in boxes on the floor. Ethan wove his way around the clutter and sat down on the windowsill. Dora was sitting in the rocker facing out, caressing the yarn hair of a Raggedy Ann.

"Drake was here tonight," she said. "He had me try everything, but nothing worked. Poor man."

Ethan was sure from the way she said it that Dora wasn't the least bit sorry. "Any news?" he said.

"He's setting up another operation on the butte west of town, where his whiskey-seller can see for two miles around who's coming.

Do you think the Masked Marauder can manage to get the drop on him?"

Ethan smiled. "He usually does."

"Cal gave me this doll," she said, holding the Raggedy Ann like a child against her breast. "Said he was gonna give me a Raggedy Andy to go with it. That was the day before Drake had Pike Hardesty shoot him." She leaned forward and grasped Ethan's thigh. Her nails bit into his skin clear through the denim. "Drake has to die. He had Cal killed, and he has to die."

Ethan put a hand on hers, forcing her to release him. "I owe you, Dora. I'd've lost my leg if it hadn't been for you. Whatever I can do, I will."

Dora's voice was barely audible when she said, "Cal wanted to marry me, Ethan. I would have been the sheriff's wife. I would have been an honest woman. Drake Bassett took that away from me. He has to pay."

For the tenth day since those Gallaghers had shown up, Patch made a bed for herself on the buffalo skin in front of Ethan's hearth. He slept in the bedroom, which was divided from the main room by a red-striped gray blanket across the doorway. Thanks to the upheaval in her life caused by the appearance of the Gallagher family, she had recently spent many a sleepless night reliving distressing incidents from the day just past.

Even now she cringed at the memory of the humiliation she had felt three days ago when her father had stripped her naked and dumped her willy-nilly into that tub of water. He had seen *everything*. She wasn't his little girl anymore. She didn't want to grow up; but her body was doing it despite her wishes.

Her stepmother had come into the house after that disastrous business with her pa and insisted on measuring her for a dress. Not that Patch would ever wear it. Not willingly, anyway. It was bad enough that her body was conspiring to make her a woman; now Molly Gallagher seemed intent on finishing the job. If that woman had her way, Patch could say good-bye to trousers forever.

She had barely gotten her long johns on after her bath when that woman had confronted her with a measuring tape in one hand and a silk dress in the other. It had certainly been a pretty dress, a kind of mossy green. And it had looked a good deal softer than the chambray and corduroy Patch usually wore. But she wasn't about to let herself be bribed into doing anything Molly Gallagher wanted. She had watched warily as the woman approached her.

"I want to see if I can cut this down to fit you," she had said as she laid the dress over the back of a chair.

Patch hadn't been able to resist reaching out and caressing the fabric. It was as soft as it looked, as sleek and silky as Rebel's underbelly.

"Hold your arms out, please," Molly said.

Patch had thought seriously about refusing, but the possibility of her father being called to enforce Molly's request convinced her to obey.

Molly measured her shoulders, the length of her arms, and then beneath them, around her budding bosom. "I'll have to take in the bodice slightly."

Patch flushed a deep red, but Molly had already gone on to measure the distance to her waist from under her arm.

"When I was a child growing up," Molly said, "my father used to spend time with me each evening, talking to me while I took my bath. He told me funny stories about the customers in his saloon. We laughed a lot, and we both enjoyed it immensely. Then a day came when I felt uncomfortable about having him there. I had changed. Things had changed."

If Molly hadn't had the measuring tape around Patch's waist, she would have bolted right then and there. But there was no escape, so she was forced to listen as Molly continued, "I didn't quite know how to tell him that I was growing up. I felt sad that I wasn't his little girl anymore."

Patch stood frozen as Molly measured the length for the hem.

"Fortunately, I had a mother to turn to. I told her how I felt, and she explained my feelings to my father. I knew everything was all right when he came to me the next night at bedtime instead of bathtime to tell all the funny stories about his customers. We hadn't lost any of the closeness we had shared before. He had simply acknowledged that I was a young woman entitled to my privacy."

Molly had finished measuring and began winding up her tape. "There. That wasn't so bad, was it?"

"Bad enough," Patch muttered. She stared with narrowed eyes at her stepmother. Her pa must have said something about what had happened here tonight. Was Molly offering to speak to her pa on her behalf? Had she already done so? Patch wanted no repeat of the embarrassment of this evening. Better to be safe than sorry. She cleared her throat and said, "I'm—uh . . . I need some privacy myself."

"Of course you do," Molly agreed. "I was just telling your father tonight that we need to make some arrangements to curtain off a portion of this room for baths."

"Uh . . . sure."

"I'll just get started on this dress." She had eyed Patch's long underwear, tapped her chin with a finger, and added, "I think some dainty underthings are needed as well."

Molly had left her standing there feeling both confused and relieved. In the past, Patch hadn't needed anybody helping her get along with her pa. Why had she been willing to let that Gallagher woman intervene now? Maybe there were just some things a girl shouldn't have to explain to her father. Patch consoled herself with the thought that she hadn't *asked* for help, she had just been smart enough to take it when it was offered.

Last night, Patch had taken a bath in absolute privacy. To her relief, her pa hadn't said a thing to her. When she found herself feeling grateful to her stepmother for the way things had turned out, she reminded herself that if Molly Gallagher hadn't married her pa, the issue of baths and privacy would never have arisen in the first place.

Anyway, the sooner that woman was gone, the sooner things could get back to normal. Patch closed her eyes, tightened her fingers in the thick fur of the buffalo robe, and imagined that everything was back just the way it had been before the Gallaghers had arrived. But even that thought didn't bring the comfort she had hoped for. Because things hadn't been perfect even then. She fingered the slightly chipped tooth she'd gotten in the fight with the preacher's middle boy. At least with the Gallaghers here, forcing her to stay around the house, she hadn't been in a fight lately.

When the front door rattled, Patch sat bolt upright. Not that she was afraid, with Ethan asleep right in the next room. But she had lived long enough in Montana to see the results of an Indian raid. And she had overheard tales of the cruelty of the small bands of Blackfoot renegades that roamed the plains. Patch rose on her haunches when the door opened just a crack, as though someone were sneaking in. She searched the room for a weapon she could use and settled on a medium-size log from the woodpile near the fireplace.

Tiptoeing, she edged her way over to a spot behind the door. As the intruder stepped inside, she raised the log over her head. It was at the top of its downward arc when she heard Whit whisper, "Patch? Are you in there?"

It took every bit of muscle she had to swerve the log so it didn't crush Whit's skull. "Durn it, Whit! I nearly smashed you flat!" she hissed.

Whit had a hand at his throat, and his eyes were wide as he confronted the raging girl. "I need to talk to you," he said, keeping his voice low. "It's important. A matter of life and death."

Phrased like that, Patch couldn't very well turn him away. She looked down at the baggy red long johns that were all she was wearing, shrugged, and said, "Come on over by the fire where there's more light. And be quiet so you don't disturb Ethan. He's sleeping behind that blanket over there."

Whit followed her, Pied-Piper style, across the room. "Golly!" he said in a hushed voice as they settled on the buffalo robe. "Is this real?"

Patch snorted disdainfully. "What do you think?"

"Golly!" Whit repeated. "This is great. Look

at those antlers over the fireplace. I've never
seen the like. That must have been a huge
deer!"

"It was an elk," Patch corrected impatiently. "Did you come here to talk or to admire the furnishings?"

Whit sat cross-legged, and he pounded a
fist against his knee. "I came because I have
to get out of here. I have to get back to New
Bedford—to the sea."

"Why are you telling me? If you want to
leave, just go. And good riddance!"

"I wish I could. But I need your help to get
to Fort Benton. I figure that from there I can
stow away on a steamboat downriver, then
hide on a train heading back east."

Patch was a little in awe of Whit's resolve.
"Aren't you scared to go all that way alone?"

Whit sat up a little straighter. "Naw. It'll be
easy," he said with bravado.

Patch's eyes narrowed speculatively. Get
rid of the boy, and the mother and that baby
were sure to follow. "All right," she said. "You
heard my pa say he's going to be taking a
buckboard into Fort Benton tomorrow. I'll
help you hide in the wagon. How does that
sound?"

"Fine. Except, how will I find my way to
the levee once I get there?"

Patch rolled her eyes. "Someone who's planning to cross the whole country by himself ought to be able to find his way across one little town."

"Well, I don't think I can! So are you going to come along and help me or not?" Whit demanded.

Patch shrugged. "Sure. Why not?" Then she had a sudden thought. "For a price."

Whit frowned. "I don't have any money."

"I don't want money. I want to know the secret of how you and your pa got that ship into that bottle."

"I can't tell you that."

"Then I can't help you."

"Aw, come on."

Patch crossed her arms resolutely. "If you want my help, tell me how it's done."

Whit grimaced, then leaned over and cupped his hand beside Patch's ear and whispered to her.

"Why, even *I* could do that!" she exclaimed when he was finished.

Suddenly the front door creaked open.

Patch's eyes rounded at the sight of the tall, dark figure in the doorway. "I thought you were in bed asleep!"

Ethan grinned ruefully. "I could say the same thing about you." As he stepped into the room, he removed his hat and hooked it on an antler on the wall beside the door. "What are you doing up? And what is Whit doing here?"

"Uh . . ." Patch couldn't think of a logical reason why Whit would have come to visit her. After all, they had barely spoken to each other since she'd given him a bloody nose.

"I wanted to see where you lived," Whit volunteered.

Ethan cocked a disbelieving brow. "In the middle of the night?"

"*He* keeps me too busy working in the day-time to do much of anything else," Whit retorted bitterly.

"It's late," Ethan said. "You'd better get on home before your ma comes looking for you."

"That's not my home!" Whit said. "But I'll be going." He gave Patch one last surreptitious look before crossing the room and letting himself out the door.

Ethan sat down in the wooden rocker beside the fireplace. He leaned back and hooked the ankle of one leg across the knee of the other. "What was that all about?"

"Oh, nothing." Patch knew that Ethan wasn't going to stop asking questions until he'd wormed the whole story out of her. She needed something to distract him from that purpose. Her nose wrinkled when she noticed a pungent odor surrounding him. "Is that whiskey I smell?"

She followed her nose, and it led her to Ethan's navy wool shirt. "You stink like a saloon on a Saturday night." She rose up on her knees to sniff his breath. Surprisingly, there was no whiskey smell. Her brow furrowed. That didn't make any sense at all. "How come your clothes smell like whiskey but your breath doesn't?"

Ethan set his foot down from his knee and started the rocker in motion. "I dropped by the Medicine Bow planning to have a drink. Before I could order, a freightman stumbled and spilled his drink down the front of me. Then Dora came up to wipe me off and"—he grinned—"my plans changed."

Patch made a moue of distaste. "Consarn it! I don't see why you or Pa want to have anything to do with that Dora Deveraux. That red-headed floozy is a—"

Abruptly, Ethan caught Patch by the chin and said, "Don't be calling names, Patch. It's not something a lady does."

Patch recoiled at Ethan's rebuke. She jerked herself out of his hold and scooted over to where she'd made her pallet. She turned her back on him and pulled the quilt up over her shoulder. As she stared into the fire, her eyes blurred. Her chest felt achy deep inside. It hurt to swallow.

Why did Ethan's disapproval always seem so much worse than Pa's? And he had used that word again. *Lady.* Dora Deveraux wasn't a lady, but both Pa and Ethan gave the dang woman plenty of attention.

"I heard tell you're going to be getting a new dress," Ethan said.

"I got measured for one," she admitted.

"That's something I'd like to see," he mused. "I bet you'd be a sight all gussied up."

Patch rolled over to face Ethan. "A dress won't make me a lady," she said, "if that's what you're thinking."

"I was only thinking that you'd be awful pretty in a dress," he said in a soft voice. "And it'd make your father happy."

"All right. I'll wear the stupid dress. But only for Pa's sake."

He smiled, and she was glad she'd agreed.

Ethan stood to go to bed. On his way past, he bent over and tousled her hair. He paused and let a strand or two slide through his fingers.

"Why, this is like cornsilk," he said. "What'd you do to it?"

"I washed it," Patch said, slapping his hand aside.

"You oughta wash it more often."

It was one insult too many. Patch attacked, throwing her weight against Ethan's legs and tripping him. Ethan just laughed as he rolled into the fall. She quickly pinned him down on his back by sitting on him. The harder he laughed, the madder she got.

Patch hit at whatever part of him she could reach with her fists. "Durn you, Ethan! Smelling like you do, how dare you say that *I* need to bathe more often."

He did little to defend himself, just parried the worst of her blows and laughed. "If the shoe fits, wear it," he managed to say. Then added, "That is, if you haven't dumped them all in the river."

Even the mention of shoes was like rubbing salt in an open wound. Patch used every swear word she knew and several new ones she made up for the occasion. Ethan just roared with laughter.

"That's enough games for now, Patch," he said at last, capturing both her hands in one of his. "It's way past your bedtime."

"I'm not a child," she huffed. "I can stay up as long as I like."

"Yeah, well, you're acting awful cranky."

"Yeah, well, maybe I've got good reason."

He shoved her off onto her fanny on the floor and got to his feet. "Suit yourself. I'm dead on my feet." He ruffled her hair once more and dodged her hand when she swung at him.

Patch watched him walk out of the room without giving her a backward look. She could still hear him chuckling as his boots hit the floor.

Oh, the indignity of it all! Patch didn't understand why his cavalier treatment galled her so. She only knew it did. She felt peeved, put-upon, and provoked. But she would get her revenge. Just let Ethan try finding his boots tomorrow morning. She'd take great pleasure in telling him he could go fish for them!

The creak of floorboards in the hall woke Molly. It was still pitch dark, and she wondered who was wandering around at this time of night. She quickly rose and put on a robe to investigate. To her surprise, she caught Whit stealthily opening the door to Seth's room.

"What are you doing out of bed?"

Whit flattened guiltily against the wall. "I

was just—I just . . . I went out to use the necessary," he said.

"Oh. Well, be careful you don't wake up Seth when you get in bed."

"That's no problem," Whit said. "Because he's not in there."

"He's not?"

"He never came to bed," Whit said.

"Go on, then, and get back to sleep." Molly made sure Whit got into bed and waited to tuck him in before she left. But instead of going back to bed, she walked over to the lace-curtained window. For a long while she stood watching as the sky slowly turned from a dark cocoon into a brilliant pastel butterfly of color.

Where was Seth? she wondered. Why hadn't he said he was leaving? And why should it upset her so much to know he had disappeared without telling her where he was going? More important, did she really want to be there to confront him when he returned?

Suddenly, the door opened, and he was standing there.

"Molly? Is something wrong?"

She kept her voice carefully under control as she replied, "You tell me. Where were you, Seth?"

"I was . . . with a patient. Mrs. Gulliver."

"All night?"

"I didn't intend to be gone so long, but she was having trouble. So I stayed."

He was lying. She could see it in his eyes, hear it in his tone of voice. But why would he lie? What could he possibly have been doing that he couldn't tell her about? The possibilities were endless and distressing, to say the least.

Molly wasn't sure what she would have said next, but she was never given the chance. There was a sharp rap on the door, and when Seth opened it, a heavy-set man wearing overalls and workboots stood there. His hair was standing on end and going every which way, and he was nervously curling the brim on a battered brown hat.

"It's Iris," the man said. "It's her time."

"I'll get my bag," Seth replied. He explained to Molly, "It's Iris Marsh, our closest neighbor. She's having labor pains at last. The baby's late coming. I've got to go. We'll have to postpone our trip into town."

Molly saw the worried look on Seth's face and said, "I'll go with you. Maybe I can help."

"The children—"

"I'll wake up Whit. He can take care of Nessie. Just give me a minute to get dressed."

Seth was waiting outside with the buggy harnessed when Molly came through the front door. "Let's go," she said.

It was a quick five miles to the Marsh place, which turned out to be a sod house cut into the side of a hill. Molly was astonished when she entered to see how many people were living in the small, dark space. There were identical twin boys about Whit's age, an older girl with deep-set brown eyes who held a year-old baby in her arms, and a pig-tailed girl about Nessie's age. Five children. And Iris Marsh was expecting a sixth.

"You kids stay out of Doc Kendrick's way, you hear?" their father said. "How's that boilin' water comin'?" he asked the oldest girl.

"It's ready, Pa," she said. "Whenever Doc Kendrick needs it."

"I'll leave you to it, Doc," Henry Marsh said. "I've got some plowing to do." He called the twin boys to come with him and left the room.

Molly couldn't believe he would simply walk away like that. Didn't he want to be near his wife in case something went wrong? But then, he wasn't going far—no farther than a voice could call.

Molly had experienced childbirth with and

without her husband present. James had
been at sea when Whit was born. She had
cried out in vain for him when the pains
were at their worst. She had wept tears of joy
when she saw their son for the first time.
How she wished James had been there to
share the moment with her! Whit had been
two when James finally came home. Her son
had been frightened of James's enthusiastic
homecoming, but he had soon come to love
his father. He was inconsolable when James
took to the sea again.

When Nessie was born, James had been
home, but he had been no more a part of the
birthing process than he had when he was
gone. Oh, he had come upstairs when she
called. But when Molly saw how much her
pain distressed him, she had sent him away
again. Perhaps that was the case with Henry
Marsh. At any rate, as many times as Iris had
been through this ordeal, the two of them
must have worked out this arrangement between them.

Molly met Seth's eyes and smiled. This
must be the most rewarding part of his work,
she thought. To help bring new life into the
world.

A small portion of the room had been curtained off with a blanket hung from a rope. A constant low moan was coming from behind the partition. Molly stepped behind the blanket and was immediately drawn to the woman who lay there.

Iris Marsh was rail thin, except for her immense belly. She had a piece of leather clenched between her teeth through which guttural groans were escaping. Her hands gripped the brass bedstead above her as her body strained to disgorge its burden. Her chambray nightgown was draped at her waist, and her knees were up and widespread. To Molly's amazement, the woman's abdomen rippled under the powerful contraction.

As soon as the contraction was over, Iris let go of the bedrail, heaved a sigh of relief, and reached out to shake Molly's hand. "You must be the new Mrs. Kendrick. Heard the doc got hitched. It's a pleasure meetin' you, ma'am."

Molly responded to the woman's overture with equal warmth. "I'm pleased to meet you, too, Mrs. Marsh."

"Call me Iris. Everybody does."

"And I'm Molly. You have a lovely family, Iris. Are you wishing for a girl or a boy?"

"Henry wants a boy. But I'd like to have me another little girl. Heard you brought a couple kids with you. How are they taking to the west?"

Molly looked up at Seth, wondering where all this information had come from, but he just smiled and shrugged. "The children are adjusting very well," she said. If it was a lie, it was in a good cause.

"I know you ladies would like to chat some more, but there's some business needs tending," Seth said. "Molly, see if you can find a clean sheet to put under Iris. And get me some of that boiling water for my instruments. I don't think it's going to be long now."

Molly did as she was told. But long after the sheets had been changed and the boiling water had cooled, the child still had not been born. More than five long hours had passed since they had arrived. Molly now knew more about Iris Marsh than she had learned about Aunt Hattie in the six months she'd lived with her.

She knew Iris and Henry had come west from a farm in Kansas trying to escape memories of atrocities that had occurred in their town during the war. That Henry preferred suspenders to a belt and that he wore false teeth. That Iris had always wanted a red satin dress and had dreamed of performing on a steamboat traversing the Missouri. That they had named their girls after flowers—Rose, Amaryllis, and Daisy—and their boys after trees—Ash and Alder. This baby would be called Lily if it was a girl, and Birch if it was a boy.

If Molly had even suspected something might go wrong, she wouldn't have let herself get so involved with the other woman. But it had seemed when they arrived that everything would be over very quickly. The baby's head had crowned some time ago, yet it refused to be born. Molly didn't dare voice the fear that had been growing over the past several hours because she didn't want to frighten Iris. But in that, she had underestimated the older woman.

"Something's wrong, Doc," Iris said. "I been straining, but the babe just won't come. Ain't there something you kin do?"

Seth took the woman's hand in his to check her pulse. It was weak; Iris was tiring. "I can try using forceps to pull the baby out. Don't know if it'll work. But it's all I know to do."

"You won't crush its skull or nothing like that, will you, Doc?"

Molly saw Seth swallow hard. "I'll be careful, Iris. As though it were my own child."

"I trust you, Doc," the exhausted woman said as her eyes fell closed. "Don't know how much longer I can hang on. Better go ahead and give it a try."

"Don't give up," Molly said as she squeezed Iris's hand.

"Don't you worry none about me," Iris murmured. "I ain't forgot you promised to throw me a christenin' party at your place."

In fact, they had planned the entire party down to the date and the guest list. Molly only hoped there would be a reason to celebrate.

"I'll need your help," Seth said to Molly. "I'm going to try and situate the head a little better for what I need to do. And I may have to cut a little. Be ready to hand me the scalpel and forceps."

Molly saw Seth's hands trembling, and she realized suddenly the tremendous courage it must take to play God. What followed happened mercifully quickly. He made a small incision, and the forceps did what all Iris's hours of pushing hadn't. Moments later, the baby was lying on the sheet between Iris's legs. Molly watched with growing respect for Seth's skill as he cleaned the mucus from the baby's throat and gave it a slap on the rump that forced out a lusty cry.

Molly felt the sting of joyful tears as she met Seth's jubilant gray eyes. She wondered at that moment what it would be like to have Seth's child, to see the joy on his face at the moment of birth.

"You have a daughter, Iris," Seth said. "Lily looks just fine."

Seth cut the cord and laid the baby beside her mother, while he waited for the after-birth and disposed of it. He made sure there wasn't any additional bleeding, then stitched up the cut he'd made.

Iris was too tired even to open her eyes to look at her new daughter. But Molly saw her feel the tiny fingers and toes, and smile when she realized they were all there.

"I guess I owe you that christening party," Molly said. "I'll take care of sending out the invitations."

Iris just nodded and kept on smiling.

A moment later, Henry appeared at his wife's bedside. He looked harried, worried, and Molly realized that even though he hadn't been present in the room, he had never really left it.

"She looks awful pale, Doc," Henry said.

"It was a hard birth," Seth said. "But give

her a little rest, and she'll be fine. By the way, you have a daughter."

Henry grinned, exposing the full set of false teeth. "She's purty as her mama, ain't she, Doc."

"Sure is, Henry. Guess we'll be going. I hoped to get to town today. May still be able to make the trip if I hurry."

It was shortly after noon, and Molly felt wrung out. And exhilarated. As Seth headed the buggy back toward home, Molly put her arm on his sleeve and said, "I don't pretend to know much about you, Seth Kendrick. But you aren't a coward. That was the most courageous act I've ever seen in my life. I am so proud of you, and proud to be your wife. You saved Iris's life. And you brought Lily into this world whole and healthy."

Seth was more moved than he could say. Molly's belief in him was a balm for his battered soul. He wanted to reward her confidence in him by telling her everything. The first words were on his lips when he bit them back. He couldn't tell her the truth. Not without taking the chance that she would despise him for it.

And now that he'd had a taste of it, he wanted, craved his wife's admiration. So he sat still and stolid and saw her expression cool when he didn't respond to what she had said.

"Do you still want to go to town today?" he asked.

"Why, yes, if we have the time before dark."

"You aren't too tired?"

Discouraged, yes. Tired, no. "I'll be fine. Besides, I'd like to get a present for the baby."

"All right. We'll drop by the house and exchange the buggy for the buckboard and then go on."

Molly removed her hand from Seth's sleeve and folded it together with the other one in her lap. She looked at Seth from under her lashes, trying to decipher the expression on his face. But his features were stony. There was nothing to see.

Only now, Molly was more curious than ever about the man she had married. She had a thousand things she wanted to ask Seth but couldn't think how to begin the conversation. At long last she simply said, "Tell me about Patch's mother."

At first she thought he wasn't going to answer. Then he took a deep breath and said, "What do you want to know?"

"What was her name?"

"Annarose."

"What was she like?"

"She was blond and blue-eyed. Tall. And her left cheek dimpled when she smiled." Which had been often.

Molly tucked a strand of hair behind her ear that had blown loose in the wind. She pulled her straw bonnet down and retied the bow a little tighter under her chin. "That's what she looked like. Tell me something else about her."

For a long time he just stared off over the grassy plains. At last he said, "She was terrified when she found out she was going to have a child. Her mother had told her that birthing a baby was a painful ordeal. But as the baby grew inside her and started to move, she became fascinated and excited by the whole idea.

"As she grew more confident, I became more terrified. I didn't want to lose her. Annarose had become the light of my world, my happiness, my heart. It turned out that I was right to be afraid. It was a hard birth."

Seth cleared his throat and continued. "After Patch was born, Annarose's skin was white as chalk, she had lost so much blood."

"Is that how she died? In childbirth?"

He shook his head. "Annarose cheated the

Devil. Two days later, she was on her feet. She took to mothering like a kid to hard candy and nursed Patch for almost a year. I never got tired of watching. I learned what it meant to be father and husband. I was their protector; it was up to me to keep them safe from harm."

"It must have been a comfort to have all that knowledge of medicine."

"I wasn't a doctor then," he said flatly.

That surprised Molly. "What did you do?"

He hesitated, then said, "It doesn't matter. That's all in the past."

Molly had opened her mouth to ask just how and when Annarose *had* died, when Seth cut her off.

"Anyway, it's my turn to ask some questions." He looked her straight in the eye and said, "Tell me about James—and I don't mean what he looked like."

The first words out of Molly's mouth surprised her. "He was hardly ever home." They sounded resentful, even to her ears. She hadn't felt that way at the time—or had she? She tried to explain away the condemning inflection in her voice. "He was the captain of a whaling vessel, you see, and had to be gone for years at a time."

Seth cocked his head to look at her. "You say that as though he had no choice."

"He didn't, really. The men in his family had been whalers for a hundred years. He was born and bred to it. And he loved it."

"More than he loved you?"

Molly drew in a hissing breath. "I don't think that's a fair question. He loved me, and he loved whaling."

"So he had both a wife and a mistress."

Molly frowned. "I don't understand."

"You and the sea," Seth said.

"He loved me more," Molly insisted.

"But he always chose the sea."

Molly was silent for the rest of the trip home. In the eleven years she had been married, it had never occurred to her to question the fact that James had spent seven of those years at sea. Gallaghers were whaling men. They came home to unload the whale oil in their holds, to impregnate their wives, and to spend what they'd earned. Then they repaired their ships, restocked them with provisions, and set sail again. It had never occurred to her to be jealous of the sea. Until now. When it was much too late.

Maybe with Seth she ought not to take things so much for granted. Maybe this time around, she should not be so indulgent of her husband. Maybe on the trip to Fort Benton, she would just have to ask Seth where he had gone last night, and demand an honest answer.

9

"That damned Masked Marauder has been at it again!"

Drake Bassett kicked at one of several broken whiskey kegs that littered the ground. Pike Hardesty had brought him up to the butte overlooking town to see for himself the damage that had been done. Drake was used to opposition; he had learned how to crush it. But this Masked Marauder was turning out to be as hard to pin down as campfire smoke.

The man Bassett had hired to sell whiskey to the Blackfeet lay on the grass groaning. He hadn't been shot—just forced to drink a great deal of the alcohol-turpentine-tar mixture he'd been selling. The poor sot might have been better off dead, Bassett thought. The whiskey concoction had blinded him.

"Get him into town and see if Doc Kendrick can do anything for him," Bassett told his henchman.

Pike leaned against a scrub juniper, cleaning his teeth with a broken twig. "Sure, boss. Whatever you say."

"I want you to find a way to stop this Marauder," Bassett said. "He's costing me a fortune, dumping whiskey faster than I can make it. I'm paying you for protection, Pike. If you can't do the job, I'll get someone who can."

Pike scratched the stubble under his chin with the twig he'd been using on his teeth. "Just can't figure out who this Marauder fella could be," he said. "Isn't a man in town I can name with the balls to do a thing like this."

"It's damned certain somebody was here. I want him caught."

"That Masked Marauder don't hang around long enough to get caught," Pike protested.

"That's your problem," Bassett said. "Clean up this mess. And I don't want to see that ugly face of yours again until you've come up with a way to get rid of that damned Masked Marauder!"

The instant Patch saw her father drive up in the buggy, she sought out Whit. He was just pulling his suspenders up over his shoulders after leaving the outhouse when Patch intercepted him. "Come on. It's time."

In the bright light of day, Whit had begun having doubts. He dragged his feet as she hauled him toward the buckboard. "I'm not so sure—"

"Look, when I talked to you last night, you said you wanted to run away. Now do you, or don't you?"

Whit's brow furrowed. "I do. But I've been thinking. Maybe I need to plan some more. What if I get hungry on the trip?"

"I'll pack you a tin full of sandwiches and some dried apples. That ought to hold you till the steamboat's a fair distance from Fort Benton. Then you can let the captain know you're on board and work your way to St. Louis."

Whit thought of the severe punishment for a stowaway on board a sailing ship and wondered if the same treatment applied on the river.

"Do you want to stay here in Montana for the rest of your life?" Patch asked.

"No."

"Then what are we waiting for? I thought you wanted to be a sailor—and get back to the sea," she taunted.

"All right," Whit said, his jaw firming as she whipped at his pride. "Let's go."

Patch hid Whit under the canvas tarp that

covered the bed of the buckboard, then went to the kitchen to pack a lunch for him. She thought the game was up when Ethan caught her wrapping sandwiches in brown paper.

"What are you doing?"

"I'm—uh . . . packing some food for me and Whit. We're going fishing. Is that all right with you?" she asked with just enough belligerence to back him off.

Ethan stuck his thumbs in the front of his jeans. "I think it's nice of you to take Whit under your wing like this."

"Who said I—" Patch cut herself off. Let Ethan think what he wanted. The truth would be out soon enough. "I gotta go. Tell Pa where we are, will you?"

"Sure, be glad to." He grinned and added, "By the way, you might see if you can hook your shoes while you're at it."

Patch grimaced and looked down at her bare feet. After Ethan had retrieved his black leather boots that morning, he had retaliated for the trick she'd played on him. Her oldest, most worn-out—most comfortably worn-in— pair of shoes had been pitched into the pond. She had newer shoes, but on general principle she chose not to wear them. It wasn't the first time, and wouldn't be the last, that she had gone barefoot.

Patch wasn't even out the door when she saw Ethan pick up Nessie and rub noses with her. That baby definitely had to go! She hurried to the wagon, looked around to make sure she wasn't observed, then slipped underneath the canvas to join Whit. A second later the dog-wolf, Maverick, jumped under the tarp to join her. Standing up as he was, the dog's figure was clearly outlined under the canvas.

"Hey! What's he doing here?" Whit demanded. "He's going to ruin everything."

"Go away, Maverick," Patch said, shoving at the dog's haunches. He didn't budge.

"Come here and help," she ordered Whit.

"He'll bite me."

"No, he won't. Come on, hurry. Before they come."

The two of them shoved with all their might, but the most they accomplished was to get Maverick to lie down.

"This is just great," Whit said in a voice that made it clear that he thought it was anything but. "What do we do now?"

"This isn't really such a bad thing," Patch said. "Nobody's gonna come around asking us any questions in town with Maverick along."

Whit pursed his lips. "Yeah, maybe you're

right. Just make sure you keep him quiet till we get there."

Patch lay down with her head on Maverick's fur. She settled herself none too soon. A moment later, she heard her father helping Molly up onto the buckboard.

"What an awful message to find waiting for you," Molly said. "Do you think you'll be able to help that poor man who was blinded?"

"Won't know till I see him. You sure you still want to go along? We're liable to end up spending the night."

"Yes. I just wish I'd had a chance to talk to Whit," Molly said. "I wanted to ask him to help Ethan with Nessie."

"Don't worry. Ethan'll take care of everything. Look at the bright side. Patch and Whit are doing something together for a change."

If only he knew, Patch thought, eyeing Whit in the shadows across from her. *If only he knew.*

Indeed, if Seth and Molly had realized their children were hidden in the back of the buckboard, they might have guarded their conversation more carefully. As it was, Patch's ears burned, and Whit's face turned scarlet as their parents exchanged humorous yet personally revealing stories about their children.

"I'll bet you'd never guess how Patch got her nickname," Seth said.

"I thought it was a shortened name for Patricia."

Seth grinned. "It could be, but it isn't. Ethan gave her the nickname when she was just three."

"Uh-oh," Molly said with a smile. "I think I know where this story is heading."

"Patch had this habit of crawling up on Ethan's chest when he was sleeping. Every time he woke up, there was this patch on his long johns where Patch's wet bottom had been. He took to calling her Patch, and the name stuck."

"That's almost as bad as how Whit got his name," Molly said.

"What's Whit short for?" Seth asked. "Whitley? Whittaker, Whitcomb?"

"Whittling."

"You're kidding."

Molly grinned and shook her head. "When we were first married, James spent time every evening after dinner sitting on the back stoop whittling. He was gone to sea when I found out I was expecting a child, and I had no idea what I should name the baby. The one thing I knew James loved was—"

"Whittling," Seth said with a laugh.

Whit rolled his eyes, and Patch grimaced back at him. They didn't think their parents were the least bit funny. To make matters worse, the heat was stifling under the canvas. Ticklish rivulets of sweat inched their way down into embarrassing places that couldn't be scratched with someone else watching. When Maverick started to stand up halfway through the trip, it took their combined weights, and overlapping body parts, to hold him down. By the time they reached the town limits of Fort Benton, neither Patch nor Whit could look the other in the eye.

Meanwhile, several times during the conversation, Molly had been on the verge of confronting Seth about where he'd spent the previous night. But the mood between them had been so pleasant that she couldn't bear to spoil it. Maybe he had been telling the truth. The least she could do was give him the benefit of the doubt.

What was more worrisome to her was how to deal with the fact that she and Seth would be spending the night together—alone. Her ambivalent feelings toward the man confused her. She admired his courage as a doctor; his physical cowardice baffled her. She desired Seth; she did not love him. She had pledged to love James forever; Seth was her husband and wanted her to be his wife in every way.

With James, everything had been so simple. Love and desire had walked hand in hand. With Seth, she felt adrift in a turbulent sea without oars or a sail, or even a rudder.

"I think it might be a good idea to go ahead and get a room at Schmidt's Hotel when we arrive," Seth said. "That way you'll have a place to rest while I pick up the plate glass for the windows at Carroll & Steell."

Molly refused to think ahead. She would take each step as it came. And do what felt right. She cleared her throat and said, "That sounds just fine."

Seth left the buckboard at the livery, and he and Molly headed for Schmidt's Hotel. While most of the town's businesses were constructed of adobe and logs, or housed in tents, Schmidt's had been the first building made from lumber hauled by bull train from Helena. Jacob Schmidt met them at the front desk. The German was known to have a volatile temper. He had once gotten angry and closed down the dining room just because a freightman had tugged on his coattail and demanded service.

"I'd like a room, Uncle Jake," Seth said.

"For you and the missus?"

"Yes," Seth said, drawing her forward to meet the German. "Molly, meet Jacob Schmidt."

"Call me Uncle Jake," the fat little man said, taking her hand and shaking it once. "I give you best room in the house. Big bed. You like it."

"Th-thank you, Uncle Jake," Molly said. She couldn't get used to the frankness of westerners. They said what they were thinking and seemed to have no sense of modesty. Seth saved her from having to say anything more by leading her past Jake and up the stairs to their room.

Uncle Jake hadn't lied. The room was lovely, with a big old maple four-poster covered with a star-patterned quilt and a matching maple wardrobe in which to hang their clothes, a brick fireplace, and a dry sink with a flower-patterned pitcher and bowl for washing. From the window she could see most of the levee, including several steamboats pulled up to load freight and disgorge passengers. Molly turned back to Seth, uncertain what to expect from him now that they were alone.

Seth slowly walked over to her. His fingertips caressed her palm as he handed her the key to the room. "I need to go check on that blinded whiskey-seller and run my errands. I'll meet you back here later. Uncle Jake can give you directions to I. G. Baker & Co. They probably have the largest selection of cloth goods."

Then he kissed her.

He took his time about it, kissing one side of her mouth, then the other, then running his tongue along the seam of her lips, slipping it inside for just a taste. He lifted his head and looked at her, and she saw the barely leashed desire that raged in him. He took a step back from her, and another. Then turned without a word and left the room.

Molly realized she was panting. She put a hand against her heart to still its pounding. Her tongue slicked her lips—and found the taste of Seth. Enervated, she sank down on the edge of the bed. Once again, she had yielded to his kisses. Her whole body had responded to the mere touch of his mouth. With very little effort, he had made her want him.

Molly couldn't understand what had happened. When he touched her, all thought of resistance fled. He didn't have to fight her for what he wanted. She willingly surrendered in his arms. Molly wasn't sure whether she felt guilt or euphoria at the prospect of the coming night. She settled the matter by admitting she felt both.

While their parents were otherwise occupied, Patch and Whit had little trouble sneaking out of the livery with Maverick. Patch led Whit up and down alleys heading toward the levee. Everything might have gone as planned, except that when they were passing the back window of one of Drake Bassett's warehouses, Patch clearly heard the words *"Masked Marauder."*

She halted in her tracks. Whit bumped into her, started to complain, and was immediately shushed by Patch. "They're talking about the Masked Marauder. Shut up so I can hear."

Whit hadn't the foggiest notion who the Masked Marauder was, but Patch was captain of the ship, and he had no choice but to follow her orders.

Patch listened only with the expectation of hearing more of the Masked Marauder's heroic exploits. But the more she listened, the wider her eyes got. The men inside weren't praising the Marauder—they were planning to ambush and kill him!

They were just beginning to discuss the details of the plan when Maverick, for no good reason that Patch could see, bared his teeth and growled ferociously. She grabbed the dog's snout, but she was too late to avoid discovery.

"You out there! What are you doing? Hey! That's my dog!"

"Run!" Patch yelled. She gave Whit a shove and took off.

Whit wasn't expecting the push. He stumbled a couple of steps to the end of the alley and fell face-first into the street. Patch came running back to grab him by the seat of his trousers and yank him to his feet. That delay allowed the men inside to reach the street in front of the warehouse.

Whit took off, but rough hands captured Patch. A second later, Maverick attacked the man holding Patch, barking excitedly and snapping at whatever flesh he could reach.

"What the hell? Get down, you damned mongrel!" The man holding Patch lashed out with a boot and gave Maverick a vicious kick in the ribs. Yelping in pain, the dog-wolf tucked its tail between its legs and slunk away.

Outraged, Patch struggled against the man's hold. "Durn you! Leave my dog alone! You pig-faced yellow-belly. You—"

"Shut up, kid," the man snarled. "Who are

you? What were you doing listening at the window?"

Patch wasn't about to tell her name. If her pa found out she was in town, she'd be in trouble for sure. Instead of answering, she bit the hand that held her.

Whit hadn't stopped running, figuring Patch was right behind him. When he heard the man howl, he looked back just in time to see Patch being slapped. Whit stopped, not sure whether to run back to help her or go in some other direction for help. The size of the man who held Patch decided him. He whirled to run and collided with a solid object. The force of the impact toppled him into the dirt.

Solicitous hands helped him up. "Where are you going in such a hurry, son?"

If Whit hadn't been so frightened for Patch, he might have been terrified at the grim features on Seth Kendrick's face when he suddenly realized who had just run into him.

Before Seth could say anything else, Whit blurted, "You have to help Patch. There's a man hitting her. Over there. He—"

"Where?"

Whit pointed.

"Your mother should still be at Schmidt's Hotel. Find her and stay with her. Go! Now!"

Seth didn't wait to see whether Whit obeyed him, just headed on the run for Patch.

"That's my daughter you're holding, Pike," Seth said when he was within calling distance. "Put her down."

Pike Hardesty peered at Seth through narrowed eyes. "This brat's yours, Doc?" he asked. "You oughta teach her not to listen at windows."

Patch jerked ineffectually against Pike's grip on the front of her shirt. "Pa, he's planning to—"

Pike shook Patch to shut her up. "Keep your mouth shut, kid. You didn't hear nothin'. Understand?"

"Why not try picking on someone your own size?" Seth said.

"Why, Doc. Didn't know you was a fightin' man." He let Patch go, and she scampered to Seth's side.

Seth's hand traced the growing bruise on Patch's face, and his jaw tautened. "Go find Molly at Schmidt's Hotel. Stay there till I come for you."

"But, Pa—"

"Don't argue with me, Patch. Get out of here."

Patch called Maverick to her side and hurried down the street. She went just far enough away to be out of her father's line of sight, then stopped to watch what was about to happen.

At last! she thought. *He's going to fight at last. My pa is* not *a coward.*

"Come on over here, Doc, and we'll see how you handle yourself," Pike said.

Seth looked over to the doorway of the building and saw Drake Bassett leaning against the portal, smoking a cigar. Though he was a relatively young man, Bassett had snow-white hair and a salt-and-pepper moustache and brows. His features were ordinary: dark brown eyes spaced wide, a nose that hooked a little, thin lips, and a sloping chin. He was dressed plainly in a gray wool suit, and he wore a single watch fob across his vest. He was a picture of honesty and prosperity.

Drake Bassett was prosperous, all right, Seth thought. It was the honesty he was lacking. The man was so crooked, he could eat nails and spit out corkscrews. Bassett was the brains and Pike was the brawn of what had become a very dirty business. People had begun to gather, and Seth was guessing Bassett wouldn't like calling attention to himself. "Call off your dog, Drake. This has gone far enough, don't you think?"

"Your kid started the trouble," Bassett said, eyeing the growing crowd.

"My daughter meant no harm. She—"

"Figured you'd try to wiggle out of fighting, Doc," Pike said. "Admit it. You're just plain yellow."

Seth felt the eyes of the crowd on him. He had chosen this path, and he had known it wouldn't be easy. But it was hard to endure the disgust and disdain in all those faces. "Think what you like. Just don't ever touch my daughter again."

Pike laughed in his face. "Ooh. I'm scared. What you gonna do to me, Doc? Rap my knuckles with a stick?"

The crowd laughed along with Pike, and some began calling Seth names. Seth just stood there, enduring their raucous jests. He had made a vow, and as hard as it was, he would keep it. He turned and began walking away.

He hadn't taken two steps when a blur came racing past him and leaped onto Pike's back. "Take that, you varmint!"

The crowd went wild, yelling and screaming encouragement to Patch as she attacked the man who had forced her father to back down. Her assault had surprised Pike, so she was able to box his ears and yank his hair before he reached up, grabbed her by the arms, and threw her over his head onto the ground.

Patch landed so hard, all the air came out of her in a huff. Then she lay still.

The crowd quieted instantly and looked at Seth to see what he would do.

Seth knelt beside Patch and checked the pulse at her throat. Although fast, it was strong and steady. She opened her eyes, and he saw she was only dazed.

"Pa?" she said. "I couldn't let him say those things about you."

"It's all right, Patch," he said. He lifted her in his arms and carried her over to Red, who was part of the crowd. He handed her into the other man's arms and said, "Take care of her."

Then he turned to face Pike, who was leering at him.

"Whatcha gonna do now, Doc?"

Seth pulled off his suit coat and draped it over the hitching rail. Then he undid his string tie and pulled it off. Finally, he unbuttoned the throat of his shirt and turned up his cuffs. "All right, Pike," he said. "Whenever you're ready."

Pike grinned at the crowd. "Looks like the doc's finally decided to fight." He put his hands up in fists like a boxer to protect his face. "Here I am, Doc. Come and get me."

Seth took Pike at his word. He marched up to him and put a fist in the burly man's stomach, folding him in half like an empty wallet. He followed that with an uppercut to the chin that straightened Pike back out again.

Pike's fists were still out there in front of him, but somehow they didn't seem to be doing him much good. Seth showed no mercy, hitting Pike in the face, choosing his punches. A right to the eye, another under the chin. A quick left opened a cut in his cheek; another jab widened it.

Pike's right eye was already swelling closed, and his left cheek was dripping blood like a faucet. Pike couldn't understand what had gone wrong. He swung hard, and Seth stepped out of his way. He swung again, and Seth simply wasn't there. He charged and caught Seth in a bear hug. Bigger and stronger, he tried crushing the other man.

But Seth got a hand under Pike's chin and forced his head back. Pike either had to let go or get his neck snapped. As soon as he did,

Seth hit him in the solar plexus, knocking the breath clean out of him.

Pike dropped to his knees.

Seth didn't have a mark on him. "I warned you not to touch my daughter. You lay a hand on her again, and I'll finish the job."

Pike heard the crowd murmuring and felt the nausea rise in his stomach at the thought of being beaten by a man everyone knew was too scared to fight. Slowly, his hand inched toward the gun tied down on his leg.

Molly had left Whit at the hotel and come looking for Seth. She had found him in time to see everything. When Seth had refused to fight, she had felt ashamed; when he had effortlessly whipped Pike, she had been astounded. She was shoving her way toward him through the crowd when she saw Pike Hardesty reaching for his gun.

"Seth!" she cried. "Look out behind you!"

Molly was watching Seth when she heard the gunshot. In that instant she realized that her feelings for him were much stronger than she had ever imagined. If she'd had a gun, she would have shot Pike Hardesty herself.

Seth jerked when the bullet hit him, but he didn't fall right away. He shook his head slightly, swayed, then crumpled to the ground.

Molly was the first to reach Seth and dropped to her knees beside him. The gorge rose in her throat when she saw the blood streaming from the wound on his head.

When Patch saw her father fall, she tore herself from Red's grasp and ran toward him. She halted when she realized Molly had gotten there before her. She stood back, feeling shut out. "Pa. Oh, Pa!"

Pike pushed his way clumsily to his feet and crossed to stand over Seth. He grunted when he saw his bullet had gone high and wide, merely creasing Seth's left temple instead of hitting him in the heart.

Bassett was watching the crowd and realized their mood had turned ugly. "You remember that business we talked about, Pike? I think you'd best be on your way."

Pike shoved his way through the crowd, which parted like the Red Sea as he approached them. There was no law in Fort Benton, and no one wanted to face him down. When he saw Patch, he made a detour that took him close to her.

Patch shrank away from the scarred man in horror.

"Keep your mouth shut, kid," Pike warned in a low voice, "or next time, I'll kill him."

Patch gasped, but before she could say anything, Pike Hardesty was gone.

Molly ripped some of her petticoat into strips and used it to try to stop the bleeding. Once her initial shock was over, she was able to see that the wound was not as serious as she had thought. She was greatly encouraged when Seth groaned and raised a hand to his head.

"Don't move," Molly said in a soothing voice. She looked around for a familiar face and spotted Red Dupree. "Could you help me move Seth to Schmidt's Hotel? We have a room there."

"Sure, Mrs. Kendrick," Red said. "Some of you fellas come over here and lend a hand. Take Doc Kendrick over to Uncle Jake's place."

Molly wrung her hands helplessly as she followed behind the men who jostled Seth toward the hotel. Patch had hold of her father's hand and walked beside him.

"Ain't but a crease," Red reassured Molly. "He'll be right as rain in no time."

"Why did it happen at all?" Molly demanded. "Why doesn't somebody arrest that man? How can he get away with shooting an unarmed man like that?"

"Ain't nobody around here as fast with a gun as Pike, ma'am. And he's mean enough to eat raw liver. Closest army is at Fort Shaw, and they're tied up with the Sioux. Got no choice except to put up with him, if you see what I mean."

Red made sure Seth was settled on the four-poster bed before he shooed everybody out of the room and left Molly, Patch, and Whit in peace.

Molly hurried to Seth's side. He started to say something to her, then groaned and lost consciousness again. She took the time to bathe away all the blood on his face. When she was finished, she noted his breathing was shallow but his pulse was steady.

She turned her attention to the two children who were sitting on ladderback chairs that had been brought in and placed in the far corner of the room.

Molly walked up to Patch and waited until the girl looked up at her. "You nearly got your father killed," she accused.

"I know," Patch replied in a frightened voice. "I didn't mean for anything like that to happen."

"It's as much my fault as hers," Whit said.

"Is that so?" Molly asked.

Whit nodded.

"What were the two of you doing in town? How did you get here?"

"It's a long story," Patch said with a sigh. "Are you sure you want to hear it?"

"Every word."

Patch and Whit exchanged worried glances.

"You can start whenever you're ready," Molly said, eyeing first Whit and then Patch. "I'm listening."

10

When Seth awoke, he thought he was alone. A moment later, a shadowy form materialized beside him on the bed.

"Is that you, Molly?"

"It's Dora Deveraux."

Seth put a tentative hand to his head and winced as he tried to sit up.

Dora pushed him back down and said, "Stay flat. Believe me, you'll feel better. How'd you let Pike get the drop on you like that?"

"My mistake," Seth said dryly. "I should have asked for Marquess of Queensbury rules."

Dora grinned. "I knew somebody would go a step too far with you someday. What did Pike say to make you mad?"

"He struck Patch."

Dora's face lost its humor. "That bastard. You should have killed him."

"Someday I will."

"Look, we don't have much time before your wife comes back."

"Where is she?" Seth asked.

"She took your kids downstairs to the dining room to get something to eat. I saw them come in and snuck up here. I had to tell you, it looks like Bassett is already back in business selling whiskey to the Indians. Same place as before, if you can believe it."

"That man can't take a hint," Seth said.

"Also, three gold miners are coming in on the stage from Virginia City at the end of the week. Think the Masked Marauder will be able to give them an escort?"

"It's a possibility," Seth said. "Thanks for the information, Dora."

"Anytime, Seth. So how do you like that new wife of yours?"

"I like her fine."

"Too bad. I miss you." Dora brushed Seth's hair back from his forehead. She trailed her fingers down the side of his face and passed her thumb across his lips, which parted at her touch. She leaned over to kiss his mouth, but he turned aside at the last second so her lips met his cheek instead.

When the door clicked shut, Dora slowly straightened and looked over her shoulder.

Molly was standing there white-faced, holding a tray in her hands.

"Who are you?" Molly asked. "What are you doing here?"

"I'm Dora Deveraux, Mrs. Kendrick. I was just visiting Seth," Dora said, cool as ice. "We're old friends."

Old friends, indeed! More like *kissing cousins*! It was painfully apparent the two of them were very well acquainted.

Molly guessed from Dora's clothing what kind of woman she was. Her full skirt only came to her knees, and the form-fitting bodice left most of her bosom and shoulders bare. Her auburn hair was pinned up in curls, and she wore a garish green feather that matched the color of her spangly dress. The woman sat on the bed snuggled up next to Seth and had a possessive hand on the pillow beside his head. She didn't seem in any hurry to leave. Molly decided to give her a nudge.

"Seth needs his rest," she said, crossing to the table beside the bed to set down the tray.

"Well, he certainly knows how to make the best use of a bed," Dora said, shooting a sly grin in Seth's direction.

Seth flushed. "Dora was just leaving," he said firmly.

Molly wanted to know why the woman had come in the first place. But it was apparent that she wasn't going to get any answers from Dora Deveraux. The woman made a point of touching Seth as she resettled the blankets around him. Then she crossed the room past Molly and stopped at the door to look back toward the bed.

"Come see me when the newness wears off," she said to Seth. She didn't bother to close the door when she left the room.

Molly wanted very much to slam it after her. She resisted the urge and walked over and closed it very carefully and quietly.

Tension sang in the room. Seth pursed his lips and shook his head. "Dora and I aren't . . . that is, we haven't—"

Molly turned and leaned back against the door. "But you did," she said with certainty.

Seth shrugged. "I'm a man, Molly, not a monk."

"She still wants you."

"I can't control what she wants."

Molly didn't realize what she was going to say until the words were out of her mouth. "I won't share you, Seth. I know what it's like to have a husband with a mistress. I won't suffer the same mistake twice. Make a choice, and make it now."

"You don't understand—"

"There's nothing to understand. Do you want her, or do you want me?"

Seth grinned. "I like you when your dander's up, Molly. It makes your eyes sparkle."

"I'm serious, Seth."

He sobered. "I choose you, Molly. Today, tomorrow, always."

For a moment it was hard to believe she had won. The extent of her relief was disturbing, because it meant she cared more than she ought. After all, they had both agreed they could never love each other. They had both agreed this was a marriage of convenience. It shouldn't matter whether he had a mistress. It shouldn't matter whether he was committed to her and her alone.

But it had. It had mattered tremendously whether he chose her or Dora. So maybe her feelings for Seth Kendrick weren't as nonexistent as she had thought.

Molly was very much aware of Seth's eyes on her as she rearranged the pillows behind him to make a backrest. She helped him to sit up, noticing the grimace of pain when he was finally upright. "How does your head feel?"

"Like someone's in there knocking around with a hammer."

"Be thankful for the pain," Molly said with

a smile. "It means you're alive." She sat down beside him where Dora had been, and tucked a napkin under his chin. "You could have been killed, Seth."

"Thanks to you, I wasn't." He took her hand in his and squeezed it. "You saved my life, Molly."

Molly looked down at his bruised and torn knuckles and then back at his untouched face. "Why did you let the whole town—and me—think you were afraid of Pike Hardesty, when you could have whipped him anytime?"

He rubbed Molly's palm with his thumb, not consciously seducing but obtaining that result all the same.

"I have my reasons, Molly. That's all I can tell you."

Molly tried not to feel hurt by his secrecy. After all, they had been husband and wife for less than two weeks. She knew he was telling her to drop the subject, but she persisted. "Why don't you carry a gun, Seth?"

His grip tightened on her hand. "I can't give you an answer to that question. Yet."

He was shutting her out. The walls were there, reminding her that however her feelings for Seth might be changing, he was holding to his side of the bargain. Molly didn't know what to say, so she said nothing.

She pulled her hand from his and busied herself setting up the tray on his lap. She expected Seth to make a fuss if she tried to feed him, but for whatever reason, he didn't. He opened his mouth and swallowed a spoonful of the broth she offered him.

"What did you do with Patch and Whit?" he asked.

"I didn't drop them down the bottom of a well, if that's what you're wondering," Molly said with a wry smile. "Although I very much wanted to. Those two rapscallions were in the back of the wagon the whole way into town!"

"I can understand why Patch would hitch a ride, but why did Whit come along?"

Molly paused with the spoon in midair, took a deep breath, and said, "He was running away."

"Patch was helping him?"

Molly nodded.

Seth forked a hand through his hair and winced when he got too close to his wound. "I suppose I should have seen it coming. Whit and I haven't been getting along very well."

"It isn't your fault," Molly said. "Whit never wanted to come here in the first place.

If anybody's to blame, it's me, for bringing him here against his will."

They were both silent, thinking about what they had hoped to achieve through this marriage, and how far short of their expectations they had fallen.

"Where do we go from here?" Seth asked.

Molly knew he wasn't only talking about Whit and Patch but about their own relationship as well. She took a deep breath and said, "Maybe we made a mistake getting married."

"No!" Seth replied sharply. "I admit I hadn't bargained on so much resistance from Patch and Whit. But I'm willing to try to wear them down if you are. I'm betting we can outlast them and turn the five of us into a family."

"I don't think you realize what a Herculean task that will be."

"Wouldn't the results be worth the effort?"

Molly imagined them all sitting down to a supper table together, talking about what each had accomplished during the day, sharing their joys and their sorrows. It was a goal worth striving for. But she had her doubts about whether they would ever succeed. "Just how do you suggest we accomplish this miracle?"

Seth grinned. "First of all, we don't let

Patch and Whit provoke us into arguing with each other over them."

"Were we doing that?"

Seth just stared, and Molly conceded, "All right. What else?"

"We stop jumping apart and feeling guilty when they see us together. In fact, I'll even go a step further and suggest we act like genuine, couple-in-love married people whenever they're around."

Molly stiffened. "How will that help?"

Seth chose his words with care. "If they see that you and I are committed to each other, that there is no hope that their machinations can succeed, they'll stop trying to push us apart. At least, I hope they will."

The loud knock at the door brought Molly to her feet. "That'll be Patch and Whit," she said. "I left them having dessert in the dining room." She took the tray from Seth's lap and set it on the table beside the bed.

He caught her wrist and said, "What do you say, Molly? Do you want to give it a try?"

"Yes," she said. "Yes, I do."

"Then sit here beside me."

Slowly, Molly sat back down beside him. She allowed Seth to draw her palm up to his mouth, where he kissed it.

"All right," he said. "Are you ready?"

Molly nodded.

He raised his voice and called, "Come in. The door's open."

Patch and Whit tumbled excitedly into the room and drew to a quick halt when they saw the intimate picture their parents presented together on the bed.

Patch frowned.

Whit grimaced.

Seth and Molly exchanged amused glances.

"Come on over here where I can see you both," Seth said.

Reluctantly, Patch and Whit crossed to stand beside the bed.

"I think you two have some explaining to do," he said.

Patch spoke first. "I'm sorry, Pa. I didn't mean for anything bad to happen. Whit made me come along."

Whit stared in disbelief at Patch. It was true he had asked for her help. But he hadn't forced her to come. He turned to his mother and said, "*She* was the one talked *me* into coming. I was having second thoughts about the whole idea of running away when—"

"If you've changed your mind about leaving," Seth interrupted, "then you'll be going back to the ranch with us tomorrow. Is that right?"

Whit stuck his hands in his pockets and scuffed the floor with the toe of his shoe. "I guess so."

"Then you'd better get a good night's sleep. You and I have a lot to get done tomorrow before we leave town."

Whit's eyes narrowed suspiciously. But if that was the extent of the punishment he was to receive, he wasn't about to complain.

"I'll stay here with you tonight, Pa," Patch volunteered. "Whit can get a room with his ma."

"No," Seth contradicted. "You and Whit can get another room. Molly and I will sleep here."

Molly opened her mouth to object, saw Seth's brow rise a fraction, and remembered their discussion. They must present a united front to their children. Their entire future depended on it. She caressed Seth's jaw and said, "I want to be able to keep an eye on your father tonight, Patch."

"But, Pa—"

Seth never took his eyes off Molly's face. "You go talk to Uncle Jake, Patch. He'll make sure you and Whit get settled in," Seth said.

Patch watched her father reach up to push a stray curl behind Molly's ear. With a snort of disgust she turned to Whit and said, "Let's get out of here," then marched out the door. Whit followed her without a backward glance.

Once the two children were gone, Molly let out the breath of air she had been holding. She reached up to grab Seth's hand, which had begun to tease the lobe of her ear. "Patch isn't going to give up without a fight."

"I never expected she would," Seth said. "I'm glad you agreed to have the children take another room. I've wanted to be alone with you for a long time." His hand encircled her nape and drew her toward him. He kissed the edge of her mouth with the enticing beauty mark on it, then groaned and leaned back against the pillows.

Seth's eyes closed, and his hand fell to his side. "Of all the nights to have a headache."

Molly laughed. "This isn't exactly how I pictured us spending our first night together, either." She rearranged the pillows again, helping him to get comfortable.

"Will you lie down with me, Molly, so I can wake up beside you in the morning?" he murmured.

"All right, Seth." Molly stepped behind a screen in the corner and changed into the warm flannel nightgown she had packed earlier in the day. When she was ready for bed, she blew out the lantern and Seth held the covers so she could slip beneath them. He curled a strong arm around her and nestled her back into the niches created by his muscular frame.

It felt different from lying close to James. Seth was leaner, and an inch or two less tall, so when their bodies spooned together she could just feel the rough bristle on his jaw against her face. His warm, moist breath on her nape made her shiver.

"You're cold," he said, pulling her more snugly against him. "Let me warm you up."

Molly felt as if she were on fire, but she wasn't about to tell Seth that when he had just admitted his head ached. There was no sense starting something they couldn't finish. Instead she asked, "What brought you to Fort Benton?"

His hand absently caressed her waist as he spoke. "I was looking for somewhere I could start over fresh. There are wide open spaces in this country where a man can carve out a place for himself."

"Start over from what?"

Seth smiled in the darkness. "You don't miss a thing, do you, Molly? All right, if you want to know, I'll tell you. I was a surgeon for the Confederacy. By the end of the war,

I'd seen enough of death and done enough mutilation in the name of medicine to last me a lifetime. I wanted to escape from anything and everything that would remind me of those brutal years. I couldn't do that by going back to Texas. People there will be fighting the war in their hearts and minds for years to come.

"So I headed north with Patch. I ended up taking a steamboat from St. Louis to the end of the line—Fort Benton. I built myself a house here two years ago and started breaking horses for the army. I hadn't intended to let anyone know I was a doctor. But someone got shot once when I was in town and—the rest is history."

"You didn't mention Ethan. I thought he came here with you."

Seth shook his head. "Ethan and I met in Texas before the war, when he was still just a kid. He showed up in Fort Benton last year, just before winter took hold. Ethan's life is his own, Molly. If you have questions you want answered, you'll have to ask him."

Molly made up her mind to do just that. Maybe Ethan would be able to tell her more about the man she had married than Seth was willing to reveal about himself. She was silent, thinking about what Seth had said. He still hadn't told her what he did for a living before he became a doctor.

But when she opened her mouth to ask, she yawned instead.

"Close your eyes, Molly," Seth said, reaching up to gently do it for her. "And get some rest. Morning comes early."

Molly snuggled back against him. The worries of the past weeks and months seemed somehow far away. She felt safe and secure. In moments, she was sound asleep.

Seth's arm tightened about Molly's waist as he felt her body relax. He fought sleep because he wanted to enjoy this moment. He smiled as he thought of how she had demanded that he give up Dora for her. If only she knew! But maybe it was better that she didn't. He didn't expect her to understand why he had done what he'd done. He didn't expect her to care for him.

All the same, he liked the feeling he had gotten when she'd insisted she wouldn't share him with another woman. He hadn't felt like that since Annarose had demanded he take his eyes off the hurdy-gurdy girl at the county fair. He bent over to kiss the petal-soft skin of Molly's nape. Of course, he would never love Molly the way he had loved Annarose. But he had to admit he was starting to care. That wasn't a bad thing. As long as he didn't let it get out of hand.

Confident in his ability to manage his feelings for the woman in his arms, Seth closed his eyes and drifted off to sleep.

Meanwhile, Patch was having nowhere near so easy a time finding peace. It was unsettling to realize that her father had sided with his new wife over his daughter. To add insult to injury, she was stuck spending the night with a stepbrother she loathed. Even now, Whit was twisting and turning restlessly in the twin bed across from her.

"Consarn it! Can't you stay still?" she cried at last.

"This bed feels strange. I can't get comfortable," Whit retorted.

"I can't believe I agreed to come to town with you," Patch ranted, "and got myself in trouble for no good reason that I can see."

Whit bolted upright. "Wasn't my fault you stopped to listen at that window! That's when all the trouble started."

"Yeah? Well, it's a durned good thing I did! Those men are planning to ambush the Masked Marauder."

"So who the heck *is* the Masked Marauder, anyway?" Whit asked.

"Only the bravest, most heroic man on the

face of the earth," Patch replied. "Of course, nobody really knows who he is because he wears a black mask."

Whit snickered. "Sounds like you're in love with him or something."

"That's ridiculous! I admire him. Who wouldn't?"

"What'd he do that's so special?" Whit asked.

"Somehow he finds out when the stage is going to be attacked by Indians, and he rides to the rescue."

"So why would those two men want to kill him?" Whit asked.

"From what I heard, the Masked Marauder destroyed some kegs of whiskey those men were selling to the Indians. They don't want him interfering with their business anymore. So they figure to ambush and kill him."

"Golly!" Whit exclaimed. "And you heard their plan? What are you going to do?"

Patch frowned thoughtfully. "If I knew who the Masked Marauder was, I'd tell him, of course. But that fella Pa fought with, that Pike—he said if I tell anyone what I heard, he'll kill Pa."

"How would he ever know you said anything?" Whit asked.

"I suppose if the Masked Marauder didn't

fall into their trap, he'd know—or at least suspect," Patch said. "And I can't take the chance. Pa doesn't carry a gun. He wouldn't have a chance if Pike decided to shoot at him again."

"On the other hand," Whit said, "if you warned the Masked Marauder, he'd probably shoot Pike."

"On the other hand," Patch said, "how can I possibly warn the Masked Marauder when I don't know who he is?"

Patch froze as she recognized the significance of something the two plotting men had said. "Wait a minute. Maybe I *do* know who it is!"

"You do?"

"I didn't realize it until just now, but I know the identity of the Masked Marauder."

"So who is it?" Whit demanded.

"Ethan Hawk."

Whit's jaw dropped. "Naw. Really?"

Patch sat up in bed. "Remember when you came to see me the other night, and Ethan came in from outside when he was supposed to be sound asleep in bed?"

"Yeah?"

"*That* was the night those whiskey kegs were supposedly broken to pieces."

"So?"

"Ethan's shirt smelled of whiskey that night, but he hadn't drunk any. He told me somebody spilled whiskey on him, but don't you see? He must have gotten whiskey on himself when he broke up all those kegs!"

"I've never seen Ethan wearing a gun," Whit pointed out.

"But he has one," Patch said. "I've seen it in his cabin. And another thing," Patch said, her voice getting more excited as she became more certain she was right. "The Masked Marauder appeared for the first time about six months ago. Right after Ethan came to live here."

"So are you gonna tell Ethan about the plan to ambush the Masked Marauder?" Whit asked.

Patch thought about it. She was drawing a pretty big conclusion from pretty flimsy evidence. If she was wrong, Ethan would be sure to tell her father. And she didn't want to think about the results of such an eventuality.

However, if she secretly followed Ethan whenever he left the ranch from now on, she would not only be there to warn him about the ambush, but she could also be there to see the Masked Marauder in action.

"I'm going to have to ponder this a little

longer," she said, "and decide what I should do. In the meantime, don't you blab anything to anybody."

"I won't," Whit promised.

"Now lie down and leave me be so I can think."

Whit lay back down and covered himself, but soon he began shifting again.

"Garn!" Patch said. She rolled out of bed, stomped over to Whit, and tucked the blanket tight under the mattress all around so he couldn't move. "Now go to sleep!" she ordered.

Whit smiled and did as he was told.

11

The first few days home after the disastrous trip to Fort Benton were busy ones for Seth and Molly. He worked with Ethan and Whit to finish the third bedroom. She cooked and cleaned and sewed diligently on a dress for Patch.

On the day the dress was finished, Molly talked Patch into trying it on to surprise the men when they came inside for supper. Nessie watched from the four-poster in Patch's room as the transformation began.

Molly started with Patch's straight blond hair, brushing all the tangles out and taking the scissors to the ends to crop them just below her shoulders. Then she cut a fringe of bangs that fell just above Patch's brows. Finally, she combed Patch's hair back from the sides and gathered it at the crown, securing it with a black grosgrain ribbon, leaving the rest to fall down her back.

Once Patch's hair was done, Molly started

from scratch and added layers of clothing. A white chemise with pink ribbons and lace-trimmed cotton drawers came first. Unfortunately, that was as far as Molly got before Patch balked.

Pointing to the corset in Molly's hands, she said, "I ain't gonna put that blasted thing on."

"Every lady wears one," Molly said.

"I ain't a lady."

"Do you want to be one?"

Patch's lids dropped to lay feathery crescents on her cheeks. "Don't matter if I do," she said in a quiet voice. "Ain't got the know-how."

"I'm here to teach you," Molly said.

Patch fidgeted with the ribbon on her chemise, liking the softness of it and the delicate pink color. She kept remembering how Ethan had said she'd look pretty in a dress. She wanted to please him, and to please Pa. But was that instrument of torture really necessary? "Do I hafta wear that durned thing?"

"It'll help your posture and make the dress fit properly."

"All right," Patch said in a resigned voice. "Do your worst."

Molly slipped the white coutil garment over Patch's head and settled it into place before tightening the laces.

"Take a deep breath," Molly ordered.

Patch gasped as Molly pulled the corset laces tighter. "You're squeezing me to death!"

"Just let me tie this off," Molly said, breathless from exertion. "There. All done. Now, hold your arms up and I'll bring this petticoat down over your head. One more."

Molly watched Patch's face in the oval dressing mirror and saw the mulish thrust of her lower lip. She had to work fast, before open rebellion broke out. "Arms up again. Let me slip this dress on." She put a hand against Patch's outthrust hip. "Stand up straight."

Patch uncocked her knee and drew her shoulders back in an exaggerated pose. "Is that straight enough for you?"

"Yes, fine," Molly answered. She disregarded Patch's sarcasm, attributing it to the anxiety that was its source.

Molly had cut off her striped silk dress so it came to midcalf on Patch, revealing a pair of black kid boots trimmed with ribbon. The leftover moss-green-striped material had become a sash for the waist. She had added an overskirt of plain green silk bought at I. G. Baker & Co., caught up at the sides with matching rosettes.

Once she finished buttoning up the bodice

of the dress, Molly straightened the sailor collar over the girl's tense shoulders and puffed out the long sleeves. She stood behind Patch and brown eyes met blue in the silvered mirror before them.

"You look lovely, Patch. Every inch a lady."

"Looks can be deceiving."

Molly laughed. "You'll do fine."

Patch tried to sit on the bed in her normal way, but the corset kept her from bending. "Just like I thought. Can't hardly move in this getup."

"You'll learn. Now let Nessie and me get gussied up, and we'll treat the gentlemen to the presence of three ladies for dinner."

Molly couldn't have said who was more nervous when they heard the men washing up on the back porch, she or Patch. But Molly wished she could have had a tintype of Seth's face when he first saw his daughter, to save and show him in the years to come. His gray eyes glittered with emotion as he walked up to Patch and took her hands in his to hold her at arm's length. Seth's eyes met Molly's, and she saw it was a powerfully bittersweet moment for him.

"You look like your mother," he said to Patch. He let go of one hand and held the other over her head so she could turn in a circle for him. "I wish she were here to see you, Patch."

Seth felt grateful to Molly for the metamorphosis she had wrought in Patch. But Annarose should have been the one to dress Patch like this. Annarose should have been the one to share the glorious sight of their daughter looking like a proper young lady.

Patch was pleased at her father's approval. But it was the reaction in a set of bright green eyes that she sought. Ethan didn't disappoint her. His glance was warm with admiration and approbation. She stood still for his inspection as he took her hand from her father. His eyes widened slightly at the small bosom revealed by the fitted bodice of the dress.

"You're quite the young lady," he said with a grin.

Patch flushed. "Do you think so?"

"You're going to be a beautiful woman someday, Patch. Take my word for it."

Patch felt a fluttery feeling in her stomach, sort of like a butterfly inside. Before she could identify its source, he let go of her hand and picked up Nessie.

"Look at this little lady," Ethan said. "Aren't you the pretty one."

As Patch watched Ethan with Nessie, she

experienced a startling and most unpleasant revelation. Ethan was using exactly the same tone of voice—and approximately the same words—to praise the four-year-old that he had used with her. She had wanted to look grown up for Ethan. It was agonizing to realize that to him she was just another little girl.

Patch just wanted to get away, to get out of the room and out of these foolish clothes. But as she started to back out of the room, her pa pulled out a chair for her and said, "May I have the pleasure of seating you, Miss Kendrick?"

His eyes glowed. His smile was so broad, it made her throat ache. How could she disappoint him by running away? She swallowed her bitter letdown and allowed her father to seat her at the table.

The heels on Patch's shoes had only raised her a couple of inches to match Whit's height. But the total visual effect of styled hair, corseted body, and tailored silk dress left Whit feeling that Patch had somehow far outgrown him in a single afternoon. He felt bereft.

"I liked you better in pants," he said flatly as he sat down beside her.

Soon they were all seated at the table, with Nessie in a special raised chair that Seth had constructed for her. Molly had used her rose-patterned china, and with the ladies dressed as they were, supper had a festive air that belied the problems they were dealing with on a daily basis.

"Whit's bedroom ought to be finished by tomorrow," Seth announced. "I figure we can move his things in there by late afternoon. Patch can start sleeping in her own bed again."

Patch opened her mouth to object, but a piercing look from Ethan caused her to shut it again.

Molly glanced at Seth and saw that his gaze was intent on her. Tomorrow they would truly become man and wife. But it was too soon. She needed more time. The patient man had somewhere misplaced his patience.

"By the way," Seth said to Molly, "since we'll be finished with the room tomorrow, I thought maybe you'd like to have your first riding lesson later in the afternoon."

"I—I suppose so," she replied. "What should I wear?"

Seth's brow furrowed. He had planned to teach Molly to ride astride because he didn't have a sidesaddle. "I don't suppose you have a split skirt?"

Molly shook her head.

He grinned. "Then I guess you'll have to wear some of my pants."

Molly laughed. "I'd look ridiculous."

"You'll look adorable," Seth countered in a teasing voice.

"A pair of my pants would fit better," Ethan said. "You're welcome to them."

Patch shook her head in disbelief. Why on earth had her pa gone to such lengths to get her into a dress, when he thought Molly would look *adorable* in a pair of his pants? She would never understand grownups if she lived to be a hundred. "I'm gonna get out of this rig and go frog-hunting down at the pond," she said in disgust. "Anybody want to come along?"

"I do!" Nessie said.

"Me, too," Whit joined in.

"I think I'll help Molly with the dishes," Seth said.

Ethan raised a surprised brow, but when Seth winked at him, he quickly rose and said, "I'll keep you kids company."

"I have to help Patch and Nessie change out of their dresses," Molly said to Seth. "You can clear the table while you're waiting for me."

Seth pursed his lips and looked around at the table. Ethan grinned and scooted out the door after Whit. "Have fun!" he called over his shoulder.

By the time Molly returned, Seth was elbow deep in dishwater. "I'll finish those for you," she said.

"I'm almost done. Why don't you sit down and relax? You've put in a hard day."

"So have you." She set a plate of bones down for Maverick, absently patting the dog-wolf on the head as she did. She picked up a towel and began drying dishes and putting them away.

"I've been meaning to tell you, I have to go into town again later this week."

"Oh?"

"It's Mrs. Gulliver again."

Molly glanced at Seth from the corner of her eye. Was there really a Mrs. Gulliver? She hadn't thought so. But surely Seth wouldn't have brought her up again if she didn't exist. "What's wrong with Mrs. Gulliver, anyway?"

"Bowels," he said.

That was an intimidating enough subject that Molly shied from pursuing it. She lifted Bandit, the raccoon, off the counter, where he had just finished eating a plate of scraps, and set him on the floor. Then she leaned out the open window and set a bowl of milk on the back porch. "Here kitty, kitty," she called. The mountain lion came running.

"How long will you be at Mrs. Gulliver's?" Molly asked as she resumed drying dishes.

"I don't expect to stay the night. But it depends on how poorly the old lady's doing."

"I'll keep a light burning for you," she said.

"I'd like that." Seth leaned over and gave her a quick kiss on the mouth. "Thanks."

"What for?"

"For turning Patch into a lady."

Molly smiled. "I have a ways to go yet."

"Maybe. But getting her into a dress is a major miracle as far as I'm concerned."

Molly focused on the china coffee cup she was drying. "I haven't wanted to mention this, Seth, because I know how attached you are to Patch. But if you really want to make a lady of your daughter, she needs to go to school."

"She attends school in town every fall."

Molly folded the damp dishcloth and laid it over the back of a kitchen chair to dry. She turned to face Seth and said, "I mean she needs to go away to school—to a finishing school for young ladies."

"No."

Molly put a hand on Seth's arm. "It wouldn't be forever. And it would open up a

whole new world to her that isn't possible
here. Just think about it. Will you?"

"No."

Molly didn't press him further.

"I think I'll go see if I can catch up to the
kids," Seth said. "Do you want to come
along?"

"I need to change my clothes. And it has
been a long day. Why don't you go on," Molly
said.

She wasn't surprised when Seth turned and
left her without another word. It was a lot to
spring on him in one night—to see his daughter as a young woman, and then to tell him
that he had to send her away.

But Molly knew there was only so much
she could accomplish with Patch. Seth's
daughter had been forced to become inde-
pendent at a very early age. It wasn't easy for
Patch to take advice or direction from anyone. Molly could polish off the rough edges,
but Patch very likely wouldn't allow more
change than that.

Seth got no farther than the back porch
when he spied a figure huddled near the
woodpile. "Who's out there?"

"It's me, Whit."

Seth crossed over to sit down beside the
boy on a pile of split logs that was stacked to

be cut for firewood. "What are you doing out here?"

Whit held up a stick in one hand and a knife in the other. "Whittling."

Seth perused the knife Whit held out to him. "Mighty fine knife. Sharp."

"My da gave it to me. He taught me how to whittle. Said it helps a sailor pass the time at sea."

Seth pulled a Bowie knife from the scabbard at his belt. "My pa taught me to whittle too," he said. He searched around till he found a stick the right size, then began to shave the bark from it. "It does a fine job of passing the time around the campfire, too."

"When you whittle, you don't have to think about anything," Whit said.

"Nope," Seth agreed.

"And however you're feeling, why, you can take it out on the wood."

"Yep," Seth agreed. Wood shavings began to pile up in front of him.

"My mother says it's silly to whittle. 'Cause you don't have anything to show for it when you're done."

"Shows how much she knows," Seth muttered under his breath.

"What?"

"Nothing."

"I especially like whittling 'cause I can do it alone," Whit said.

"Me, too," Seth agreed. "But I'm glad you let me join you tonight."

"Yeah, well, I'm getting kind of used to having you around."

Molly had stood by the kitchen window and listened shamelessly to the conversation by the woodpile. Seth Kendrick was a kind, caring man. What woman wouldn't fall in love with him?

A grieving widow.

Clamoring voices announced the return of Patch, Nessie, and Ethan. Molly pulled her robe more closely around herself and stepped out of the kitchen door to join them on the back porch.

Nessie came running up to her and held out both hands. "See my frog, Mama?"

Molly bent down just as Nessie opened her hands. The frog she was holding leaped straight up in the air, actually grazing Molly's cheek on its way past. She yelped in surprise, to the accompaniment of laughter from everyone on the porch, including Nessie.

Molly collapsed in a heap on the porch step and pulled Nessie into her lap with a breathless laugh of her own. "I nearly had a seizure!"

The dog-wolf, Maverick, and Rebel, the mountain lion, soon appeared to stalk Nessie's frog, which was finding the porch a much less safe place than the pond.

Molly sat quietly and held Nessie while she listened to Patch tell her father about the huge bullfrog she had almost caught.

"But he got away," she said at last. "No thanks to Ethan."

"I didn't think your pa'd want you to go swimming in the dark," Ethan said.

"I ain't afraid."

"Never said you were," Ethan replied. "But it'd be a shame to get that pretty hair of yours all wet."

Patch reached up and patted the ribbon in her hair, as though to make sure it was still there. "Yeah, well, it would have dried."

"I think maybe it's time for you kids to get to bed," Seth said.

"I'll be waiting for you, Patch," Ethan said as he headed off toward his cabin.

In a tradition as old as the ages, Seth's and Molly's children wheedled and fought against the end of the day as their parents readied them for bed. Molly insisted on removing the ribbon and brushing Patch's hair fifty strokes before she would allow the girl to escape to Ethan's cabin. Whit and Nessie had passed the stage of exhaustion, yet they resisted the pull of sleep that sought to claim their consciousness.

At long last, the bedroom lamps were out, the children tucked in and kissed and told they were loved. And Molly and Seth were alone, and awake, and very much aware of each other.

"Would you like to go for a walk now?" Seth asked. "Or just sit and talk?"

Molly began to back away from him. "I really ought to go to bed. I—"

"Please don't go."

Seth reached out and grasped her hand.

Molly felt a slow warmth travel up her arm and spread throughout her body. She looked up into Seth's eyes and found them avid with desire. His nostrils were flared for the scent of her, and his body was taut with need.

"Come with me," he said.

"Where?"

"To the stable. You can see the mare you'll be riding tomorrow."

And make love to me.

Seth didn't say the words, but Molly heard them all the same. Somehow she found herself following him. When they reached the stable, he lit a lantern and hung it at the head of a stall. A pretty black mare with a white diamond on her forehead stuck her nose out over the half-door and nuzzled Seth's shirt.

"I usually have something for her—a dried apple or a carrot."

Molly patted the mare's silky nose. "She's beautiful."

"She's also very gentle."

I can be too.

"You don't have to worry about getting thrown," Seth said.

Molly looked up into Seth's eyes and read his thoughts.

It's all right, Molly. I won't hurt you.

"Would you like to see the hayloft?" he asked.

It's more private up there. We won't have to worry about being interrupted.

"All right," she said.

Seth took the lantern and climbed up the ladder ahead of her. Molly saw he must have been thinking about this for a while, because in the corner of the loft lay a quilt she had last seen packed away in the top of the wardrobe in Seth's room. He set the lantern down on an empty crate and spread the blanket on a crunchy bed of hay. Then he turned and faced her.

You can still say no. We can stop here and now.

Molly took a step toward him. It was all the response he needed. She was swept up in his arms and pulled into a strong embrace. His mouth found hers, his tongue seeking entrance.

She groaned once in despair—or desire—and parted her lips.

His tongue was gentle but thorough, reaching behind her upper lip for the sensitive flesh there. He searched the ridged roof of her mouth before drawing her tongue into a duel with his and asking—demanding—that she return the favor.

He untied her robe and impatiently pushed it off her shoulders, then stopped and looked at her in the shadowed light of the lantern. Her nipples had peaked beneath the soft flannel gown and were clearly visible. He slowly unbuttoned the gown, kissing his way down, making her flesh catch fire from the warmth of his lips.

"Molly, Molly. I want you so much!" His voice was guttural with need. Urgent. Excited.

Molly caught the fever in his flesh and fed upon it. She reached out a hand and unbuttoned his shirt and shoved it away from his shoulders. He quickly skinned out of his long john shirt, leaving him naked to the waist. Molly did something she had wanted to do for a long time. She put her hands around him and, leaning her cheek against the wiry hair on his chest, felt with her hands for the scars on his back.

"How did you get these?" she asked.

"They're gunshot wounds, Molly. Part of my past."

He didn't let her ask another question, just covered her mouth and took what he needed.

Molly's knees refused to hold her, and as she felt herself falling, Seth caught her and lowered them both to the quilt. His hands caught the hem of Molly's nightgown and slipped up under it, pushing it out of his way as he caressed her calves and the insides of her thighs, coming ever closer to the heat of her, yet not touching. Waiting.

Molly shivered.

Seth took her hand and placed it over the front of his jeans. "Feel that, Molly. That's what you do to me."

Molly shivered.

"You're cold, sweetheart. Let me warm you." He mantled her body with his, fitting his hips into the cradle of her thighs, letting her know how much she was wanted.

Molly thrust her hands into Seth's hair and pulled his head down to kiss him. She breathed his name. "Seth."

She teased his lips, playing a game of taste and touch, but never staying in one place so that he could put his tongue in her mouth and mime the dance of lovers.

Abruptly, Seth grabbed her gown at the neck and edged it down, revealing her breasts but trapping her arms. Slowly, as though he had all the time in the world, he leaned over and kissed one breast, then the other. He caressed her with his mouth, sucking and biting, and then soothing with more kisses.

"Seth," Molly begged. "I want to touch you."

He stopped long enough to pull the gown down to free her arms, then pulled it off over her feet. He stopped again to look at her.

Molly felt self-conscious. No man had ever seen her thus. Not even James. She was grateful for the dim light that she hoped would hide the marks left by the children she had borne.

But Seth's eyes saw only perfection. "You're beautiful, Molly." He laid a hand reverently on her womb and let it trail down to the nest of dark hair between her legs.

Molly started to close her eyes, but Seth said, "Look at me. I want to see what you're feeling."

So much. She was feeling so much. Molly groaned as Seth slid a finger inside her.

He lay beside her, and his mouth found hers and tasted honey as he gloried in the feel of her mouth on his.

Molly arched toward him, opened to him, felt him put another finger inside her.

She put her hands on his face and ended the kiss. "Seth. Stop. Please."

He gasped with the effort, but he did. "What's wrong?"

Molly reached down to the buttons on the front of his jeans. "Take off your clothes. So I can touch you."

Seth's entire body tautened at the thought of her hands on him.

Molly smiled at the haste with which Seth's trousers and long johns found their way to the bottom of the quilt to join her nightgown. She put a hand on his flat belly and trailed her fingers down the crease between his thigh and the place where his desire for her was abundantly evident. She surrounded him with her hand, surrounded the heat, the softness, and the hardness.

Molly drew him toward her and led him inside.

Seth sighed with pleasure as he pushed deep inside Molly, all the way, until there was none of him that was not a part of her. He felt her heels grasp his buttocks and pull him tight against her. He began to move, slowly, and mimed with his tongue in her mouth what his body did below.

Molly's fingernails made crescents in Seth's flesh as she clutched him and held on, while her spirit soared and her body shuddered with its release.

Seth's face looked more in agony than ecstasy, but his final cry was one of triumph as he spilled his seed in her and made her his wife.

12

Patch was nearly asleep on her pallet in front of Ethan's fireplace when she heard him moving stealthily through the room. She opened her eyes just a crack and saw in the banked light of the fire that he was dressed in dark clothes. She tried to remember whether the Masked Marauder had ever rescued anyone at night. She didn't think so. But she couldn't take any chances.

As soon as he was gone, she dressed quickly and followed after him, riding bareback with a halter she'd grabbed at the corral because she thought he would get too far ahead of her if she stopped to saddle her horse. After an hour of following him, Patch still hadn't figured out where Ethan could possibly be going. Patch looked on that as a positive sign that he must be the Masked Marauder. Why else would he be wandering around in the dark?

He changed direction again, and this time

Patch saw in the distance the soft yellow glow where Fort Benton was situated. He continued on through town, beyond the last warehouse on the levee to a wooden barnlike building. Patch pulled her horse to a stop in the shadows and watched nervously as Ethan went inside the darkened building. A few moments later, he came out leading a large, coal-black horse on a halter and carrying a small saddle roll. He mounted again and, leading the black, rode back the way he had come.

Patch slipped into a nearby alley and stared with eyes rounded big as saucers as he rode past her.

Ethan really was the Masked Marauder!

She wondered why he kept the big black in town, where it might be found. Although the townspeople would hardly think to look for the Masked Marauder's horse right under their noses. At least, they hadn't so far.

Patch wanted to confront Ethan with what she knew and beg him to allow her to go along on his next adventure. But if Ethan wouldn't let her go swimming in the pond after dark, he would hardly be likely to take her along when there was real danger. She didn't dare let him know she had found out his secret.

Although he took a circuitous route, Ethan ended up right back at the ranch. Patch followed him to a copse of pine not far from his cabin, where a lean-to stood. She had never even known it was there! When he took the horse and the saddle roll inside, she turned and left, racing for the corral to return her horse before he returned and discovered it missing.

She headed back to his cabin on foot, stripped off her clothes, lay down with her back to the door, and covered herself with the quilt. A few minutes later, she heard the door squeak as Ethan pushed it open. She marveled at how quietly he made his way across the room.

To her surprise, he made a detour over to her. She held her breath, then realized that was sure to give her away. She forced herself to take slow, deep, even breaths as Ethan knelt beside her and pulled the covers up over her shoulders. He brushed aside her bangs, his hands gentle, his touch slow and easy, so as not to disturb her sleep.

Patch nearly died when she felt the touch of his lips on her forehead. She fought to keep from opening her eyes to look at him. Whyever had he done such a thing? Fortunately for her thudding heart, a moment later he stood and walked away. Patch wondered if he had ever done anything like that before. She didn't understand what she was feeling, but it upset her to think that Ethan felt free to just kiss her like she was some baby or something.

She couldn't confront him about it without revealing she was wide awake—a fact for which she had no easy explanation. Patch lay there and fumed about it for a while, until she decided what he'd done wasn't so terrible and maybe best forgotten. Except she didn't really want to forget it. In fact, she was probably going to remember it for the rest of her life.

Patch fell asleep thinking about the best way of saving the Masked Marauder from the ambush that Drake Bassett and Pike Hardesty were planning for him. All she really knew was that the ambush was supposed to happen on the butte west of town where the two men had set up a whiskey-selling operation. She wondered whether she at least ought to let that information slip to Ethan. She decided to sleep on it and make her decision in the morning.

Only when she woke up in the morning, Ethan was gone. And so was the big black stallion.

Patch realized she couldn't take the chance that Ethan might slip away like that sometime and end up getting ambushed. So when he returned, she immediately confronted him.

"I know you're the Masked Marauder, Ethan."

His eyes never blinked. He never moved at all. "What makes you think that, Patch?"

"Don't try to pretend. I saw you go to town last night and get your black stallion. I saw the saddle roll—which probably has your mask inside. The reason I'm telling you I know is—"

"You're wrong about the stallion, Patch. Your pa is paying for the use of that black for stud. That's where I was this morning. I took him up to service the mares in the box canyon."

"What about the saddle roll?" Patch queried.

"Just some tack for the stallion."

"Tell me the truth, Ethan. It's important. Are you the Masked Marauder?"

"You'll have to look elsewhere for a hero, Patch. I'm not the man you're searching for." He turned and walked away.

Patch had been so sure it was Ethan that the letdown was tremendous. Now she was no closer to knowing who the Masked Marauder was than anybody else in town. But she had information that was vitally important for the Masked Marauder to know. What on earth was she supposed to do now?

Molly was worried about Patch. Seth's daughter had been wandering around all morning with a hangdog expression. Right now she was sitting at the kitchen table with an uneaten sandwich from lunch in front of her, turning her glass of buttermilk in circles on the tablecloth. Nessie was down for her nap, and Whit was putting the finishing touches on his room with Seth. Ethan had gone scouting for more wild horses that could be captured and sold to the army.

"Is there anything you'd like to talk about?" Molly asked.

Patch shook her head no.

"Do you want to go outside for a while?"

Patch shrugged. "I guess so." She rose and scuffed her way out the door.

Molly decided Patch's distraction was probably due to the fact that she would be moving back into her own bedroom tonight. When she did, Nessie would still be there. It was going to be an adjustment for Seth's daughter to share her room with somebody else. If Molly could have arranged things differently, she would have. But Seth had said it wasn't practical to build a fourth bedroom for Nessie when the two girls could easily share. Molly could sympathize with Patch because she had a difficult situation of her own to face this evening.

Last night, after she and Seth had made love, they had lain for a long while in each other's arms. At first, Molly had felt content. Making love to Seth had felt right and good, and it had been more than just a little wonderful. But soon she had begun to think of all the things Seth hadn't told her about himself . . . and to wonder.

Who had shot him in the back? And why? What had he done before he became a doctor? How had Annarose Kendrick died? Why had he allowed the town of Fort Benton to think him a coward? Where had he learned to be so handy with his fists? What kind of relationship did he *really* have with Dora Deveraux? And why did he want to keep so much of his past a secret from her?

Molly had learned a great deal about patience from being married to a man who was gone to sea for years at a time. It should have been a simple matter for her to let Seth's secrets unfold over time. But the existence of a dark, unknown side to her husband frightened her. She had already surrendered her body to the stranger beside her. Molly was haunted by the fear of committing her heart and soul to a man who was not worthy of them. She was determined to know what Seth seemed equally determined to keep to himself.

Molly cleared her throat and said, "Seth, I think we need to have a talk."

Seth lazily ran his fingertips across the crest of her breasts. "I'm listening."

Molly grabbed his hand to still its sensuous journey. "I want to know what you did before you became a doctor. And I want to know how Annarose died."

He tensed. "I've told you those things aren't important."

"They are to me."

Seth tried distracting her by nibbling on her ear.

Molly jerked away. "Seth, please. I want some answers."

Seth sighed and lay down flat. He raised an arm to shield his eyes. "Why do you want to know?"

"I want to understand who you are."

"By finding out what I used to be?"

"Yes. By finding out everything I can about you."

He sat up abruptly and leaned over her, his eyes fierce and smoldering in the light of the lantern. "What if I told you I've killed men, Molly? Not just a few. What if I told you I'm good with a gun—fast. What if I told you Annarose died a violent death? Will those answers satisfy you?"

He lurched to his feet and began stuffing his legs into his pants. He yanked on his boots and threw his shirt and long johns over his shoulder. "Come on, get dressed."

Molly grabbed at her nightgown and hurriedly poked her arms into the sleeves. She stood and began gathering the quilt.

"Leave it," he snarled. "I might need a place to bed down sometime."

As Molly followed Seth down the ladder, she realized that much of his fury had been directed at himself. Was he regretting what he had been? What he had done?

Unfortunately, the answers he had given her had only raised more questions. Tonight, when she joined him in the bedroom they would be sharing from now on, she had to decide whether to ask for more answers. Or whether to simply go forward from here, accepting and loving the man Seth was—the man he had become, shaped by the violence in his past.

Molly had been staring out the kitchen window, and she saw Seth come out of the barn headed for the house.

She had completely forgotten about her riding lesson! She was still wearing the dress she'd put on first thing this morning. Ethan had brought her a pair of his jeans earlier in the day, and she ran to Seth's bedroom now to put them on. She hurried because she didn't want him coming into the bedroom after her.

"Molly? Where are you? Are you ready to learn how to ride?"

Molly was embarrassed by the way Ethan's pants conformed to the contours of her hips and legs. But she hadn't time to find something else to wear. She furiously rolled up the hems and pulled on a pair of boots Seth had bought for her in town. She checked to make sure Nessie was still sleeping soundly and moments later arrived breathless in the kitchen doorway. "I'm here."

Seth whistled appreciatively. "Those jeans do more for you than they ever did for Ethan."

Molly smoothed her hands down over her hips. "I'm hoping to get a riding skirt sewn in

another day or so. But I've been planning
and cooking for the christening party tomorrow for Iris's new baby. I just haven't had
time—"

"You look fine. Don't worry about it. Come
on."

The black mare, Star, hadn't looked particularly large when Molly stood beside her in
the corral. However, the view was somewhat
different from atop the animal. Molly was
very much aware of how far off the ground
she was. She clutched the saddle horn for
dear life while Seth adjusted the stirrups.

"You're going to do fine," Seth assured her.
"Just relax."

With Seth's hands positioning her, touching her at the waist, on her back, at the knee
and the ankle, that was impossible.

"Just walk Star around the corral so you
can see how it feels. Let your body move with
the rhythm of the horse."

At first Molly was stiff, but with Seth's encouragement she was soon surprisingly comfortable. "This isn't so bad," she said.

The trot was more difficult, but she soon
mastered it, and finally the canter, which although it was a faster gait, was smoother.
Molly was loping Star around the corral, con-

fident in her ability to control the animal,
when Bandit darted across Star's path.

Molly was thrown up on Star's neck as the
mare went stiff-legged, shying away from the
raccoon. Just as Molly regained her seat and
her footing in the stirrups, Nessie crossed
practically under Star's feet, oblivious to the
danger, intent on catching Bandit.

This time Star reared. Nessie froze, suddenly aware of the animal towering over her.
Molly sawed on the reins, hoping to turn Star
so the animal's hooves would not come down
and crush her daughter. Star backed sideways on her hind legs and jerked against the
reins. For a moment it appeared the mare
would lose her balance and topple over backward.

Molly's mouth was open, but the scream
was caught in her throat.

Seth was halfway across the corral when
he realized he wasn't going to get there in
time. His heart was in his throat. Everything
seemed to move in slow motion. There was
nothing he could do to prevent the tragedy
that was about to occur.

The mare's hooves were on their downward arc when a blur of color—Patch!—
rolled under the lower rail of the corral,
grabbed Nessie, and kept on rolling. Even so,

Star's hooves struck a glancing blow on Patch's shoulder.

Suddenly everything was moving at full speed again. Molly and Seth reached the two girls almost at the same moment. Nessie was sitting in the dirt beside Patch, crying. Molly dropped onto her knees and scooped her daughter into her arms. She squeezed Nessie tight, reassuring herself that the little girl was whole and safe.

Patch lay sprawled on the ground where she had landed. She inched her shoulder up slightly and groaned.

"Is she all right?" Molly asked Seth in a choked voice.

With shaking hands, Seth felt for broken bones and torn skin at the point where the mare's hoof had landed. He lifted Patch's right arm to see the range of movement, and she groaned again.

"I don't think her shoulder's broken, but she's good and bruised," he said. He gently lifted Patch into his arms and carried her inside to her bedroom. Molly came along and pulled the covers down and took off Patch's shoes before Seth laid her down.

"Get some cool water," Seth ordered. "A compress will help ease the bruising."

Molly picked up Nessie, unwilling to let

her out of her sight, and headed into the kitchen.

Seth sat down beside Patch and started unbuttoning her blouse. He put a hand behind her and sat her up so he could take her shirt off. When he saw the pink ribbons on her chemise, it occurred to him that he might be embarrassing her—again.

Patch's eyes were closed, her face flushed. "I'd leave you to do this for yourself," he said in a constricted voice, "but I expect you won't have much use of that shoulder for a while." He skimmed the shirt off her, had her turn over on her stomach, and covered her up to the waist.

Molly returned with a bowl of cool water and several cotton cloths which Seth used to ease Patch's pain.

"Good thing I was wearing pants," Patch mumbled against the pillow.

"What's that?" Molly asked.

"Couldn't've made it to Nessie in time if I'd been dressed up like a lady."

Molly met Seth's eyes. "No, I guess this country isn't made for ladies," she said. She smoothed the bangs back from Patch's face and said, "I want to thank you for risking your life for Nessie."

"Woulda done it for anybody," Patch said

ungraciously. She didn't know herself why she'd risked life and limb for that little intruder. But she didn't want praise for doing it. She just wanted everybody to go away. She closed her eyes and shut them out.

"I think she's sleeping," Nessie said, leaning close and peering into Patch's face.

Molly took Nessie by the hand. "Let's leave her alone and let her rest." She put a comforting hand on Seth's shoulder as she passed by him.

"I think I'll sit with her for a few minutes," he said.

As Molly turned to leave the room, Whit arrived in the doorway, having just put the finishing touches on his new room. "What's going on?" he asked. "Why is Patch in bed?"

"Star almost kilt me," Nessie said importantly. "But Patch saved my life."

"Golly!" Whit said. "I miss all the fun!"

When Ethan showed up at suppertime, Whit treated him to an embellished version of Patch's heroic efforts to save Nessie from Star's thundering hooves. The object of all this praise was, of course, still asleep in bed.

After supper everyone marched out to Whit's new room, which had its own outside entrance as well as a door cut through to

Patch's room, which connected it to the rest of the house.

Seth had made a bed with rope springs, and a table and chair. The table already held a lantern, several books Whit had brought from Massachusetts, and a pitcher and bowl for washing. There were pegs on the wall for his clothes. It had a dirt floor right now, but Seth eventually planned to cover it over with wooden planks. A stone fireplace graced one wall and was necessary to heat the room through the frigid winter.

Molly's contribution was green-checked gingham curtains for the glass windows. Right now they were tied back to allow the last of the sun's rays to light the room.

Molly left the three men talking about whittling while she ushered Nessie through the connecting door into Patch's bedroom. "You be careful not to roll over during the night and hurt Patch's shoulder," she admonished her daughter as she tucked her into bed.

"I won't hurt Patch," Nessie said. "I *love* her."

Molly looked to see whether Patch might have heard this confession, but Seth's daughter seemed still to be sleeping. "I love her, too," she whispered to Nessie. "Now go to sleep."

After Molly left the room, Patch's eyes blinked open in the darkness. All this talk about love was getting pretty sickening. That Gallagher woman and her kid hardly knew her. How could they care? Only, Patch had to admit the little girl had a way of getting under your skin. When she had seen Nessie under Star's hooves, she hadn't hesitated to risk her life for the kid. It was all pretty confusing, actually.

Patch froze when she felt Nessie's fingers curl around her hand and squeeze gently. Patch grimaced. The little intruder had a way about her all right. She closed her eyes and sighed and gently squeezed back.

Molly had stepped into Whit's bedroom in time to catch Seth tucking her son—toes and all—under the covers. Ethan had already gone to his cabin. She quickly kissed her flustered son good night in front of Seth, followed Seth outside, and closed the door behind her.

"He's excited about having his own room," Molly said as they walked around to the kitchen door. "You did a wonderful job with all the furniture."

"I'm glad you're feeling so charitable with

me, because I'm afraid I have some bad news for you."

"Oh?"

"Ethan dropped by Fort Benton while he was gone. Seems Mrs. Gulliver can't wait. I'm afraid I have to go see her tonight."

"Oh." Molly hadn't realized she would feel so disappointed. But she did. "Maybe you won't be gone long."

"I hope not," he said. "But don't wait up for me."

Molly managed a smile. "I'll leave a light in the window for you."

"Thanks, Molly." He pulled her into his arms and kissed her hard. And just as quickly let her go. "I'll be back as soon as I can."

Pike Hardesty had been watching in hiding for the better part of a week, waiting for the Masked Marauder to show his face. The Blackfeet had been coming and going every day, buying their firewater, with no sign of any masked rider on a big black horse. It had seemed so provoking an act to begin selling whiskey again in the exact same place that he had been sure the Masked Marauder would be back. But he hadn't come.

There was a campfire over by the kegs, where the whiskey-seller could warm himself. But Pike was hidden up a hill behind some rocks. It was damned cold. This was the last night he planned to sit out here all alone waiting. If the Masked Marauder didn't show up tonight, he would just have to come up with some other plan to get rid of him.

When a rider suddenly appeared in the eerie light of the campfire, his black cloak flowing out behind him, Pike's skin crawled. A mask covered the man's face from the nose up, and a black hat sat low on his brow. Pike saw the metal gleam of two guns, one tied down on each leg.

Pike realized the man had picked his moment carefully. The only Indians near the campfire had already passed out from the whiskey they'd drunk. The whiskey-seller already had his hands up. If Pike hadn't been there, a repeat of the past destruction most certainly would have occurred.

But Pike was there. He raised his rifle and sighted on the Masked Marauder's heart. The way the man was silhouetted in the light of the fire, he couldn't miss. Just pull the trigger, and it would all be over. But Pike had spent a week in the cold to catch the Masked Marauder, and he ought to at least get to watch the man squirm before he died.

The Marauder had already tied up the

whiskey-seller and taken an ax to the first of the barrels of whiskey when Pike came sauntering down the hill with his rifle trained on him.

"You might want to stop what you're doing for a minute," Pike said, "and think about meetin' your maker."

When the Marauder started to drop the ax from his right hand, Pike said, "Don't make a move. I'm going to shoot you anyway, but if you're real careful, I might let you live a little longer."

"Well, well, Pike. I always thought this day would come," the Marauder said.

"How do you know my name?"

"Everybody knows you, Pike. You make a habit of shooting unarmed men. Only, I guess this'll spoil your record, seeing as how I'm wearing a gun—two guns."

Pike lifted the rifle and sighted along the barrel. "You're gonna die."

"Everybody's gotta die sometime."

Pike was getting nervous. He had the rifle aimed right at that Marauder, had the drop on him plain as red paint, but the masked devil wasn't showing scared. What kind of man was he? More to the point, who was he? "Take off that mask," Pike ordered.

"Can't do that, Pike."

"I'll shoot if you don't."

"You'll shoot if I do."

Pike knew he ought to just shoot the Marauder and get it over with, but he wanted the man to grovel before he killed him. "I figure you're all gurgle and no guts," Pike said. "So I tell you what I'm gonna do. I'm gonna start shooting at parts of you, and when you decide to take off that mask, you just tell me and I'll stop."

"I expected as much from you, Pike. Your kind—"

Pike was listening, watching the Marauder's mouth move as he spoke, so he was startled when a gun magically appeared in the man's left hand. Pike pulled the trigger on his rifle as soon as he saw it, and he knew his bullet hit the man. But the Marauder shot at the same time.

Pike saw the yellow flash before he heard the six-gun roar. He stumbled backward—his jaw dropping in surprise—as a bullet smashed into his rifle, splintering it and driving the weapon out of his grasp.

The Marauder dropped the ax and pulled his other gun faster than Pike had ever seen anyone move in his life. But the masked man didn't shoot. He just stood there with both guns aimed at Pike.

Pike felt the sweat break out on his brow. His stomach curled up and forced bile into his throat.

"I ought to kill you," the Marauder said. "But I'll give you a warning instead. Get out of town, Pike. Get out of Montana. Because if I ever see you again, I'm going to put a bullet through your black heart."

Pike watched impotently as the Marauder backed away into the darkness. A moment later, he heard the thunder of hoofbeats as the Marauder made his escape. Pike grabbed the Colt in his holster and shot into the darkness, hoping he would get lucky, but knowing he was just wasting bullets.

Pike ranted and raved for several minutes after the Marauder was long gone. Not only had he failed to kill the masked man, he'd been made to look a fool in front of the whiskey-seller, who was bound to spread the story in Fort Benton. Drake Bassett wasn't going to be happy when he heard what had happened here tonight. Hell, he wasn't too damn delighted himself!

First the defeat at the hands of that yellow-bellied doctor, and now this! Pike was in a mean mood by the time he hit the outskirts of Fort Benton. He headed for the Medicine Bow Saloon and stomped over to the table in the corner he considered his own private property, bullied the men sitting there out of their seats, and proceeded to drink three glasses of rye in brooding silence.

What he needed was a woman, Pike decided at last. And only one woman would do. He searched the smoky saloon for Dora Deveraux, and when he didn't see her, he headed up the stairs to her room, knowing full well she was probably with another customer. It was going to mean a fight, but he was itching for one.

He twisted the doorknob planning to walk right in, but the damn thing was locked. "Open up, Dora, and let me in!" Pike yelled.

Dora came to the door, but instead of opening it she spoke through the wood. "I've got a customer, Pike. Come back later."

"Send him on his way, Dora. Or I'll do it for you."

"Wait your turn. I'll make it worth your while."

"I don't wanta wait. Now open this damn door before I kick it in!" he shouted at the top of his voice.

When Dora opened the door, Pike shoved past her, wanting to get his hands on the man he knew would be in her bed. He stopped, gape-mouthed at what he found. A slow red flush worked its way up his neck. For there in Dora's bed, with pillows plumped up behind his back and covered only in a sheet, sat his nemesis—Doc Kendrick.

"Evening, Pike," Seth said. "Sorry to inconvenience you, but I got here first."

Pike took one step toward the bed before he heard the snick of a gun being cocked. He stopped dead. The doc held both hands up and wiggled his fingers to show he was unarmed. Pike turned and saw Dora standing with a small derringer. It wasn't much as guns go, but she couldn't miss at this range, and even a small slug was enough to kill a man if it landed in the right spot. Dora was holding the gun aimed right between his eyes.

"Get out, Pike. And don't come back tonight," Dora said.

Pike looked from the gun in Dora's hand to the amused expression on Doc Kendrick's face. "Hiding behind petticoats this time, Doc?"

Seth shrugged.

"Bet that new wife of yours'd sure be interested to know where you are right now."

The doc didn't bat an eyelash, but his face paled, so Pike realized he'd hit a nerve.

"Yeah," he said. "Next time I see her, I 'spect I'll just have to have a little talk with her."

"Stay away from my wife," Seth said in a deadly voice.

"Whatever you say, Doc," Pike said. He looked from the unwavering gun in Dora's hand to the doc and back again. It wasn't worth dying just to get laid by Dora. He'd use one of the other girls.

But he'd make Dora sorry. And Doc Kendrick would pay as well.

Pike tipped his hat and said, "Be seein' you, Doc." Both his eyes and his voice hardened when he added, "And you, too, Dora."

13

Seth returned in the early hours of the morning. Molly awoke immediately when she heard him moving around in their bedroom.

"Seth?"

"Go back to sleep," he said.

She turned over and sat up in bed, watching as he undressed. His movements were weary. "You must be exhausted," she said.

"I am." He stripped down to his white long-john shirt and drawers and eased into the bed beside her, releasing a hissing breath as he did.

Molly waited for him to reach out for her, to pull her into his arms. When he didn't, she wondered whether he might still be angry from the incident in the loft. "How is Mrs. Gulliver?" she asked.

"What? Oh, fine."

Molly turned over and inched closer to him. She tentatively put a hand on his side.

He grabbed her wrist and held it away from him.

"Seth, you're hurting me."

Abruptly, he released her. "Leave me be," he said. "I'm whipped, Molly. It's been a long day."

Molly knew she shouldn't take his rejection to heart. After all, he was used to coming back to this room and being alone. Even though he had known she would be there, it still must be an adjustment. Besides, the man had been up all night nursing a woman with troubled bowels. That was bound to make anyone grouchy and brusque.

Molly made all the excuses for Seth she needed to feel better, then made up her mind to turn over and go to sleep. She flipped the covers up over her shoulder—and distinctly smelled perfume.

At first she thought she must be mistaken. She lay there and inhaled slowly and deeply. There was something in the air, all right. She inched over to face Seth again, leaned a little closer, and sniffed the shoulder of his long johns. Just honest male sweat there. But as she lifted her face, her nose brushed against the back of his head. His hair reeked of the pungent female scent.

Blood thrummed in Molly's veins as she

absorbed the implications of what she had
discovered. Was it possible that the reason he
had wanted nothing to do with her tonight
was that he had already lain with another
woman? Had he really been with Mrs. Gulliver, as he had claimed? Or had he been with
Dora Deveraux?

Molly hated herself for being so suspi-
cious. Probably Mrs. Gulliver was one of
those eccentric old ladies who smothered
herself in expensive colognes. So why not
just ask him why he'd come home from nursing an old lady smelling like a French doxy?

Molly had opened her mouth to confront
Seth when she heard a loud snore. He was
asleep. Was it the sleep of the guiltless? Or the
sexually sated? For certain, it was the sleep of
an absolutely exhausted man. If he wasn't
guilty, she would feel like a fool for waking
him up.

Maybe now was the time for some of that
patience she had learned over the years. All
she had to do was wait and watch to see how
Seth acted in the morning. She would know
if he had been with another woman. Surely
the truth would be written all over his face.

Besides, the mysterious Mrs. Gulliver had
been invited to the christening party tomorrow for Iris Marsh's new baby. If Mrs. Gul-

liver showed up, all Molly's questions might be answered.

Unfortunately, Mrs. Gulliver sent her regrets through her niece, Mrs. Biddle, who came and brought her five-year-old daughter to play with Nessie. Molly had also invited Red Dupree and Jacob Schmidt to the party. Everyone else present had been suggested by Iris, including members of the Methodist congregation in Fort Benton where Iris and Henry attended. Among them were the saddler and his wife, the proprietor of I. G. Baker & Co., the tinsmith and his wife, and three freightmen.

That many people wouldn't have fit in the house comfortably, and Molly was glad the day had turned out sunny and warm, because she could hold the party outside. She had talked Seth into making a table out of a few split logs and two sawhorses and covered it with a piece of the same checked gingham material she had used to make Whit's curtains. Everyone had been asked to bring a covered dish and dessert for the table and a blanket to spread out in the shade of the cottonwoods near the house. Besides her own covered dish and dessert, she was providing iced tea and lemonade for everyone.

Molly noticed that the wives liked Seth and

spoke cordially to him. The men nodded politely, but they didn't willingly include him in their circles of conversation. Doc Kendrick was a necessary man to have around when they were ailing, but otherwise, they knew little about him. In the west, one didn't ask questions; information had to be volunteered. Over the past two years Seth had remained aloof from them. Molly saw the strain around her husband's mouth and eyes as he smiled and pretended their indifferent treatment of him didn't matter.

But there was no reason why Seth's relationships with his neighbors couldn't be improved. Molly walked right up to the tinsmith and said, "Your wife tells me you're thinking of adding another room to your home, Mr. Grimbald. I'm sure Seth would be willing to lend a hand if you need it."

Mr. Grimbald tugged at the neck of his collar and said, "Why, I wouldn't want to impose."

Molly looped her arm through Mr. Grimbald's and walked him over to where Seth was talking with Ethan.

"I was just telling Mr. Grimbald that you'd be glad to help him build the extra bedroom on his house," Molly said with a bright smile on her face.

Seth's face looked ominous, and for a moment Molly thought Mr. Grimbald was going to pull her arm out of the socket trying to escape. But she held on as a slow smile spread across Seth's face. He took off his hat, forked a hand through his black hair, and settled the hat again.

"Look, Doc," Grimbald began in a effort to ease the tension, "I never said I wanted you—"

"I'd be glad to help you, Isaiah," Seth said. "Matter of fact, I just added a bedroom on here."

"You did?" Grimbald said. "How'd you cut the door through to the rest of the house?"

"If you want to come with me, I can show you."

Molly smiled as Grimbald wandered off with Seth.

When she turned to join the rest of the party, Ethan blocked her way.

"Neatest thing I ever saw," he said with a grin.

"What's that?"

"Don't play dumb with me, missy. I saw you grab Grimbald. And I saw him nearly jumping out of his drawers to escape your clutches. That's as smooth a manipulation of two men as I've ever seen."

Molly lifted her chin. "If these people knew Seth, they wouldn't ignore him like they do."

"I couldn't agree with you more. I just never thought I'd see the day when Seth would rejoin the human race."

"I didn't know he'd ever left it!" Molly responded tartly.

"Maybe not in body, but in spirit he resigned himself to being alone a long time ago. You're good for him, Molly. He won't thank you for dragging him back among the living, but I will."

Molly relaxed. "You're a good friend, Ethan. How did Seth ever find you?"

He smiled sardonically. "I found him. Come on over and sit down with me out of the sun, and I'll tell you about it."

Once they were settled on a quilt under a shady cottonwood, Ethan said, "I was fifteen and on the run from the law when I met Seth for the first time."

Molly's eyes widened. Was Ethan an outlaw?

He leaned close and whispered, "Yes."

"Yes what?"

"I'm still wanted by the law, Molly. Not here in Montana," he reassured her. "Back in Texas."

"What did you do?"

"I killed a man who deserved to die. I was wounded in the shoot-out. Dora dug the bullet out of my leg, but—"

"Dora Deveraux?" Molly asked in amazement.

Ethan grinned. "Small world, huh?"

"I'll say," Molly muttered. "Go on."

"Anyway, Dora dug the bullet out, but I was still losing a lot of blood when I saw what I thought was an abandoned line shack. I managed to slide off my horse and get myself inside. Turned out Seth was there. He had Patch with him. Lord, she was only about three years old then and tiny as can be."

"What was Seth doing there? Was he hurt?"

"Drunk."

"*Drunk?* Seth?"

"And looking at the moon through the neck of a bottle."

"I can't believe it. And Patch was there while he was in that condition? Was she all right?"

"Curled up on the bunk and sleeping like an angel."

"What did you do?"

"Took the bottle and the guns away from Seth and laid him on the bed with Patch."

"*Guns?* Seth?"

"Two of the nicest Colts you ever saw. Found me a comfortable spot on the floor and went to sleep. Come morning, woke up to find Patch sitting on my chest. Saw the kid was hungry and fed her. Figured I couldn't just leave her there with Seth passed out like that. I hung around till Seth woke up, then hung around a little longer till I convinced him he owed it to the kid to stay sober."

That wasn't the whole story, but Ethan didn't feel he could say more than that without revealing Seth's secrets.

"I stayed with Seth and Patch for almost six months while my leg healed—at least as much as it was ever going to. Then the family of the man I'd killed found out Seth was hiding me. I didn't want to put him or Patch in any danger, so one night I lit out.

"I saw Seth again during the war, when he was doctoring. It turned out the family of the man I'd killed had hired detectives to watch Seth in case I showed up, and they came after me again. I had to run. I've been running ever since. I came here last fall because Dora said she needed my help. I'll stay until I have to move on again."

"I thank you for helping Seth," Molly said. "And I hope you don't ever have to leave."

Ethan grinned. "I hope so too. I kind of like

it around here. Besides, Patch needs looking after as much now as she ever did."

Molly saw Iris gesturing to her and realized it was time for the christening ceremony to begin. "I've got to go," she said. "Thanks again for taking care of Seth, Ethan." She leaned over and kissed him lightly on the cheek and then ran to join Iris.

The christening itself was lovely. Iris and Henry Marsh had asked Molly and Seth to stand as godparents for their sixth child. Molly held the baby while the Reverend Adams baptized her. Then she and Seth took their vows as godparents to the baby, and the celebration began.

Of course everyone fawned on Lily. But the main topic of conversation at the party was the Masked Marauder's encounter with Pike Hardesty the previous evening.

Drake Bassett's whiskey-seller had come running back into town and spread the word at the Medicine Bow Saloon. He had seen it all, he said. How Pike Hardesty had the Masked Marauder dead in his rifle sights, and the Marauder had drawn his gun and beat Pike "slicker than butter on a teaspoon." However, the rumor was that the Marauder had been wounded.

"Anybody asked you to treat a gunshot wound lately, Doc?" Grimbald asked.

"Not lately," Seth replied. "Maybe the Marauder didn't get shot after all. Could be that's just brag on Pike's part. Or maybe it was only a scratch, and he took care of it himself."

"Could be," Grimbald agreed, and turned to discuss the possibilities with someone else.

This was the first time Patch had been dressed up in company, and Molly kept a close eye on her to see how she was managing. It was comical to see Patch come face to face with Ferdie Adams, the preacher's middle boy. Ferdie's eyes nearly bugged out of his face. He yanked his hat off his head and rolled it nervously in front of him. His eyes remained glued on Patch's two small feminine accomplishments.

"What're you looking at?" Patch demanded, fists on hips. "Didn't you ever see anybody in a dress before?"

"Ain't never seen *you* in one," Ferdie pointed out.

"Yeah, well, watch what you say about it. Just 'cause I'm all gussied up don't mean I can't use my fists if I have to."

"Yes, ma'am," Ferdie said.

Patch snorted in disgust. "I ain't a ma'am, Ferdie."

"Whatever you say, Patch." He put a finger into his collar, which seemed to have gotten tighter in the past few minutes. "You, uh, wanta go down to the pond and catch frogs?"

"Can't hardly move in this getup," she confessed. "How about a game of marbles, instead?"

"Sure," Ferdie said. "You got any?"

"I got a whole bag. I'll go get them and meet you around back."

Whit had been standing nearby throughout their conversation and asked, "Can I play too?"

"Who're you?" Ferdie asked.

"That's my dumb old stepbrother," Patch said.

"Name's Whit."

"You any good at marbles?" Ferdie asked.

"I was a champion player in New Bedford."

"Patch is the best player around here," Ferdie said. "You better than she is?"

Whit met Patch's eyes and said, "Could be. Don't really know."

Ferdie's eyes gleamed as he sensed the possibility of a challenge. "Go get your marbles, Patch, and let's find out."

Molly started to follow after them, to intervene if necessary, but she was waylaid by Mrs. Gulliver's niece.

"I want to think you for inviting me," Mrs. Biddle said. "We don't have many entertainments in Fort Benton. I hope this is just the first of many."

Molly smiled. "I'm glad you could come. I'm only sorry Mrs. Gulliver isn't here." At least now she knew the woman really existed.

"Aunt Judith didn't feel well enough to leave the house today. Your husband has been a godsend, Mrs. Kendrick. Why, Doc Kendrick sat with my aunt for an entire half-hour last night, bless his soul."

"A half-hour?"

"Can you imagine such a thing? And him such a busy man, with a family of his own to come home to now."

Molly felt sick to her stomach, but her facial expression didn't change a hair. In a perfectly pleasant voice she said, "Did he say where he was going when he left your aunt's house last night?"

"Why, no he didn't. Home, I expect. Where else would he go with a pretty wife like you waiting for him?"

Where else, indeed? Molly very much

feared she knew the answer. She'd seen for herself that Dora Deveraux didn't think much of Seth's marriage vows. But she couldn't understand what he found so attractive about the woman.

"I'd better go check on my daughter," Mrs. Biddle said.

Molly didn't see the woman leave, though she was staring right at her. She had turned her glance inward.

"Penny for your thoughts?"

Molly was jerked back to reality by Iris's voice. "You wouldn't much care for them, I'm afraid."

"I noticed you frowning after you talked to Mrs. Biddle. Bad news?"

"No. Yes. Not really."

Iris smiled. "You seem to be perfectly clear on that."

Molly laughed. "I wish you lived closer. I could use someone to talk with who could make me laugh."

"Come visiting anytime. It gets a mite lonesome without someone to talk to. Not that my oldest girl isn't a comfort to me, but sometimes a woman just likes to have another woman to share her thoughts with. You know what I mean?"

"I know exactly what you mean," Molly said.

"Anyhow, I been wanting to tell you what a good job you've done with Patch. Never seen her look so pretty nor act so nice. She's turning into a real little lady. Why—"

"Fight! Fight! It's the doc's brat, Patch, she—"

Molly didn't hear the rest. She was already running toward the back porch. When she rounded the corner of the house, it wasn't the preacher's middle boy rolling around in the dirt with Patch—it was Whit.

Both their faces were red with exertion. Whit had a swollen eye. Patch had a split lip. Their arms and legs were tangled together, and it was hard to see where one began and the other ended. As Molly arrived from one direction, Seth arrived from the other. He reached down, hauled Whit up by the scruff of his shirt, and grabbed one of Patch's arms —the one with the sore shoulder, from the yelp she let out—and held both children at arm's length.

"I'm not a cheater!" Whit yelled.

"You durned sure didn't win fair and square!" Patch yelled back.

"Shut up!" Seth shouted over both of them.

Both Patch and Whit seemed to realize at

the same time that they were surrounded by adults watching with various levels of amusement. The two adults that mattered most— her father and his mother—weren't laughing.

"Whit! How could you?" Molly cried.

"Just look at yourself!" Seth said to Patch.

"He started it!" Patch said.

"She hit me first!" Whit argued.

"You're both to blame," Seth said. "And I'm ashamed of both of you."

"I hate him!" Patch cried.

"I hate her back!" Whit shouted.

"Stop it, both of you!" Molly said. She turned her back on the children, in hopes of concealing their misbehavior behind her skirt, and met the eyes of the crowd. "Just a little family squabble," she said with a crooked smile. "We'll have it settled in no time. Why don't you all go see what kind of dessert is on the table."

No one moved for a moment, until Iris said, "Come on, folks. Let's give this family some privacy so they can settle their differences."

The preacher breathed a sigh of relief that Ferdie was not involved, as he laid a hand on his middle son's shoulder and ushered him away from the fray. Ferdie looked back over his shoulder and grinned at Whit. "You sure showed her," he whispered to the other boy.

"I'll take Nessie with me," Iris said to Molly. "She can play with Amaryllis."

A few moments later, only Ethan remained to watch the confrontation of parents and children.

Molly looked at the remains of the dress she had so lovingly sewn for Patch. The sash was gone. One sleeve was ripped from the shoulder, the hem was down, and there was a tear in the skirt. A fine powdery dust covered the whole of it, and blood from Patch's cut lip stained the bodice. The ribbon had come undone in her hair, and one blond curl hung down over her eye.

"What am I going to do with you?" Seth said. "Look at you. Look at your dress."

Patch's fingertips covered the tear in her skirt and fitted the material back in place. When she looked up again, Ethan was staring at her with pity in his eyes.

Molly's heart went out to Patch when she saw the stricken look on the girl's face.

"I just ain't cut out to be a lady, Pa," Patch said in a woeful voice. "And I don't care if I never become one."

She tore herself from her father's grasp and ran off in the direction of the pond. Seth started to go after her but realized he still had hold of Whit. "What do you have to say for yourself?"

"It wasn't my fault!" Whit retorted. "I hate her. I hate you. And I hate living here! Let me go!" He jerked himself free and ran toward his room.

A moment later, Molly heard the door slam.

Ethan took his hat off, forked a hand through his hair, and put his hat back on again. He cleared his throat and said, "I think I'll go see if I can find Patch," then turned and walked away.

Seth stood across from Molly, unyielding, stony-faced. Molly had absolutely no idea what he was thinking. If she had felt secure in her relationship with him, it would have been easier to contend with the upsetting scene she had just witnessed. She would have gone to Seth for succor and given it as well. Enfolded in his strong arms, they could have laughed over this perfectly normal incident of sibling rivalry and reassured each other that everything would be all right.

But Molly didn't take a step toward Seth and was thus denied the consolation they could have provided each other. She was frozen in place by the certain knowledge that her husband had lied to her about where he had been last night.

Molly was very much afraid that she had made a horrible mistake in coming to Montana. That she had made a mistake in marrying this secretive man with his violent past. That was not the worst of it. The biggest mistake of all was that she had fallen in love with a man who did not—could not—love her back.

Molly gritted her teeth to still her trembling chin. She balled her hands into fists and hid them in her skirts. "I'm going to return to our guests," she said in a controlled voice. "Do you want to come with me?"

"Do you want me to come?"

"I can face them by myself. But it would be easier if you came with me."

"Then I'll come with you." Seth took her elbow in his hand to lead her around to the shade of the cottonwoods. "Smile," he said.

Molly put a bright smile on her face.

"Everything all settled down?" Henry Marsh asked as they approached.

"It's quiet for the moment," Seth said. "But with kids you never know what's coming next."

Henry grinned. "You said it. The wife and I sure do appreciate your having this party for us, Doc, Mrs. Kendrick. And we're proud as punch to have the two of you stand godparents to our Lily."

"It's our pleasure," Molly said. But she wondered if she and Seth would still be together when and if the time ever came that they were needed as godparents for the child.

Molly slipped away during the afternoon to speak with Whit and found him sitting on the edge of his bed, whittling. A pile of wood shavings had collected on the dirt floor at his feet.

When he saw his mother, his lips compressed, but he didn't stop what he was doing.

"I brought a steak to put on your eye, for the swelling," Molly said. "Lie back on the bed." She didn't give Whit a chance to protest, just pressed him down. He lay with the knife on one side of his body and the whittling stick on the other. She dabbed at his eye with a cool, wet cloth, then laid the steak on. "I can think of better uses for a good steak," she said with a tentative smile.

"I'm sorry, Mother," Whit blurted. "I didn't mean all those things I said. I don't hate it here. I don't want to leave. I don't even hate Patch. I get mad at her a lot, but mostly she's okay."

"Then maybe the next time you see her, you can apologize."

Whit's chin jutted. "It wasn't my fault."

Molly brushed a lock of sweat-damp hair away from Whit's brow. "You weren't just a wee tiny bit to blame?"

"Maybe," he admitted grudgingly. "All right. I'll say I'm sorry." Under his breath he added, "But I'm only gonna half mean it, 'cause it was half her fault."

Meanwhile, Patch had found a secluded spot near the pond and was stripping off the tattered dress—and along with it all pretenses of being a lady. It was foolish even to try, she thought, when she was so certain of failing. She stood there fingering the feminine chemise and drawers while tears dripped off her cheeks and her nose began to run. Just as she lifted her arm to swipe it off, someone thrust a bandanna in her face.

Patch took it and blew her nose. Assuming her pa had come to tell her how disappointed he was in her, she kept her face hidden behind the handkerchief.

"I'm sorry, Pa. I didn't mean to cause a ruckus. It just happened. I never lost at marbles before. And when Whit beat me—well, I got angry."

Patch felt a shirt being settled around her

bare shoulders, and a pair of arms comfortingly surrounded her.

"Oh, Pa, I—"

"It's Ethan."

Patch dropped the kerchief and looked aghast through watery eyes at Ethan's sympathetic face. She shoved against his chest, pushing him away, mortified to think he had seen her standing there in her underwear. She quickly poked her hands through the arms of his shirt and tried buttoning it up. But her fingers were shaking too badly.

Ethan pushed her hands out of the way and did it for her.

Patch couldn't look him in the eye. But he wasn't content to let her suffer in peace. He lifted her chin and made her look at him.

"It isn't what you wear that makes you a lady, Patch. It's how you handle yourself around other folks. It's more than manners— although you have to learn them. It's knowing you're entitled to respect, and respecting the rights of other people. Your stepmother is that kind of lady."

Patch bristled, but Ethan didn't let her pull away. He lifted the tail of his shirt and wiped the blood from the edge of her mouth. "You don't have to keep fighting against everyone and everything. The people who care about you most are already on your side."

"I can't face Pa," Patch admitted.

"There's nothing you can do that your pa won't forgive and forget."

Patch sighed. "I hope you're right."

He pulled her into his arms and gave her a quick, hard hug. "You know I am."

She looked up into his green eyes and said, "Thanks for coming, Ethan."

He grinned. "It's a good thing I did. How were you planning to get back into the house past all those people when you're stripped down to nothing like that?"

"I guess I wasn't thinking too straight." Patch had her arms around Ethan, and it suddenly dawned on her that the only mark on his upper body was a thin red scratch. Either Pike Hardesty hadn't wounded the Masked Marauder, or Ethan wasn't him.

"Now what's wrong?" Ethan asked as he saw her perplexed look.

"Nothing. Only, haven't you ever wondered who the Masked Marauder is?"

Ethan's lids shuttered his eyes. "Sure I've wondered. Doesn't everybody?"

Patch shrugged. "I really thought it was you. I don't know how I could have been so wrong."

Ethan stiffened imperceptibly. "Come on, Patch. Let's get you back to my place and get you into some clothes."

As much as Molly wanted the party to be over and their guests gone, everyone stayed until the last possible moment, squeezing the most fun and joy they could from times spent together that were too few and too far between. It was after dark and Nessie was asleep in her bed before Seth and Molly finally bade the last of their guests farewell.

"Have you seen Patch or Whit since early this afternoon?" Molly asked as she eased down onto the front-porch step.

"Ethan had a talk with Patch. She's bedding down at his place tonight. I checked, and Whit is asleep in his bed."

Molly heaved a sigh of relief. "At least neither of them ran away."

Seth sat down on the lower step, evoking memories of the last time they had been here together. "That's counting small blessings indeed. Besides, if you want my honest opinion, I don't think either one of them wants to run away."

"I hope you're right." She pulled at a stray thread on the sleeve of her cambric dress. "Seth, do you think Pike really shot the

Masked Marauder? I mean, if he had, the Marauder would have come to you for help, wouldn't he?"

"I'll tell you, Molly, even if I'd doctored the Masked Marauder, I wouldn't have said anything today."

"Does that mean you did take care of him?"

Seth smiled. "Anything's possible."

Molly's eyes widened. A relieved smile touched the corners of her mouth. There it was—the explanation for where Seth had been last night. He had already as much as told her he knew who the Masked Marauder was. And if the Masked Marauder had been wounded, of course Seth would have had to treat him. And the perfume—why, what more perfect hideout for the Masked Marauder than some Soiled Dove's boudoir?

If Molly was grasping at straws, well, she had made herself a haystack. She didn't want to believe Seth had lied to her about Dora. It hurt too much. Because she cared too much.

She took Seth's hand and said, "Come with me." She grabbed a quilt hanging over the porch railing and tucked it under her arm. She led him away from the house, down toward the pond.

"Where are we going?" Seth asked.

"Someplace quiet. Someplace private.

Someplace where I can have you all to my-self."

Molly spread the quilt over the dew-soaked grass beneath a cottonwood. It was dark; the only light came from a quarter moon and the stars.

"Now," she said. "Take off all your clothes."

"What?"

"We'll have a race to see who can finish first."

Seth laughed and tore the buttons off his shirt as he ripped it from his shoulders. All Molly saw was flashes of white as Seth skinned out of his jeans and long johns.

"I win," he said a minute later. "Now I can help you."

Molly laughed as he began tugging at petti-coat strings that needed to be untied. She was breathless by the time he had unlaced her corset. He simply ripped her chemise down the front and skimmed it down off her arms.

She backed away from him, laughing as she pulled down her lace-trimmed drawers. When he stopped coming, she pulled them back up again. "Fooled you!"

A second later she was lying flat on her back on the quilt, and he was lying on top of her. His hand cupped the heart of her, and she could feel the warmth of him through the cotton cloth.

"Seth. Make love to me."

His mouth found hers and teased it open so his tongue could come inside and ravish her. He searched out the beauty mark on her face and kissed her there. Then his kisses went seeking and found places she hadn't known were so sensitive to the touch. A moment later, his hand was inside her lacy cotton drawers, and she moaned as he teased her with his fingertips. But soon the cotton was in his way, and he pulled the lacy garment down and off and tossed it aside.

"Molly?" Seth pulled her into his arms, and the touch of warm flesh against flesh in the cold night air was exquisite. The hair on his chest was slightly abrasive as he rubbed himself slowly against her. His mouth found the place where her neck joined her shoulders, and he kissed his way up to her ears. His breath was hot and moist, and the sensation sent shivers down her spine.

Molly wanted to return the pleasure he was giving her, so she let her hands go wandering and found the muscles across his shoulders, the crease of his spine, his taut buttocks, and his long, lean flanks. She listened for the sounds he made—the moans and groans and hissed-in breaths of air—that taught her how to please him. As she slid her fingertips down his side, he gasped and bolted upright.

"What's wrong?" Molly asked. "What did I do?"

"I'm a little ticklish," he said.

Molly grinned. "That's an awful thing to admit." She reached up to tickle him on purpose, and this time he grabbed her hand at the same time he gasped.

Only it wasn't a funny kind of gasp, it was a painful kind of gasp. "Seth?"

He took her hand and brought it back to his body, then gently ran it across a scab along his ribs. "I had an accident with an ax. I didn't want to worry you. It's just a scratch, but it's still pretty sensitive."

"You should have told me. I would have been more careful." Then Molly grinned impishly. "I guess I'll just have to find some less-sensitive spot to handle." Whereupon she reached over and cupped him in her hands.

Seth groaned. But there was no mistaking this as anything but a sound of pleasure. He didn't move, just let her touch him however she wanted. And Molly tried everything to see what made him moan the loudest.

Seth didn't last long before she was flat on her back, and he was deep inside her.

"Love me, Seth," she whispered. Her body arched into his, seeking fulfillment.

His body thrust into hers, seeking the same.

And in the darkness, under the wide Montana skies, they found the peace and contentment each had been seeking.

Afterward, Seth pulled Molly into his arms and levered a leg over her to keep her close. They were quiet for a long while, listening to the katydids and frogs. "I guess I should have listened when you said Patch needs to go away to school to become a lady. I thought— I hoped she could do all her changing right here. I can see maybe it might not be a bad idea after all to send her away."

Seth laid his head against Molly's breast, and she smoothed his hair with her hands. "It doesn't have to be right away," she said. "And it doesn't have to be for long. Don't worry, Seth." She kissed the top of his head. "Everything will turn out fine."

"Tomorrow—"

"I don't want to think about tomorrow," Molly said, kissing Seth's eyes closed. "I want to enjoy tonight."

It was nearly dawn before they crept back into the house, wrapped together in the quilt and giggling like children.

14

It had been nearly three weeks since the christening party, during which time Seth had gone into town twice to treat Mrs. Gulliver. Both times, he had come home very late. Both times, he had made love to Molly after he slipped into bed. He had never again smelled of a tart's perfume. But Molly couldn't help wondering why he was gone so long, and where he went when he wasn't with Mrs. Gulliver. She might have ignored her nagging unease except for one thing: Molly was fairly certain she was pregnant.

The signs were there: tenderness in her breasts, a slight dizziness if she stood too fast, fatigue, and most telling of all, she had missed her monthly course. She wasn't sure how she felt about having another child. The thought of having a baby—Seth's baby—was wonderful. But were they—all of them—ready for another addition to the family?

Patch and Whit were speaking again, although *snarling* would be more descriptive of their communication. Patch seemed to tolerate having Nessie in her room well enough. But every night at supper, Molly waited for an eruption of the tempers that never seemed far beneath the surface.

That was why she had so much looked forward to the trip she was making this afternoon to visit Iris Marsh. She wanted to talk to the other woman and get some advice. When she had thought she might be pregnant, she had talked Seth into teaching her how to drive the buggy. Now she was glad she had.

Seth didn't want to let her go on her own. "You might get lost. Or lose a wheel. The horse might bolt. There are always Indians around. Or—"

Molly had interrupted, "I'll be fine. The trail you use to reach the Marsh place is easy to follow. And the distance is short enough that if I lose a wheel, I can walk home or to the Marshes' whichever is closer. You taught me to drive, so you know I can handle the rig under any circumstances. And you must admit the likelihood of anything else"—she specifically did not mention an Indian attack—"happening is slim."

It was slim, but it was there. When Seth

frowned, Molly put her arms around him and kissed him on the mouth. "You have work to do here. I'll be fine."

Reluctantly, he had agreed.

Whit and Patch decided to stay home to help Seth and Ethan with gentling a couple of wild horses that were scheduled to be delivered to the army later in the summer. Molly settled Nessie beside her on the front seat and waved at them all as she cheerfully drove away.

Molly felt pretty proud of herself when she pulled the buggy up in front of Iris's sod house. Iris was outside leaning over an elevated tin tub, scrubbing clothes on a washboard. Her oldest daughter was working a wringer and hanging the clothes on a line that had been strung between two trees. The pig-tailed girl, Amaryllis, was sitting at her mother's feet playing with several calico kittens. The older baby, Daisy, had inched her way to the edge of a blanket and was eating a handful of grass. Molly's godchild, Lily, lay in a wooden cradle placed in the shade of the hill. Molly assumed the twin boys were with their father working in the fields.

"Why, what a surprise!" Iris said, wiping her hands dry on her apron as she approached the buggy. "Step down and come inside for something cool to drink."

As soon as Nessie was out of the buggy, she raced over to play with the kittens.

"Rose," Iris called to her oldest daughter, "keep an eye on things out here while I go sit and visit with Mrs. Kendrick."

"Yes, Mama."

Molly made a detour to admire Lily before she followed Iris into the sod house. The coolness of the earthen room was a relief after the heat of the afternoon sun. It took Molly a second to get her bearings in the dimness before she settled into a chair Iris held for her at the table. Iris poured them each a glass of sun-brewed tea and sat down across from Molly.

"Now, what brings you visiting in the middle of the week?" she asked.

"Do I have to have a reason for coming?"

"Most people do."

Molly smiled. "You're right. I wanted some advice."

"Ain't much I know about you don't know better yourself," Iris said. "But fire away."

"It's about Seth."

Iris smiled. "Guessed as much. There's more to that man than meets the eye."

"Do you think he would keep a mistress in town?" Molly blurted.

Iris was silent for a moment before she asked, "What makes you think such a thing?"

Molly explained that Seth had gone to town to check on Mrs. Gulliver, but that Mrs. Biddle had said he didn't stay there very long. "But he's usually gone from home the better part of the evening," she finished.

"And you think he's seeing another woman?"

Molly nodded. "Dora Deveraux."

"Tell me, when he comes home these nights he's gone, does he make love to you?"

Molly flushed. "Yes."

"Does he take his time?"

"Yes."

"Then I don't reckon it's another woman. Which leaves you looking for another reason why he stays in town," Iris said, tapping her chin thoughtfully. "Any thoughts?"

"He might be meeting the Masked Marauder."

Iris's eyes widened. "Does he know who it is?"

Molly leaned forward eagerly. "From things he's said to me, I think so. I just wish I knew for sure one way or the other what he's doing in town. Because . . . because I think I'm pregnant."

"Lordy, lordy, girl. That's great news!"

"I don't know," Molly said with a worried frown. "Patch and Whit are having enough trouble accepting things the way they are."

Iris took a swallow of tea to give herself time to think. "I see what you mean. But maybe a new baby is exactly what your family needs."

"It is?"

"How can they not love the baby? It'll be Patch's kin through Seth, and Whit's kin through you."

Molly smiled. "I knew there was a reason I came to see you, Iris. You talk such good sense."

"Glad you think so, Molly. You'd better get going so you're home in time to make supper for that man of yours."

Molly hadn't gone very far when she got the idea to go to town before she drove back to the ranch. The more she thought about it, the better she liked it. She could buy some material to make Patch a new dress and pick up a pair of trousers for Whit. And she would buy something special for Seth, a present to give him when she told him about the baby. At the crossroads, instead of continuing east toward the ranch, she turned north toward Fort Benton.

Pike Hardesty could hardly believe his eyes when he saw Doc Kendrick's wife come driving into town perched up on top of that buggy seat. He looked for the doc on horseback following her, but unbelievable as it seemed, she was alone. Well, well, maybe he was going to get a chance to get back at Doc Kendrick sooner than he'd thought.

Molly found everything she wanted at I. G. Baker and was feeling quite pleased with herself when she walked out of the store, loaded down with packages. She was conscious of someone following too close behind her and looked over her shoulder to see who it was.

Pike lifted his hat and said, "Afternoon, purty lady. Let me help you with those packages."

Before Molly could protest, he had taken the parcels out of her hands. There was nothing she could do without making a scene. She took Nessie's hand and, with her back stiff, and chin high, began walking toward where she'd left the buggy.

Pike walked beside her. "Been wondering when you'd come to town, purty lady. Guess that yellow-bellied husband of yours was scared to show his face."

"My husband seemed to come away well enough from his last encounter with you," Molly said. She had arrived at the buggy. "I'll take those packages now."

Pike dumped them in the buggy.

Molly lifted Nessie up into the front seat, but when she tried to join her daughter, Pike stepped in front of her, barring the way.

"Seems kinda strange you defending the doc after what he done to you."

"And what is that?" Molly asked.

"Caught him myself in Dora Deveraux's bed, not more'n two weeks after you was married," Pike said.

Molly's face blanched. "You're lying."

"Come along and ask Dora yourself if you don't believe me."

Pike had hold of Molly's arm and wouldn't let go. He started dragging her away from the buggy toward the Medicine Bow Saloon, halfway down the street.

"Wait here for me, Nessie," Molly called over her shoulder. "I'll be right back."

Molly looked around at the townspeople they passed, for someone she knew, someone who would help her. But when Pike glared at them, they all looked down at the ground. Molly wasn't sure what Pike had in mind for her, but the thought of going upstairs in the

Medicine Bow Saloon with him sent her heart into her throat.

She wasn't without hope. She was sure that if Red Dupree saw her come into the saloon with Pike, he would intercede. Only Pike didn't go in the front door. When they reached the shadowed alley alongside Bassett's saloon, he headed through it to the back of the building.

It was then that Molly realized that if she was going to escape, she had to do it on her own. Just as they reached a set of back stairs to the second floor, she stomped on Pike's foot and yanked hard to free her arm. He was so surprised at her attack that he let her go and grabbed his foot.

When Pike saw her start to run toward the street, he came after her. Molly had nearly reached sunlight when she was caught from behind. Pike grabbed her by the shoulder and swung her around so she slammed against the wood-slatted building. His fisted hand swung around and hit her hard in the chin. Everything went black as Molly slid down the side of the building onto the ground.

When she came to, Molly was terrified, because she was in a strange bed. A quick look at her surroundings left her confused. The entire room was littered with dolls. A cherubic doll with a ceramic face lay on the pillow next to her. Molly sat up and put a hand to her sore jaw, working it carefully until she was sure nothing was broken. She heard voices arguing outside the room—a man and a woman—and looked around for a weapon. She opened a drawer in a bedside table and found a small gun. At first she was afraid to touch it, but as the voices got louder and angrier, she took it out and held it in her hand.

When the door opened, the derringer was pointed at Dora Deveraux.

"It's not loaded," Dora said. She walked over to Molly and took the gun out of her hand. Then, to Molly's chagrin, she unloaded the bullets into her palm and dropped both gun and ammunition onto the bedside table.

Molly stared wide-eyed at the woman, wondering what her part was in this kidnapping.

"I sent Red out to keep an eye on your kid," Dora said. "You wanta tell me what you're doing in town without Seth?"

"I came to get some material for a dress," Molly said, "and to get a present for Seth. I wanted to surprise him."

Dora put a hand on Molly's chin and

turned her bruised face to the light. "He's gonna be surprised, all right."

"Were you arguing with Pike Hardesty?" Molly asked.

Dora clucked her tongue in disgust. "Stupid fool. If any of those men down there knew he'd hit you, they'd lynch him to the nearest tree. Don't know that Seth won't kill him anyway when he sees what Pike did to your face. I told Pike he oughta get out of town for a while. He didn't like gettin' advice from a woman. But at least he wasn't dumb enough not to take it."

Molly very much feared it was Seth who would be killed in any encounter between the two men. Pike had already shot at Seth once. The next time, he might not miss. She would just have to come up with some story about what had caused her bruise that didn't involve Pike Hardesty.

"Please don't tell Seth about this," she said to Dora.

"He's gonna find out."

"Not if you don't say anything."

"Why did Pike wanta haul you up here, anyway?"

Molly cleared her throat. "I called him a liar when he said Seth was here in bed with you right after we were married."

"Ain't that a sack of hell," Dora said. "I told Seth he should've explained to you about that."

All the blood drained from Molly's face. "Then he *was* here?"

"Why, sure he was, honey. But that's because—Hey! Don't you go fainting on me now." Dora put a hand on Molly's head and forced it down between her knees.

Molly felt dizzy. She could hear a buzzing sound in the background that she knew must be Dora talking, but she couldn't understand any of the words. Her chest hurt. And her eyes burned. And her stomach felt nauseous.

"I'm going to throw up," she said.

"Now, now—"

"I'm going to throw up," Molly repeated.

Dora ran to get a basin from the dressing table and held it while Molly was sick. She dampened a cloth with water from the pitcher and wiped Molly's mouth.

"You don't look so good. Maybe I better ask Red to drive you home."

"No!" Molly knew there was no way she would be able to explain things to Seth if Red came along. "I'll be fine." She got to her feet and was none to steady. "I think if I could just have a sip of water, I'd be fine."

"Haven't got any more water, honey. But

how about a little shot of something stronger? Probably be just what you need."

Molly nodded and held out her hand for the shot glass full of whiskey Dora poured for her. She took a tentative sip and felt it burn all the way down. It warmed her inside, where she was so terribly, terribly cold. She sipped again, but got too much, coughed, then swallowed the rest. She handed the empty glass back to Dora and said, "Thank you."

Molly walked very carefully, though unsteadily, to the door. When she got there, she turned and said to Dora in a perfectly calm voice, "Stay away from my husband. If you go near him again, I'll scratch your eyes out."

She left the room, then realized she had no idea which door led to the back stairs. She opened Dora's door again and asked, "Which way to the stairs?"

The beautiful Soiled Dove was grinning ear to ear when she said, "Last door on your left."

When Molly got back to the buggy, Red took one look at her and said, "Son of a bitch. What happened to you?"

Molly had yet to think of what reason she was going to give Seth for her bruised face.

What popped to mind was, "Some yard goods fell on me from the top shelf at I. G. Baker."

"Lordy mercy. Looks like that smarts," Red said as he helped her up into the buggy. "You gonna be able to get home all right?"

"I'll be fine," Molly said.

And she was. In fact, she was so dead inside that she didn't even feel the pain of her jaw. When she arrived home it was after dark, and every lantern in the house was lit. As soon as she drove up, Ethan, Patch and Whit came running out to greet her.

"Where have you been?" Whit demanded anxiously. "I got worried when you didn't come home."

"Where's Seth?" Molly asked.

"He went looking for you after it got dark," Ethan said. "I expect he'll be back when he doesn't find you somewhere on the road between here and the Marsh place."

"I decided to go to town to get some things."

Ethan didn't say anything, just looked at her in a way that spoke volumes. Molly nearly fell as she got down from the buggy. Ethan caught her in his arms and carried her inside.

"Mother!" Whit cried. "Is she all right?"

"I think she's just worn out," Ethan said.

"Why don't you go help get Nessie to bed and then you can come say good night to your mother."

Ethan laid Molly on Seth's bed and reached down to take her shoes off. Her eyes were closed when he started undoing the buttons on her dress. They flashed open in alarm, and she grabbed at his hand.

"Figured you better loosen the laces on that corset you're wearing," he said.

Molly tried to get up to go behind the screen to change and slumped back down again. Tears slid out of the corners of her eyes. "Go ahead," she said.

Impersonally, deftly, Ethan unbuttoned Molly's dress. He lifted her and slipped the bodice off her shoulders, then turned her over and untied the laces on her corset. Molly sighed in relief. He put his hands on her shoulders and began to rub the tension out. "Would you like to talk about how you got that bruise on your face?"

"It happened in town," Molly said.

"I figured that. How?"

"Some yard goods fell on me."

"Uh-huh."

"Did you know Seth was seeing Dora Deveraux?"

Ethan's hands froze. "Who told you that?"

A shuddering sigh escaped Molly. "I had it right from the horse's mouth."

"You saw Dora?"

"Thanks to Pike Hardesty."

"What does Pike have to do with this?"

"He's the one who told me Seth was seeing Dora."

Ethan swore under his breath and began to rub Molly's shoulders again. "Everything isn't always what it seems, Molly."

"I should hope the hell not," Seth said from the doorway.

Molly pushed herself up on her hands, realized she was only half-dressed, and pulled her dress up to cover her chemise as she scrambled into a more presentable position on the bed.

"What are you doing in my bedroom with my wife?" Seth demanded in a cold voice.

"Molly wasn't feeling well when she got home. I carried her in here."

"And took half her clothes off? That was mighty considerate of you."

Ethan stood and said, "Listen, Seth—"

"Get out of here, Ethan."

Ethan's lips pressed flat. He looked from Molly to Seth and back again.

"It's all right, Ethan," Molly said. "I'll handle this."

"You're a fool, Seth," Ethan muttered as he stalked out the door.

Seth closed the door behind Ethan and turned to Molly. "Where were you?"

"I went to town."

"Without telling anyone? Do you know how dangerous that is?"

"I do now. I'm sorry, Seth. I—"

"Sorry?" Seth grabbed her by the shoulders and shook her hard. "Do you have any idea how I felt when you didn't come back before dark? Do you have any idea what kind of crazy thoughts went through my head when Iris said you'd left hours ago? Do you?"

"Seth! Stop! I'm going to be sick."

Before he could do anything to help, she leaned over the side of the bed and heaved. But she had lost everything in her stomach at Dora's. Molly retched and retched until tears squeezed from her eyes, but nothing came up. At last her body released her from the awful spasms, and she slumped forward, sobbing.

Seth lifted her up in his arms and pulled her face to his chest. When he did, she cried out and grabbed her jaw. For the first time he saw the terrible bruise that had previously been hidden in the shadows created by the single lantern.

"What happened to you? Who did this?"

Molly knew that Seth's life might depend on how well she told her story. She tried to keep her voice casual and light as she explained, "It was just a silly accident. I was buying material for a new dress for Patch at I. G. Baker. A heavy bolt of material fell from the top shelf and hit me in the jaw. Really, it looks worse than it feels."

Molly held her breath for a second, waiting to see whether Seth would accept her story. When he pulled her tighter into his arms, she let out a silent sight of relief and closed her eyes.

"I was so worried about you, Molly. If anything had happened to you . . ." He smoothed the hair back from her face and kissed her eyes closed. It frightened him to see her so pale. "What made you sick, Molly? Do you know? Was it something you ate?"

He had given her the perfect opening to tell him she was sick because she was pregnant with their child. But how could she tell him that joyous news in light of what she had learned this afternoon? "I didn't have anything to eat today," she said. "I guess I was just exhausted."

He hugged her tight. Seth had discovered something in those awful hours when he had searched for her that had at first astonished him, then left him terrified. How awful it would be to find out he loved Molly, only to lose her before he had a chance to tell her so. Now look what he had done. He had accused his best friend of having taken advantage of his wife. And instead of being glad that Molly was home safe, he had shaken her within an inch of her life. She had been so sick! Lord, his body ached for the wretchedness he had seen in her face.

"Molly, I just wanted to tell you—"

"Not tonight, Seth. I'm so tired. I can't talk anymore tonight."

There were several knocks on the door, and it opened to reveal Whit and Patch.

Whit crossed to the foot of the bed. "We just wanted to see if you're all right, Mother."

"I'm fine," Molly said. "I'll tell you both all about everything in the morning."

"Let's go, Whit," Patch said. "Your mother needs to rest."

"I know that," Whit snapped. "I was just leaving."

The two of them left the room arguing over which one of them was being more considerate of Molly's feelings.

Seth finished undressing Molly and laid

her carefully in bed. He joined her and pulled her into his arms. First thing tomorrow morning, he would tell her he loved her. And they would start over from there.

15

When Seth woke up early the next morning, Molly still had dark circles of exhaustion under her eyes. He decided it didn't make sense to wake up an exhausted woman to tell her he loved her. He was careful to be quiet in the kitchen as he made coffee so as not to wake anyone, but as he turned from the stove, Nessie stood at the kitchen door.

"You woke me up," she accused. The very next words out of her mouth were, "Where's Mama?"

Seth hurried over to scoop Nessie up in his arms. He laid a finger across his mouth and said, "Shh. Your mother's still sleeping. She's tired from her trip into town."

"I went to town too," Nessie said.

"I know."

"I didn't like the bad man."

Seth froze. "What bad man?"

"The man with the hurt on his face. Here." Nessie laid her hand against Seth's cheek.

"What did the bad man do?"

"He took Mama away. But she didn't want to go."

"Where did he take her, sweetheart?"

"I don't know. Mama told me to stay in the buggy. I got scared."

"But you were a good girl and stayed in the buggy?"

"Uh-huh. Red came and said Mama would be coming in a minute. But it felt like a whole *hour*," Nessie said. "And when she came back, she had a hurt on her face too. Here." Nessie put her hand on Seth's jaw, which had tautened as the little girl spoke.

Seth set Nessie down and said, "I want you to go get back in bed with Patch and stay there until your mother wakes up."

"But Da—"

"What did you call me?"

"Uh . . . Seth?"

Seth gave her a quick hug. "I like Da better. Now do as I said, Nessie."

She made a face but said, "All right, Da."

Seth crept into his bedroom and sat down on the bed beside his sleeping wife. His fingertips lightly grazed the bruise Pike Hardesty had put there. His face paled with fury. "I'll kill him this time," he whispered.

He rose and silently left the room.

* * *

Molly swatted at the itch on her face for the second time. When it came back again, she opened her eyes. Nessie was sitting beside her on the bed. She had a strand of Molly's hair in her hand and was using it to tickle her mother under the nose.

Molly rolled over and said, "Go away, Nessie, and let me sleep. It's too early to be up."

"Da is up."

Molly squinted over at the other side of the bed. "So he is. Did you just call Seth 'Da'?"

"Uh-huh. He said I could. After I told him about the bad man."

Molly tensed. "What bad man?"

"The bad man who took you away."

Molly sat up and pulled Nessie into her lap. "What did you tell Da?"

"That you didn't want to leave me, but the bad man made you go away."

Molly set Nessie on the bed and started dressing, yanking on the new split riding skirt she had made for herself. "What did Da say when you told him that?"

"He told me to go back to bed."

"Where is Da now?"

"I don't know."

"Patch!" Molly shouted as she ran into the next room. "Patch! Wake up!"

Patch sat bolt upright at the sound of her name being screamed through the house. A second later, Molly arrived in her bedroom doorway.

"Go get Ethan, quick!"

"What's the matter?"

"Your father's gone to town to fight Pike Hardesty again."

"Why would he do that?"

"Because Nessie told your father that Pike put this bruise on my face."

Molly turned her head, and Patch gasped at the black and blue mark on Molly's jaw.

"Garn! You look awful!" Patch said.

Molly tried not to sound as frantic as she felt. "We have to go after your father. Pike doesn't fight clean, and he doesn't fight fair. He'll kill Seth."

"I'll be back with Ethan in the flick of a horse's tail. He'll know what to do."

Molly woke up Whit and told him to watch Nessie while she was gone to town. When Ethan arrived at the house moments later, she explained the facts to him as quickly and calmly as she could.

"Now he's gone to meet Pike. We have to stop him."

To Molly's surprise, Ethan seemed reluctant to go after Seth. "He can handle himself.

He doesn't need you in town. And I don't think he'd appreciate you coming after him."

"I don't care what he'd appreciate," Molly retorted. "I am not going to let this baby be born without a father!"

"Baby?" everyone said at once.

Molly closed her eyes and clenched her teeth. "I wanted to tell Seth first. But yes, I'm going to have a baby."

"I guess it couldn't hurt to go and keep an eye on things," Ethan said. "But *I'll* go. The rest of you stay here."

Molly wrung her hands in indecision.

"There's nothing you can do in town that I can't. You're exhausted. You have to take care of yourself. Think about the baby," Ethan said.

For the baby's sake and no other reason, Molly nodded.

Patch and Whit exchanged looks. They hadn't agreed to anything. The instant Ethan was out of sight, they slipped out of the house to the barn and saddled their horses.

"We gotta be there," Patch said. "Pa might need us."

"Right," Whit said. "We can warn Da in case there's an ambush or anything."

Patch arched a brow at Whit. "He ain't your Da."

"He is so. You wanta make something of it?"

Patch tightened the cinch on her saddle. "Ask me again when I have more time to argue."

Nessie was watching out the front window when Whit and Patch rode away. "There they go."

Molly was sitting at the kitchen table with her head in her hands. "There who goes?"

"Whit and Patch. They're riding *fast.*"

Molly jumped to her feet. "They're what?"

Nessie pointed. "See."

"I'll wring their disobedient little necks!" Molly grabbed Nessie by the hand and ran all the way to the barn. She harnessed the buggy and shoved Nessie up into the front seat. "Hang on," Molly said. "We're going to town!"

Pike had stayed out of town for twenty-four hours and figured that was long enough. Nobody was going to come after him for hitting Doc Kendrick's wife. They were too scared of him to do anything. Dora had just said that to get rid of him. He still owed Dora for that business with the doc. Now was as good a time as any for her to pay.

Despite Pike's belief that there was no danger for him in town, it never hurt to be careful. He used the back way upstairs to Dora's room.

Dora was just ushering a customer out, and Pike waited until she was closing the door to shove his way into her room.

Dora turned and walked away from him. "Hello, Pike."

"Don't touch nothin', Dora. I ain't forgot how you pulled a gun on me."

Dora draped herself across the bed and pulled her black negligée aside to show off her red satin chemise and drawers. She pulled a knee up and adjusted the red garter on one of her black silk stockings. "You come here for a reason, Pike?"

"I figure you owe me some time under the covers, Dora. I'm here to collect."

"You know I never turn down a payin' customer, Pike. Only, before you drop your drawers, maybe you'd like to know the Masked Marauder is waiting for you downstairs."

"What?"

"Came in about three hours ago. Been sittin' at your table downstairs playing solitaire ever since."

Pike felt the sweat break out on his brow. "What's he want with me?"

"How should I know, Pike? Why don't you go downstairs and find out?"

Pike thought seriously about sneaking out the way he'd come in. Then he thought again. The Marauder would be expecting him to walk in the front door of the saloon, not to come down the stairs. He'd have the drop on that masked devil this time for sure. He'd lay all that talk to rest about him getting outgunned by the Masked Marauder when he shot that sonofabitch dead.

By now, the town of Fort Benton knew there was going to be a showdown of some kind. A crowd had gathered in the saloon, although no one had worked up the nerve actually to speak to the Masked Marauder. There was a constant irritating noise, like a mosquito buzzing an ear at bedtime, as they talked low amongst themselves. Most of the speculation centered on why the Marauder had finally decided to show himself in public. And whether he would, at last, reveal his identity.

The Marauder had ridden up to the Medicine Bow Saloon on a big black stallion looking more sinister than anyone had expected. His shirt, pants, and boots were all black. He wore a black leather vest with the outline of a Texas star stitched in red on the pocket.

Movement on Front Street came to a standstill as he dismounted. He was tall, broadshouldered, and slim-hipped. Tied-down twin Colts rested in tooled black leather holsters that looked well used. His black mask was tied in a knot behind his head and covered his face down to his nose, with only slits for his eyes. It wasn't even possible to tell the color of his eyes because his high-crowned black hat was pulled low and shadowed his face. He sported no beard or moustache, but he had a strong jaw and a grim-lipped mouth. An aura of danger and mystery surrounded him.

It was hard to believe this man might be someone they knew, someone who worked beside them day to day. Try as they might, it was impossible to imagine any one of their ordinary friends as this mythical hero. Yet here he was in their midst. The Masked Marauder had come to life.

Men had stepped aside as he shouldered through the batwing doors of the saloon and looked around. Apparently he hadn't found whoever it was he'd been looking for, because he sauntered over to the table against the wall—Pike Hardesty's table—and sat down. He had asked Red in a low, raspy voice—obviously disguised—for a deck of cards and a glass of rye. Since then, he had played solitaire and ignored the rest of the room.

When Pike started down the stairs, a hush settled over the saloon. Hardesty had his Colt revolver drawn and aimed at the Marauder. He walked right up to the masked man and said, "This time I aim to find out who's under that mask."

"You will, Pike," the Marauder said.

Since all eyes were focused on the confrontation across the room, it was easy for Patch and Whit to slip in under the batwing doors of the saloon. They sidled along the wall trying to be inconspicuous.

"I don't see Pa," Patch whispered, searching the barroom.

"Maybe he ain't here yet."

Patch shot Whit a look of disdain. "We're here. And he left before we did."

"Maybe he's upstairs," Whit suggested.

At that moment Patch caught sight of the Masked Marauder. She grabbed Whit's arm and said, "He's here."

"Where? I don't see him."

"Not Pa, you idiot! The Masked Marauder!"

Whit's eyes rounded when he spied the masked man dressed all in black. "What's he doing here?"

"Looks like he's facing down Pike Hardesty."

Patch looked up the stairs. If Pa was up there, he'd be with Dora. She didn't think he'd had much to do with Dora since Molly came along. If she went upstairs, she could warn Pa not to come down. But if she left the barroom, she might miss the Masked Marauder in action. She finally decided to station herself at the bottom of the stairs. That way, she'd be able to warn her pa if he showed up.

Patch's heart was thudding as she watched the Masked Marauder play his game of solitaire, despite the gun trained on him by Pike Hardesty. She could see him talking but couldn't hear what he was saying.

I don't care what he told me. The Masked Marauder has to be Ethan, she thought.

He had left the ranch right after Pa, riding to the rescue. He could have stopped to get his mask from the warehouse at the edge of town. Why else would the Masked Marauder have appeared in public like this and forced Pike Hardesty into a confrontation, except to save her pa?

"Why don't you take off that mask and let all these fine folks see who you are?" Pike said.

The Marauder turned another card. "Does it really matter who I am, Pike?"

"Naw. I'd just like to see your face when I kill you," Pike said with a grin. "Now get up slow and easy, and keep your hands where I can see them."

Everyone in the saloon held their breath, waiting to see if the Marauder would go for his guns. There was a murmur of surprise when he stood up, just as Pike had ordered.

Abruptly, Red spoke from behind the bar. "Do your killing outside, Pike. I've laid down enough fresh sawdust on your account."

Pike slowly backed away from the Marauder to bring Red into his line of sight. The bartender had a shotgun aimed at him. "Whatever you say, Red. Just don't go gettin' an itchy trigger finger."

"Come on, you," Pike said, gesturing the Marauder out from behind the table with his gun. "Outside."

Patch and Whit melted into the wall as the Masked Marauder passed by them. Patch could have reached out and touched him, he was so close. It wasn't until he had nearly reached the batwing doors that Patch realized he didn't have Ethan's hitching gait. But if the Masked Marauder wasn't Ethan Hawk, who was it?

"That's Da," Whit croaked.

"What?" Patch hissed.

"Da is the Masked Marauder!" he hissed back. "Look at him. At his hands. At his mouth. It's him!"

Patch's eyes rounded, and her jaw dropped. It wasn't possible. It couldn't be. Ethan was—But Ethan *wasn't* the Masked Marauder. The Marauder didn't have Ethan's limp. If Whit was right, her father was about to face down Pike Hardesty in a gunfight!

She shoved Whit ahead of her and urged, "Let's go! We have to help him if we can!"

They were caught up in the crowd that poured from the saloon into the street after the two gunmen. The onlookers backed up against the buildings on either side of Front Street, out of the line of fire. Patch and Whit found a spot behind the horse trough from which to watch the showdown.

"We have to do something!" Patch said.

"Da doesn't need our help," Whit said confidently. "He can handle this with one hand tied behind his back."

Patch stared at Whit for a moment, then out at the masked man before her, whom she now recognized as her father. Whit seemed confident that her pa could save himself despite the fact Pike Hardesty was standing

there holding a gun on him. Patch thought of
the reverence she had always felt for the ca-
pabilities of the mythical masked hero. She
cringed at the memory of all the unnecessary
battles she had fought on her father's behalf.
He was not a coward. Never had been. She
was the one who had been afraid—of what
people would think. Patch felt a welling of
emotion in her throat.

"You're right," she said to Whit. "Pa can
take care of himself."

In fact, the Marauder didn't seem the least
perturbed by the fact Pike held a gun on him.
When he reached the middle of the street, he
turned to Pike and said, "I warned you what
would happen if you didn't get out of town.
I'm willing to make this a fair fight."

Pike snickered. "I ain't."

When Molly drove into Fort Benton, she
saw the crowd gathered on Front Street. She
saw the two men in the distance faced off
against one another and knew what she had
to do.

She stopped the buggy and said, "Climb
down, Nessie, and wait here for me." She
helped her daughter out of the buggy, then
lashed the buckskin gelding with the whip,
sending him galloping down the street
straight for the two men.

Pike heard the excited roar of the crowd behind him and took his eyes off the Marauder for one second to see what had caused it.

In that moment the Marauder drew his gun and fired.

Pike saw his own shot go wide in the same instant he felt a bullet strike him in the chest. He staggered, then his knees crumpled and he fell on his face. The Marauder walked over and knelt down beside him.

"Who are you?" Pike rasped.

The masked man leaned over to whisper in his ear.

Pike's eyes widened. "Bullshit! You can't be —" It was the last thing he ever said.

The crowd converged on the Marauder, shaking his hand, patting him on the back, and begging him to take off his mask.

Molly had pulled the buggy to an abrupt stop when she heard the gunshots and saw a man fall. She sat in the buggy seat, heart pounding, hands tight on the reins to restrain the excited buckskin, and stared at the scene before her. At last she realized it was Pike Hardesty on the ground and that the Masked Marauder was kneeling beside him.

She felt relieved that Pike was dead, but where was Seth? She searched the crowd and found Patch and Whit peeking over the horse trough in front of the saloon. She would tan their hides when she got them home! She backed the buckskin up and headed the buggy toward them.

Among those watching the events on Front Street with avid interest was Drake Bassett. He was not at all happy with what he had seen. He had counted on Pike to get rid of the Masked Marauder. But usually, if one wanted something done right, one had to do it oneself. Bassett took a Winchester down off the wall mount beside his desk and balanced it on the windowsill to take aim on the Marauder. He had to wait for the shot because the crowd had converged on the masked man.

"I sort of suspected this might happen."

Bassett froze.

"If you want to live, I suggest you drop that rifle."

"Who's there?" Bassett stood as the rifle clattered to the floor.

"Turn around and find out," the voice said.

When Bassett turned, he felt his skin get up and crawl all over him. "It can't be—"

He looked out the window at the man who had shot Pike Hardesty, then back at the masked man standing in front of him—unarmed. "Is this some kind of joke? A trick? Which one of you is the real Masked Marauder?"

The masked man flashed a smile. "Both of us."

"Who are you?" Bassett demanded. "And who is he?" He pointed out the window.

"The bane of your existence," the masked man said in a hard voice.

"I don't think I—" Bassett pulled the gun he kept inside his coat, certain he could kill the unarmed man standing before him. Only, before he even had the gun out of his coat, the man had pulled a knife from behind his back and thrown it. Bassett looked down and saw the hilt protruding from his belly.

"How did you do that?"

"Lots of practice," the masked man said with a cynical twist of his mouth.

Bassett fell on his side, the lifeblood ebbing out of him.

The masked man stood there for a moment staring at the dead man before him. He tensed as he heard someone at the door, then relaxed when he saw who it was.

"Is he dead?" Dora asked.

"Yes."

"I'm glad, Ethan."

Ethan reached up and untied the mask

from his face and shoved it into his pocket. "I'll be moving on now, Dora."

"But I'm glad you came, Ethan. I'm glad you remembered, and that you came."

"I owe you, Dora. If you ever need me, Seth will know how to find me."

"Do you think you'll ever settle down somewhere, Ethan?"

"A man with a price on his head never can." Ethan looked bleakly out at the Masked Marauder being cheered by the townspeople. "I have to say my good-byes to Seth, but then I'll be on my way."

Down on the street, Molly was starting to get worried. She had retrieved Nessie, and she had Patch and Whit in tow, but nowhere did she see Seth. Where was he? Had Pike somehow gotten to Seth before the Marauder confronted him?

Patch suddenly jerked free. "There's Pa! Pa!"

Molly turned to see where Patch was pointing. Her jaw dropped as she saw the man standing in the center of the crowd, the man dressed all in black who removed his mask at last to reveal who he was.

Patch and Whit grinned at each other as sheer amazement quieted the crowd. An in-

stant later, a babble of excited voices
erupted.

"Who'd have thought it?"

"Sure had us all fooled, Doc!"

"My God, and we all thought you was a—"
Coward.

Stillness descended for a sobering instant
as they all thought the word. Then the babble
began again.

"That sure was some fancy shootin', Doc!"

"You were something else! Just something
else!"

Molly felt herself pushed forward by the
crowd, who had recognized her and the children and were anxious to reunite them with
Seth.

Seth looked sheepish. "I'm sorry I couldn't
tell you sooner, Molly," he said. "It just
wasn't possible."

"We're having a baby, Pa," Patch said.
"That is, Molly's having a baby."

The crowd laughed, and someone shouted,
"Seems like you been a pretty busy man
lately, Doc."

Molly flushed bright red.

"You gonna keep on wearing a gun, Doc?"
someone yelled.

"We need a sheriff here in Fort Benton,"
another said. "Seems you'd do a good job."

"I just want to be a doctor," Seth said in a quiet voice.

"Come on, Doc. Will you at least think about it?"

"All right," Seth said. "I'll think about it. Right now, I'm taking my wife and kids home."

"Sure, Doc, sure."

Seth wrapped an arm around Molly's shoulders. She remained stiff against him. He had known she would be upset when she found out he had been sneaking out at night to be the Masked Marauder. But he had thought she would at least see the humor in the situation.

Molly wasn't laughing. She wasn't even smiling. As he lifted her up into the buggy seat, she arched a brow and said, "When we get home, we have to talk."

Ethan joined them at the buggy with Seth's big black horse, which he tied on behind.

Patch leaned out of the buggy and asked, "Did you know Pa was the Masked Marauder, Ethan?"

"How about that!" Ethan said.

Prompted by Ethan's enthusiasm, Patch launched into a litany of accolades for the Masked Marauder.

It was easy for Seth and Molly to avoid

talking on the way home because Patch and Whit never shut up. They argued vociferously over which was the most dangerous exploit of the Masked Marauder. And whether Whit was going to help Patch build a ship in the whiskey bottle she had taken from the saloon. At last Patch said, "For a while I thought Ethan was the Masked Marauder, Pa. Can you imagine that?"

Seth turned and shared a smile with Ethan, who was riding along beside the buggy. "Oh, I can see how you might have been fooled."

When they got home, Molly took the children inside and fed them supper. Seth unharnessed the buggy and rubbed down the buckskin. Ethan joined him in the barn.

"I wanted to thank you for being a friend when I needed one," Ethan said.

"Anytime."

"That Masked Marauder idea of yours worked just fine. You should have seen the look on Bassett's face when he realized there were two of us."

"How is Drake?"

"Dead," Ethan said. "Dora's gonna make up some story about a drifter passing through to account for the stab wound in his belly."

Ethan straightened the buckskin's mane. "It's time I moved on, Seth. Especially now that the town has seen you use a gun. Eventually, they'll find out who you are. And then *they'll* know where I am."

"Maybe not."

Ethan shook his head. "Can't take the chance. Might put you and your family in danger." Ethan grinned. "Speaking of families, it looks like you're going to be a proud papa again."

Seth grinned back. "How about that?"

"With another mouth to feed, you might want to take that sheriff's job they offered you in town," Ethan said.

"I'll think about it."

"You know, Seth, the past is over and done. It was an accident."

Seth heaved a sigh. "Yeah."

"I guess I'd better go say good-bye to Patch before I leave."

Ethan found Patch sitting on the back porch. "Hello, there."

"Sit down, Ethan. I was just counting my marbles. I'm going to have a rematch tomorrow with Whit."

"I'm sorry I won't be here to see you win," he said.

"You have to go scouting for wild horses again?"

"No." He took a deep breath and said, "I'm leaving, Patch. For good."

"But you're Pa's partner. You have a cabin here. You can't leave."

"I'm a drifting man. And it's time to move on."

"Why?"

He put a hand on her shoulder. "I have my reasons, Patch. I have to go."

"No you don't!" she said, jerking away from his touch, refusing to be mollified. "You could stay if you wanted to." She damned her pride and grabbed his shirt in both fists. "Don't leave, Ethan. I love you! Someday I want to be your wife!"

"Dammit, Patch. You don't know what you're saying. You're just a kid!"

Patch recoiled as though he had slapped her.

Suddenly aware that he had hurt her feelings, Ethan sought to mend fences. "You've got your whole life ahead of you, Patch. And plenty of time to find the man who'll be right for you."

"I don't want anybody else. I want you," she said stubbornly.

He took her hand and brushed his thumb across her grimy knuckles. "I tell you what I'll do, Patch. I promise someday, when you're all grown up, I'll come back and find you. If you still think you want to marry me —" He shrugged. "Well, we'll see."

"Do you promise?" Patch said.

Ethan nodded.

"Cross your heart and hope to die?"

Ethan crossed his heart with his finger.

"Dang it, Ethan, I'm going to miss you so much!" Patch launched herself into Ethan's open arms and hugged him hard enough to last her the long years she would have to wait for him to return.

Patch didn't try to stop the tears. *Ethan was leaving. He didn't believe she loved him. He thought she was just a kid!* Well, she wasn't going to change her mind about marrying him. She would wait a lifetime if she had to! When he came back—Ethan wouldn't dare break his promise—she would be waiting. And she would be his wife.

Ethan handed Patch a handkerchief to wipe her runny nose. She started to hand it back, but he folded her fingers around the wadded-up ball of material. "Keep it for me till I come back." He stood and said, "Now I have to go say good-bye to your ma."

"She ain't my—"

"She is. And you're lucky to have her," Ethan said.

"Maybe I am," Patch agreed.

"That's the first sign I've seen that you're starting to grow up," Ethan said. "Now give me another hug and say good-bye."

Patch put her arms around Ethan's waist and held on until he removed them.

"Good-bye, Patch."

"Good-bye, Ethan. Don't forget I love you."

He smiled. "I won't."

He turned his back on her and walked away.

16

Seth's path back to the house from the barn crossed Whit's door. He knocked, and when Whit called out to him, he stepped inside.

"I thought I'd check to see that you were tucked in for the night."

"Mother was already here," Whit said.

"All right. Sleep well, then."

When Seth turned to leave, Whit said, "I wouldn't mind if you tucked me in too."

Seth sat down beside Whit and performed what had become a ritual for them over the past weeks. Then he did something he hadn't done before. He leaned over and kissed Whit on the forehead.

Whit stared at him with probing eyes. "What did you do that for?"

"Because I wanted to show that I love you," Seth said.

"I'm not your son. Why do you care?" Whit challenged.

Seth smiled. "I don't think I can give you a

reason. Love just is. I want to help you grow up to be a good man. And I want you to be happy." Seth shrugged. "I can't explain it any better than that."

Whit cleared his throat. "I might love you too."

Seth smiled again. "I wouldn't mind if you did." He leaned over and blew out the lantern beside the bed. "Go to sleep, son."

Whit turned over and did as he was told.

Seth wasn't consciously avoiding the coming confrontation with Molly. But when he headed through the connecting doorway, it seemed a good idea to stop and say good night to Patch and Nessie, too.

The instant he walked through the door, Nessie stood up on the four-poster bed and leaped for him. He barely caught her before she hit the floor.

"Whoa there, girl! What're you doing jumping out of bed like that?"

Nessie wrapped her arms around Seth's neck and laid her head on his chest. "I knew you'd catch me."

Seth's heart was still pounding from the near miss. "Just give me a little more warning next time," he said with a chuckle.

Nessie was easy to love, Seth thought, because she gave love so freely. He should have

mentioned that to Whit, but he hadn't
thought of it at the time. "It's bedtime, little
one. Lie down now and get some sleep."

He laid her down and pulled the quilt up to
her chin, then leaned over and kissed her
teasingly on the nose.

Seth looked over at Patch, who was leaning
on her elbow watching him. Before Annarose
died, when Patch was still a baby, he had
spent time with her like this every night. He
had forgotten about that until now.

As Seth crossed to Patch, she lay down flat
and pulled her own covers up, leaving nothing for him to do.

He sat down beside her anyway. He felt
awkward with his daughter, not sure how he
should treat her. She seemed too grown up
for the kind of teasing he had done with Nessie. In fact, the expression on her face dared
him to try something like that with her.
Which was how he knew that 'was exactly
what he should do.

He leaned over and kissed her on the nose,
but as he sat up, he licked his lips. "Mmmm.
Those freckles tasted distinctly of brown
sugar."

"Oh, Pa!" Patch said. "Don't be ridiculous."

"Maybe I was wrong. Let me see." He
kissed her nose again. "Definitely brown

sugar," he said. "And you know how I love sweets." He began kissing Patch all over her face, everywhere he could find a freckle.

Soon she was laughing, fighting him off— not too hard—and loving every breathless minute of it.

"What is all the noise in here?"

Seth stopped what he was doing and grinned at Molly, who was standing in the doorway. "I was just kissing all the brown sugar off Patch's face."

Molly smiled. "Pretty sweet, is she?"

Seth looked at Patch and said, "The sweetest."

Patch turned a bright shade of scarlet and pulled the covers up over her head. "Paaaa."

"Come on out, Patch," Seth whispered to the covers that hid her face.

Only her twinkling blue eyes appeared. "Huh-uh."

He held up his hand and said, "I promise to swear off brown sugar for the rest of the evening."

The blanket came down, revealing a shy smile on Patch's face.

Seth carefully tucked the blanket around her as though she weren't already a young woman with budding breasts. "Sleep well, Patch. I'll see you in the morning. I love you."

He blew out the lantern and joined Molly at the door.

"Good night, Da," Nessie said.

"Good night, Pa," Patch whispered. And then, very quietly, "I love you too."

Seth slipped an arm around Molly's waist and headed for the front door. "Let's go sit on the porch," he said. "I have some things I want to say to you."

But when they were settled on the front porch, Molly on the top step and Seth on the bottom, it was Molly who asked the first question.

"Where have you been on the nights when you were supposed to be with Mrs. Gulliver?"

"With Dora Deveraux."

Molly groaned. "Why, Seth?"

"She was giving me information about where Bassett set up his whiskey-selling operation so the Masked Marauder could raid and destroy it. Also, Bassett had someone in Virginia City tipping him off when miners carrying gold were taking the stage to Fort Benton. He'd leak that information to Blackfoot renegades, who robbed the stage. Dora gave me the same information—"

"—so the Masked Marauder could ride to the rescue," Molly said in amazement.

"There was never anything between me and Dora after I married you."

"Pike said he saw you in her bed."

"There were extenuating circumstances."

"This I have to hear," Molly muttered.

"Remember the rumor going around at the christening party that Pike had shot the Masked Marauder?"

Molly nodded.

"Well, he did. I just had a flesh wound, but it was pretty bloody. I couldn't come home to you like that. When Pike showed up at Dora's room, the only excuse I had for being there was that I was making use of her services."

Molly frowned. "So that's why you grabbed my hand that night when I touched your ribs!"

Seth grinned crookedly. "It hurt."

"Wouldn't it have been simpler if you'd just explained everything to me in the first place?"

Seth brushed at some dust on the toe of his boot. "I didn't know you very well when I married you, Molly. I had no idea how you'd react if I told you the truth."

"But later—"

"I couldn't stop until I'd finished the job. I thought you wouldn't worry if you didn't know the truth. But it looks like you worried anyway. I'm sorry for that."

"Does what happened to Annarose have anything to do with the Masked Marauder?"

"No."

"Then why wouldn't you tell me how she died?"

Seth took a shuddering breath and covered his face with his hands. "I didn't want to talk about it."

Molly scooted down to the bottom step to sit beside Seth. She laid a comforting hand on his knee. "I'm sorry. You must have painful memories. It's none of my business how she died."

Seth dropped his hands and said, "I shot her. I killed Annarose."

Seth waited for Molly to cringe away from him. But her hand stayed on his knee, and her eyes never wavered from his agonized face.

He found himself explaining, seeking her understanding and absolution from the horrible nightmare that had plagued him for the past nine years.

"Nine years ago I was a Texas Ranger, Molly."

"A Ranger!" she exclaimed. "With all that

talk of killing, I thought you'd been an *outlaw!*"

"I chased enough of them," Seth said grimly. "Once I was ambushed, shot in the back by some rustlers and left for dead. Annarose nursed me back to health and never said a word about my quitting the Rangers.

"Not that I would have. I loved the danger. I loved the challenge of tracking down desperados, of pitting my wits against theirs.

"Nine years ago, when Patch was three, I went after some Mexican bandidos who had robbed a stage and killed the driver. There were three of them. They fled toward the nearest town, a place not far from my ranch. It was dark by the time I rode into town. I knew I should have waited till morning. They had the advantage in the dark.

"But one of them started talking to me, taunting me, saying I was chicken-livered, afraid to fight. When I stepped out of the shadows, they were waiting for me.

"If I hadn't tripped, the first shot would have killed me. I fired at the powder flash and killed one of them. Then I heard someone move behind me.

"You don't forget being backshot, Molly. I wasn't about to let it happen again. I turned and fired into the darkness—toward the noise I'd heard. There was another flash of gunfire in front of me, and I turned and shot at that.

"The next thing I heard was a horse galloping away. I would have gone after him, but I was still shaking. I went to check on the two bodies I'd seen fall. One of the bandidos was dead. The other body—the one behind me—was Annarose.

"I had shot her twice in the chest, but she was still breathing. She was in town to find a doctor because Patch was sick. She'd come running toward me to warn me about the ambush."

There were tears on Seth's cheeks, and he turned away from Molly to wipe them away with his sleeve.

"It wasn't your fault," Molly said. "It was an accident."

"Yeah. I've been telling myself that for nine years. I wanted to die with Annarose. For a couple of months after that, I did my best to get killed. I'm a notorious man in Texas, Molly. An outlaw killer. The meanest, most deadly Ranger around.

"I would probably be long dead now if it hadn't been for Ethan. He convinced me I had something—someone—to live for."

"Patch," Molly whispered.

Seth nodded. "I quit wearing a gun and learned how to heal folks instead."

"So why did you create the Masked Marauder?"

Seth shrugged. "Drake Bassett and his henchman had to be stopped. I didn't want to be known as a gunman, Molly. I didn't want to be dragged back into the life I'd left behind."

"Did you have to let people think you were afraid to fight?"

He shrugged again. "I couldn't kill anyone else if I walked away."

Molly put a hand on Seth's cheek, which was rough with a day's growth of whiskers. "As I said once before, you're an unusual man, Doctor Kendrick. And for the record, I love you very much."

Seth dragged Molly into his arms and hugged her tight. "And I love you."

"Seth, I can't breathe," she laughed. "The baby—"

He turned her in his lap so he could put his hand on her womb. "Were your other two births easy, Molly? Will having this baby be hard on you?"

"I'll be fine, Seth. I get a little sick in the beginning—"

"I'll say!"

"—but in a few months I'll feel wonderful, I'm sure."

"If anything happened to you—I love you so much, Molly." He kissed her until they were both breathless.

Molly laid her head against Seth's chest and gasped for air. "Is that quilt still in the loft, Seth?" she asked.

"It was the last time I looked," he said with a crooked grin.

"Let's go." She entwined her fingers with his and led him toward the barn.

He lit a lantern, and she raced ahead of him up the ladder to the loft. She was shaking the blanket out when he lifted her into his arms and kissed her hard.

She laughed and thrust her hands into his hair to hold him close. "You crazy, crazy man! Put me down."

"I want to hold you in my arms forever."

"You're going to get awfully tired over the next nine months," she said, "as I get bigger."

Seth grinned. "I'll look forward to it."

He set her on her feet and took the blanket from her. "I'll do that."

But as he shook the blanket to spread it on the straw, he heard a growl and saw two golden eyes reflected in the lamplight.

"Is that you, Rebel?" Seth said. He started

to shoo the mountain lion away. "You may have gotten here first, but I've got the better claim."

When Rebel growled another warning, Molly put her hand on Seth's arm. "Seth, look." She lifted the lantern and held it so it shed more light on the corner of the loft. There in the corner was a litter of tiny cubs.

"Oh, Seth," Molly said. "Aren't they adorable. Wait until Patch sees them!"

Seth swore under his breath. "I had plans for that stack of hay," he muttered.

"Let's leave her alone. We can go down to the pond. It's lovely there," she said. "Come on. Grab the quilt, and let's go."

Seth hadn't forgotten their night together down by the pond, under the stars. If they couldn't make love in the loft, the soft grass by the pond was a good substitute.

They ran nearly the whole way, and Molly couldn't breathe because she was laughing so hard. She sought out the spot where they'd made love once before. Seth had both hands on the blanket, shaking it out, when Molly teasingly reached up between his legs from behind.

Seth let the blanket hang from his hands, just stood there and waited to see what she would do.

Molly cupped him in her hand and felt him growing, felt the softness pulse and harden. She put her other hand around him so she held him from before and behind.

Seth gritted his teeth to keep from groaning, but he lost the battle, and a long, low moan issued from his lips.

And was answered by a moan from the shadows under the trees.

"What was that?" Seth said.

"What? I didn't hear anything."

He pulled Molly's hands off him and put her behind him. "Who's out there?" he demanded.

Something moved out from the shadows.

"Maverick!"

The dog-wolf sat down in front of Seth, cocked his head and looked up at him.

"Scat!" Seth said, waving the beast away.

Maverick ran a little bit away and came back with a stick. And sat down in front of Seth.

Molly giggled.

"This isn't funny," Seth said.

"I know," Molly said, and giggled again.

Seth took the stick and threw it as far out into the pond as he could. "That ought to take care of him for a while. Now, where were we?"

He took Molly's hands and put them on the front of his jeans and rubbed them up and down. Then he left her to her own devices while he returned the favor.

While their hands teased, taunted, aroused, Seth leaned down and joined his mouth to Molly's. They played with each other, lips and hands, until their knees were weak. They sank to the quilt, and Seth pushed her skirt up out of the way and let his hands glide up her legs.

"Molly, Molly, let me love you."

"Seth, I—"

Maverick barked to announce his arrival. It was all the warning Seth and Molly got before the wet dog shook himself, spraying them with a whole pond's worth of water. Then he sat down beside Seth and let the stick drop on the quilt.

Molly looked at Seth.

Seth looked at Molly. He grabbed her and roared with laughter. They rolled around the quilt, laughing until their ribs hurt.

"I can't believe he did that," Molly said through gusts of laughter. "I'm soaked."

"So am I," Seth said, stripping himself out of his shirt and using it to wipe their faces dry. "I give up. Let's go inside and go to bed."

Maverick followed them all the way to the

kitchen door, but Seth shut him firmly outside. They tiptoed past Patch's door to their
own bedroom.

"Shall we light a lantern?" Molly said.

"I don't need any light," Seth said. "I'm perfectly willing to feel my way around." He
promptly demonstrated by cupping Molly's
breasts in his hands and letting his thumbs
brush the tips, which immediately hardened
into pebbled tips.

Molly gasped in pleasure. "That sounds
like a wonderful idea," she said. She leaned
over and kissed her way across Seth's chest
until she found a male nipple. She closed her
teeth around it and nipped him, then used
her tongue to soothe the hurt.

Seth mimicked her action, taking her
breast in his mouth, teasing the nipple with
his tongue, biting just enough for her to feel
his teeth, then sucking until Molly moaned
her pleasure and thrust her hands into his
hair to hold him there.

Slowly, taking their time, they stripped
each other bare. In the dark, every sensation
was magnified. They were lovers, celebrating
their love for each other. Gentle touches,
adoring caresses, teasing hands and laughter.
Lots of laughter as they searched in the dark

for the edge of the quilt and sheets and pulled them down.

Then Seth lifted Molly into his arms, held her close, and kissed her gently. "Come to bed, wife, and let me love you."

He laid her down, and Molly slipped her feet under the covers—and leaped back up into Seth's arms with a screech.

"There's something down there!"

"Where?"

"Under the covers. Something *alive!*"

Seth tried to put Molly down so he could light the lantern, but she was having no part of that. "Molly, if you'll just let me put you down—"

"I'm not setting one foot on the ground until you get that *thing* out of here!"

Seth finally managed to get the lantern lit. Sure enough, there was a lump under the covers, about in the spot where Molly's feet had been. Seth reached over and yanked the covers away in one fell swoop.

Bandit was curled up in a ball. As soon as the covers were pulled away, he began to chatter angrily.

"You think you're upset," Seth muttered under his breath. "Patch!" he yelled. "Patch, get in here!"

Enough was enough. A frustrated man

could take only so much. Then, of course, he realized that both he and Molly were stark naked. He dragged his jeans on, while Molly grabbed a robe and drew it around her.

A second later, Patch opened the door. Nessie was with her, and so was Whit. "What's wrong, Pa?" she asked anxiously.

He pointed to the raccoon curled up on the foot of the bed. "Get that animal out of here before I shoot it."

"I wondered where he'd gotten to."

She scooped the animal up in her arms. "Anything else, Pa?"

"No, just go to bed, all of you. *And go to sleep!*"

When the door closed behind the children, Seth turned to Molly. He smiled crookedly. "I guess I lost my temper."

She walked into his arms and hugged him. "I can understand why," she said. She kissed him on the chin, the cheeks, the eyes, and finally the lips.

The kiss grew, and maybe because they'd been interrupted so many times, they let their mouths say everything they were feeling. Seth took Molly's lower lip between his teeth and nibbled it, then sucked it into his mouth. His tongue teased the sensitive underside of her upper lip. Their mouths touched tentatively, as passion built slowly but surely.

"Dare we try this again?" Seth asked. He could feel Molly's smile against his lips when she answered, "Sure. Why not?"

Seth didn't waste time taking off his jeans, simply lifted her into his arms and carried her over to the bed. He laid her down, then blew out the lantern and joined her. He slipped a hand up under her robe—

And there was a knock at the door.

"Don't answer it," Seth hissed.

"We have to," Molly whispered back, straightening her robe. "The children—"

Seth levered himself off the bed and lit the lantern. Then he stalked over to the door and yanked it open. "What is it?" he demanded.

Nessie stood there, her thumb in her mouth. "I can't sleep."

Seth sighed. "Would it help if you lie down with us for a little while?"

"Uh-huh."

Seth picked her up, shut the door, and carried her over to the bed. He set her down and went back over to stand beside the door. A second later there was another knock. When he opened the door, Whit and Patch stood there.

"Where's Nessie?" they asked.

Seth pointed to the bed. "Would you like to join us?"

Patch and Whit jumped into the bed beside Nessie and scooched down under the covers.

Seth didn't try to get next to Molly, just took the space that was left on the opposite side of the bed. He sat there and met Molly's eyes over the top of the children's heads. "You realize," he said, "that this sort of thing could severely limit the size of our family."

Molly grinned. "For the next eight months that isn't a problem."

Seth groaned. "Good night, Molly."

"Good night, Seth." Molly blew out the lantern and scooted down under the covers.

Then three sets of loving hands gently tucked their parents into bed.

Dear Readers,

First, thanks so much for your support of my previous Dell book, *Sweetwater Seduction.* Your response to Eden and Burke was wonderful, and I especially loved hearing from those of you who wrote me personal letters.

The Barefoot Bride meant a lot to me as I wrote it, because as single parent I find myself searching for that special man who can also have a special relationship with my ten-year-old son and teenage daughter. In *The Barefoot Bride,* Molly and Seth marry because of their children—and find true love in spite of them.

I always appreciate hearing your opinions and find inspiration from your comments, questions, and suggestions. Please write to me at P.O. Box 8531, Pembroke Pines FL 33084 and enclose a self-addressed stamped envelope so I can respond. I personally read and answer all my mail, although a reply might sometimes be delayed if I have a writing deadline.

Take care and keep reading!

Happy trails,

Joan Johnston
January 1992

Reckless abandon. Intrigue. And spirited love. A magnificent array of tempestuous, passionate historical romances to capture your heart.

Virginia Henley

☐	17161-X	The Raven and the Rose	$4.99
☐	20144-6	The Hawk and the Dove	$4.99
☐	20429-1	The Falcon and the Flower	$4.99

Joanne Redd

☐	20825-4	Steal The Flame	$4.50
☐	18982-9	To Love an Eagle	$4.50
☐	20114-4	Chasing a Dream	$4.50
☐	20224-8	Desert Bride	$3.95

Lori Copeland

☐	10374-6	Avenging Angel	$4.50
☐	20134-9	Passion's Captive	$4.50
☐	20325-2	Sweet Talkin' Stranger	$4.99
☐	20842-4	Sweet Hannah Rose	$4.95

Elaine Coffman

☐	20529-8	Escape Not My Love	$4.99
☐	20262-0	If My Love Could Hold You	$4.99
☐	20198-5	My Enemy, My Love	$4.99